THE
REPOSSESSED
GHOST

BRIAN C. E. BUHL

Cover design copyright © 2023 by Niki Lenhart
nikilen-designs.com

Published by Water Dragon Publishing
waterdragonpublishing.com

ISBN 978-1-959804-63-5 (Trade Paperback)

10 9 8 7 6 5 4 3 2 1

FIRST EDITION

for Melissa

ACKNOWLEDGMENTS

This has been a long time coming. When I started this novel, Obama wasn't that far into his second term. Most people had cell phones, but they were not quite as ubiquitous as they are today. The world has changed so much that I considered writing a prologue just to establish when this story takes place.

It's been a long time, and I have a lot of people to thank for helping me see this through. Michael Todd Gallowglas, for example, has always believed in me, even when I had trouble believing in myself. Richard S. Crawford, Andrea Stewart, and several other writers I've worked with in critique groups, helped me shape this story into what it is today.

Most especially, I must thank Jennifer L. Carson. She saw something in this story that no one else did, when the novel was still rough and surly. She would not allow me to leave this story to rot in a drawer. Jennifer helped me see a dream come true.

Finally, I need to thank my family, Melissa, Bryanna, and Christopher, for helping me stay grounded and sane.

THE
REPOSSESSED
GHOST

1

MY NAME IS MEL WALKER, and I steal cars for a living. I tell people I'm a repo man, though technically it isn't true. I work for a licensed repo man named Marshal. He gets the jobs and sends me out. I do all the work, and at the end of the day, he pays me under the table.

In this line of business, everyone has a specialty. I prefer the classics. There isn't as much molded plastic to destroy. Some older cars, all I have to do is pop the hood and jam a screwdriver across the starter solenoid. Then I'm off, windows down and wind in my face. There isn't as much money in the older cars, but without a tow truck or specialized tools, they're just more practical.

I've stolen dozens of cars, but there is one that stands out in my memory. It was a '74 Chevy Nova, baby blue, with chrome trim and gray interior. It wanted to pull a little to the right, but it purred like a jungle cat and floated like a steamboat. I've driven way fancier cars, but I remember the Nova because the night I stole it was the night my life changed forever.

I was cruising down the Louisiana freeway between Slidell and New Orleans. I had just pulled off the easiest job of my life, thanks to everyone celebrating Halloween. My heart pounded from the thrill of the getaway. I had a grin on my face that I couldn't wipe away. The night air felt cool, and the nearly full moon lit up the sky, bright enough to illuminate the bushy trees lining the narrow highway.

Some repo men partner up. One person acts as lookout while the other grabs the car. Or, in more dangerous situations, one might offer up a distraction. I didn't work that way. For one thing, I didn't know anyone else interested in breaking the law on a regular basis. Most guys my age are either just starting college or, if they're particularly slow, finishing high school. For another, I didn't make enough money on these jobs that I could afford to split it. I lived and worked comfortably alone.

Relishing my solitary getaway, I twisted the dial of the radio. The 40-year-old speakers squawked and chirped through inches of static. Not finding anything there, I shut it off and opened a window. Sharp evening air whipped my hair back and made my eyes water. I rolled the window back up and checked myself in the rear-view mirror.

That's when I saw her. A woman, sitting behind me in the back seat. She sat perfectly still, silent as a serial killer.

"Shit!" I screamed and jumped in my seat. The wheel jerked in my hands. Tires squealed. The heavy blue vehicle hitched towards the center of the road. I used both hands to grip the steering wheel, and both feet to stomp the brakes. The Nova spun and skidded off the road. Motes of dust swirled up in front of the car, dancing in the beams of the headlights.

With the car stopped on the shoulder, I sat for several moments, breathing hard. My heart thumped against my rib cage. I'm not normally what you'd call "high strung." I speak a little slower than most and smile a little faster than the rest. As the dirt cloud settled around the Nova, I wondered what made me so jumpy. Finding a strange woman in a stolen car is startling, but it shouldn't have made me lose control. Surprises are part of the job.

I sat still, listening to the steady hum of the engine. No other sounds in the car except my breathing and my heartbeat in my ears. Did I imagine the woman? I didn't want to look in the mirror to check, but just thinking about it pulled my eyes up. My heart skipped a beat. She still sat behind me, undisturbed by our spin out.

Something about her twisted my stomach in knots. Just a young woman in a simple dress, but seeing her made it hard to breathe, like staring down from a great height, or coming face to face with a black widow. It took me a moment to realize why. I could see through her. As she sat there, patient as the grave, I could see the backseat through her transparent skin.

"Who ... Wha ..." I tried to speak, but I couldn't think straight. Pure animal panic ran through me. Had I pissed myself? I let my hand slide to the inside of my crotch. Still dry, for now.

"You can see me?" the young woman asked, still not moving.

I nodded, unable to form words. I stared into my rear-view mirror, trying to accept the reality my eyes presented.

"You just sat there, ignoring me all night. I was starting to think no one could see me."

In the dark of night, things tend to lose their color. Dark cars become universally black in the absence of light. Rainbows don't exist in shadow. The woman in the backseat looked like she'd stepped out of an old black and white movie. Colorless, medium length hair touched her shoulders. She wore a dress of white and off-white. Light and shadow defined her pale skin. I took in all of the details of her, still seeing the coal gray vinyl of the backseat on the other side of her.

Some part of my brain began to rationalize. There had to be a reasonable explanation for everything. She must have been sleeping in the backseat when I stole the car. I could have overlooked her until she woke up and startled me. And her transparency? Her unnatural lack of color? An optical illusion, created by the rear-view mirror.

She couldn't be a ghost. Ghosts weren't real.

I turned to look at her directly and found the backseat empty.

"Shit."

Had I hallucinated her? I remembered hearing that runners can get high off endorphins and adrenaline. Maybe I was having a kind of repo man's high. Or maybe someone slipped something into some of that Halloween candy I grabbed earlier at the bar. Whatever messed me up, I needed to come down off this bad trip.

I turned forward, preparing myself to put the car back on the road. I gripped the wheel and took a deep breath, trying to steady myself. I checked my side mirrors, then glanced up to the rear-view mirror. There in the backseat sat the transparent stranger.

"What is wrong with you?" she asked. Her brow drew down in an angry V, and the set of her jaw marked her frustration.

3

"No, you're not there," I said to the reflection. "You're not real. You're just in my imagination."

She reached forward to touch me. Her fingers passed through my shoulder. Cold. Unnatural, like ice water sliding beneath my skin. The hairs on my arm and the back of my neck stood up as though I'd jammed a knife in a wall socket.

I screamed. I batted at the door handle. My clumsy fingers fumbled the door open and I fell out. The ground rushed to meet me. I found rough gravel. My knee landed on a sharp rock. My jeans tore and blood ran down my leg. It hurt, but I didn't stop to examine it. I scrambled to my feet and ran. The headlights illuminated me from behind, casting my shrinking shadow into the branches of trees.

Leaning against a moss-covered telephone pole, I stopped and panted. The ache in my scraped knee throbbed in time with my heartbeat. I rubbed my shoulder, working to warm the spot where the ghost had touched me.

The cool night air chilled my nervous sweat, making me feel that much colder. I shivered, looking back towards the car. The Nova's headlights shone back at me like accusations.

I tried to take stock of my situation. I stood in the middle of nowhere on a Thursday night. I didn't own a cell phone. Other cars would eventually come by, but I didn't like my chances of getting picked up. I didn't want to have to try and explain why I left the car, still running, on the side of the road. If a cop showed up, I didn't want to explain the car at all. The repo work I did existed in a legal gray area, as far as I knew. Without a proper license of my own, any conversation I had with the cops would lead to me going directly to jail.

"Come on, Mel," I said to myself, still looking back at the car. "You don't believe in ghosts. Pull yourself together."

After a little while, I managed to cobble together a little courage. I limped back to the car. Before stepping in, I walked around it, looking through the windows to see if the ghost had disappeared. The car looked empty and abandoned, still rumbling in its throaty purr.

Careful not to look into the rear-view mirror, I sat back in the driver's seat. I took several long, calming breaths, clinging to the scraps of courage that got me back in the vehicle. With the same deliberation as ripping off a band-aid, I looked up.

The woman in the back seat stared back at me, lips pressed together in a thin line. She frowned the way my ex-girlfriend frowned whenever I forgot something important. Great. Now my ghost passenger was angry.

"Will you please stop freaking out?" she said.

A frantic little laugh escaped me before I could clamp it down. I wanted to stay calm. I just didn't see how. I felt the urge to get out of the car again, but resisted. I focused on my breathing while I kept my eyes on the reflection of the ghost.

"I'm sorry," I said. "What do you want from me?"

"I just want you to calm down and talk with me." She paused to take a deep breath. "I'm scared, and I can't seem to leave. Please don't leave me alone."

My stomach twisted in a knot, out of sympathy this time instead of fear. I turned to look at her, and again, she disappeared. In the tiny backseat window, I could see her skewed reflection, more dim and insubstantial than what I'd seen before.

I turned back to the rear-view mirror where I could see her clearly. "It's okay. I'm not going anywhere."

The ghost settled back into the vinyl and let out a brief sigh. "Thank you. My name's Kate. Kate Lynnwood."

"I'm Mel. How did you die, Kate?"

"I didn't!" she said, her eyes wide and her voice growing shrill.

I could see my breath as mist. The windshield grew opaque as the interior of the car chilled.

"Are you sure?" I shivered.

Kate relaxed her shoulders and unclenched her fists. The air in the Nova warmed a little. I flipped on the heater and put my hands in front of the vent.

"I don't know. The last thing I remember before waking up back here was leaving the library."

Car lights cut through Kate's face from behind. She melted away in a blaze of white light. The roar of tires on concrete caught up to the Nova, crescendoing then diminishing as the other car flew past. I blinked after it. As my eyes readjusted, Kate materialized in the mirror.

"Are you okay?" I asked.

"I'm fine," she said, still frowning.

I drew down my seatbelt and goosed the Nova back onto the

road. I didn't want to be sitting there when the next car came along. They might stop to offer assistance. Or worse, they might stop to show me their badge.

"You said you can't seem to leave." I glanced up at Kate's reflection.

"When you ran off, I tried to go after you, but it ... it didn't work."

"What do you mean?"

"I don't know! I went through the door. Then I was just here in the backseat again."

The air chilled. My skin crawled with goose flesh.

"Please, try to stay calm." I said, turning up the heater. I clenched my jaw to keep my teeth from chattering.

Kate took several slow breaths. As she relaxed, the Nova's heater began to cut through the cold air.

"I don't want to be dead," Kate said, her voice just above a whisper.

I've never thought much about the afterlife. My mom tried to make me go to church and read the Bible, but she had "cast her seeds on stony ground," as our old pastor might have said. I was never all that interested in my mortal soul. I didn't want to discover God's plan as much I wanted to find out what girls kept under their shirts and skirts.

Kate looked about my age. With unblemished skin and a nice figure, she looked like the kind of girl I would pursue with no hope of catching. If she weren't dead, we would have been having a completely different sort of conversation. Seeing her stuck in the backseat, knowing her life had ended, I found my heart going out to her in a different way.

"It'll be alright, Kate." As soon as the words left my mouth, I felt stupid. She was dead. Things would never be all right for her again.

We rode in silence for a while. I kept trying to think of something that I could say that would be comforting, but nothing came to mind. Occasionally, I'd feel a chill seep through my skin, cutting right to the bone. Whenever that would happen, I'd glance up to see her frowning or burying her face in her hands.

A man can get used to almost anything. As strange as the night had been, the shock of having an undead passenger in the car faded. I had a ghost in my backseat. I could live with that. I didn't feel any of the blind terror that had gripped me earlier. Even the pain of my scraped knee faded to just an itchy, dull ache.

As I drove, I studied Kate in the mirror. She looked out the window and watched the countryside go by. Ghost or not, the person I saw in my rear-view mirror was just a regular girl, sitting and waiting through a road trip.

"Where are you from?" I asked.

"I'm from Sacramento, but I've been studying in New Orleans," she answered. She said *Orleans* the way so many tourists do, with a long *e* and the accent on the wrong syllable. She talked with a West Coast accent, quicker and more clipped than my Southern drawl.

"What are you studying?"

"Officially I'm undecided." Kate leaned back in her seat, still looking out the window. "I had been leaning towards pre-law, but I don't know if I want to be a lawyer anymore. I was thinking about switching to public health, but it might be too big a shift at this point."

"You're going to school in New Orleans?"

"I'm a sophomore at Tulane."

"And the last thing you remember is leaving the school library?"

Kate closed her eyes and wrinkled her nose as she tried to remember. A cute face. I thought again about how much I would have liked to have made her acquaintance before she died.

"No," she said at last. She sounded worried. "I remember being in this car. I couldn't move. I might have been tied up, laying face down on this seat."

I pulled off the road again and drove up close to the bushes and trees lining the highway. I found an opening in the foliage. I contemplated taking the Nova through and hiding the car on the other side. I couldn't see what was beyond the bushes, though, so I backed into an opening and put the car in park. Getting the car stuck would be worse than getting seen.

"What are you doing?" Kate asked.

"Nothing." I turned on the dome light and fumbled around in the toolbox next to me in the passenger seat. "I just want to check out the backseat."

I sat up and brandished my long, black handled flashlight as though I'd drawn a magic sword. I looked back into the mirror. Kate's voice filled my ears mid-sentence.

"— a while, and I don't see anything."

"What? Kate, I can only hear you when I can see you."

She let out a sigh. "I was just saying there's nothing to see back here."

"Maybe not from where you're sitting." I got out and leaned into the backseat, resting my weight on my uninjured knee. "I just want to see for myself."

I shined the light on the floor and panned it around the seat where I thought Kate had been sitting. The carpet was a much darker gray than the vinyl. When I put my hand on the floor, I expected it to feel wet and tacky with blood. Instead it felt stiff, and a little bit gritty. I panned the light to the seat. It looked dry, but there were circular areas in the material more faded than the rest.

"I think you bled back here," I said.

I leaned further into the car. The flashlight slipped from my grip and I lurched forward to grab it. As I did, I slapped my right hand onto the seat to catch my weight.

That evening, I had stolen a car, seen a ghost, spun out, and nearly crashed my most recent repo. But that was nothing compared to what happened when my hand touched the car seat.

2

WHEN MY HAND TOUCHED the seat, a strange feeling overwhelmed me. It happened fast, like the flash from a camera. Some kind of energy rose up from the seat into my palm. It rushed into me as sudden as a static shock. I felt no pain, and I managed not to flinch away. One moment, something existed in the seat. The next moment, that thing became a part of me. It raced up my arm, crossed my shoulders, and entered the back of my neck. When it reached my brain, it felt like someone had turned on a light, illuminating parts of my mind I hadn't known were dark. I stiffened, raising my head and closing my eyes. My heart raced like an engine.

I opened my eyes. I could see Kate. She sat as far away from me as the backseat would allow. She appeared more solid than she'd been in the reflection. Her skin and her clothing possessed drab colors. Her light blue eyes stared at me, wide with horror beneath blond bangs. She clutched her hands together in front of her chest. Her skin still looked too sallow, but her dress had changed from monotones to pale yellow trimmed with white.

"I can see you," I said. My voice sounded dull and distant in my own ears. I could see her lips moving, but her voice was too faint for me to make out the words. With the light filling my mind, my senses were dimmed and distorted as if I were under water. Sounds were distant and dulled, incomprehensible.

Things became stranger after that. Instinctively, I turned to my right, though not physically. I still faced Kate, but a sensation overwhelmed me, a feeling of slowly corkscrewing in one direction. It felt like getting off the merry-go-round after being spun too fast, or laying on a bed after too many beers. The sensation of turning triggered feelings of nausea. While my senses spun out of control, and my stomach threatened to unload, my vision changed.

A second Kate emerged from the first, sliding across the seat towards where my hand still rested. Her leg passed through my arm without the sensation of coldness I felt when she touched my shoulder. The first Kate remained where she sat, staring at me with large, frightened eyes. She didn't seem to notice her double.

I continued to turn without actually turning. The second Kate leaned forward, her eyes directed at the rear-view mirror. Her mouth moved several times, but I still couldn't hear her. I let my gaze drift towards the driver's seat. My breath caught in my throat. I saw myself sitting there, looking up at the mirror.

I flinched. The sensation of turning ceased. Shaky and disjointed, I raised my hand from the car seat and put my palm to my face. The surreal moment burst like a soap bubble. My senses returned to normal. The phantom version of me in the front seat disappeared. So did the twin ghosts of Kate Lynnwood.

I moved deeper into the backseat. I shifted around, looking for a reflection of Kate. The angle of the rear-view mirror didn't give me a good view of the rear of the car, and it was too far away to reach from where I sat. I tried the back and side windows. I found her on the passenger side of the car, still trying to back away from me.

"Kate, what's wrong?"

"You were glowing!" Her voice sounded tinny and distorted, like something from a bad AM radio.

The inside of the car chilled again. The windows misted white. Kate's reflection became more distorted and obscured in window fog.

"Kate, calm down. I think you make the car colder when you get upset."

I shivered in the backseat, waiting for the air to warm back up. The mist completely blocked Kate's reflection. Whatever she saw when the weirdness came over me made her overreact. Then again, what is the proper response when you're in her position? Comparatively speaking, she'd dealt with facing the strangeness more calmly than I had.

I climbed out of the backseat and stretched my limbs. Kate's chilling effect turned the Nova into a refrigerator on wheels, and the cool October evening felt like a warm relief. I rubbed my arms and tried to find some sense in the madness.

My eyes fixed on the backseat of the Nova. I stared for several moments at the spot where the vision came over me. If I were a smart man, I would have left it alone. Maybe run away, leaving the car right there on the side of the road. Marshal might get upset over the botched repo, but he'd get over it and I'd keep my sanity.

I shook my head. What could I possibly be afraid of? I'd already met a ghost that evening. A pretty one, actually. The weird vision didn't seem any stranger than playing chauffeur to a dead woman. Why worry about the beer you spilled when your car is going over a cliff?

I leaned back into the Nova and felt around on the backseat again. An iciness pierced my hand. My knuckles ached as though I'd just punched a bag of ice.

"Ow!" I said. "Sorry if I touched you, Kate. I'm just looking around again."

I moved my hand to the center of the seat. Again, I felt something intangible. It came into me, slower than before. Light filled the back of my mind, a growing warmth rather than a flash of lightning. I closed my eyes as I'd done before, shivering with the cold and the strangeness of the feeling. When I opened my eyes, I could see Kate again.

"There you are. Am I glowing again?"

Kate started speaking. I still couldn't hear her, but it didn't matter. The first word on her lips looked like a *yes* and she nodded.

I didn't know how any of this worked, but I've always been more curious than cautious. I tried to regain that sensation of turning, but only shifted my body to the right. I tried again. My field of vision slid to one side, my eyes moving, but nothing more. I felt like I'd partially woken from a flying dream. One moment, I'd done something fantastic. The next, I couldn't remember how. I tried several times, squinting my eyes and twisting up my face with concentration, but nothing happened. I felt foolish.

I stood up. The light in the back of my mind went out. Getting back into the driver's seat, I twisted the mirror around until I could see Kate clearly.

"Sorry," I said.

"Do you really think I'm a ghost?" Kate asked. She sat stiffly, but looked calmer about the prospect than she'd been before. The car seemed a little bit warmer.

"Yeah. I think you died in the backseat. I think you bled back there, and they tried to clean it up."

I put the car in gear and drove back onto the road. If any cars had passed us while I fumbled around in the backseat, I had been too distracted to notice. I considered myself lucky that a curious cop hadn't come by and tapped me on the shoulder.

"Will you go to the police?" Kate asked.

If the air chilled for me as it did for Kate, I'm sure the Nova would have turned into a solid block of ice. I stammered a bit before I found coherent words. "I don't think that's a good idea. They'll arrest me. For stealing the car if I'm lucky. For murdering you if I'm not."

"But I can't go myself. I can't even get out of the car and use a phone. You're the only one that can help me."

"You want me to help you, even if it means going to jail?"

"They won't put you in jail. You didn't do anything wrong. Look. Just park somewhere away from them, walk in, and tell them you're worried about me."

I thought about it a moment. "How about I use a payphone and call in an anonymous tip?"

"I guess that works. As long as they take you seriously."

"If I call and tell them that I think Kate Lynnwood is dead, how can they not take it seriously?"

"Don't tell them that I'm dead." We exchanged frowns in the mirror. Then she said, speaking slowly, "How do you know that I'm dead? How are you going to answer that question when they ask?"

"You have a point. What should I tell them?"

"I don't know." Kate looked out the window as if looking for inspiration along the road. "You just have to get them to investigate."

I didn't like this plan. We drove in silence for a while. Kate chewed her lip with her arms wrapped around her. I watched with dread as the wilderness of the designated state park gave way to civilization. Trees and brush became street lights and squat buildings. The glare of the city surpassed the brilliance of the moonlight.

I pulled into a gas station and parked along the side of the store, away from the doors and windows. I had no way of knowing the time, but it must have been well past midnight. I didn't see any other cars around the store.

"I don't think I can go with you," Kate said.

I could see my breath again.

"Is this how it's going to be forever?" she continued. "Stuck in the back of this car?"

Gritting my teeth, I dug into my tools until I found my leatherman. I pulled the longest blade free, then looked back at the mirror. "Let's see what we can do about that."

I turned and stabbed the backseat. The metal bit into the vinyl with a soft ripping sound, like a zipper slowly pulled. I had a hard time making the cut. Not because of the toughness of the material, or the dullness of the blade. I've always loved cars like the Nova. I might have had an easier time cutting into my own flesh than cutting up the car. It had to be done, though. I couldn't leave Kate stuck back there. A ragged triangle of vinyl came away with my blade. I turned to look back at the mirror.

"How do you feel?" I asked.

"I don't know," she said, rubbing her belly. "Different. Hollow."

"Can you get in the front seat?"

"Maybe. Can you let me out? I don't want to climb over the seat."

"As far as I tell, you shouldn't even be able to touch the front seat. Can't you just go through it?"

The inside of the Nova became wintry in a rush. I felt like I'd been dumped in a tub full of ice water. The chill made my scraped knee ache. I clamped my mouth shut to keep from chattering, but I couldn't do anything to stop from shivering.

"I don't want to just 'go through it!'" Kate yelled. "Damn you, Mel! I don't want to be a ghost!"

My hands fled on their own to the safety of my armpits, desperate to cling onto my own body heat. I reluctantly freed one to pull the door handle and fell out into the October air. Even the pavement of the parking lot felt warm compared to the inside of the car. I crawled a few feet away before getting to my feet and looking back at the Nova. The windows were covered with frost.

"Good job, Mel," I said. "You sure know how to say just the right thing."

As I walked around the corner of the store, I realized I still had the triangle of car seat in my hand. I entered the store, gave the skinny clerk behind the counter a nod, and went into the men's room. There were other reflective surfaces I could have used, but if Kate managed to come with me, I wanted a little bit of privacy.

I checked myself out in the mirror. I flipped up the handle on the sink and plunged my hands into the water. While my hands warmed, I looked up and saw Kate materialize just behind me. I smiled.

"Looks like you got out of the car," I said, trying to keep my voice low.

Kate turned in a circle, taking in her surroundings. She frowned and said, "Am I in the men's room?"

"Yeah, but it's just you and me."

"Damn it, Mel." She turned to open the door, but her hand passed through the doorknob. She tripped and fell, disappearing through the door. I turned off the water and continued to watch the mirror for a few moments. She rematerialized behind me and brushed imaginary dust off the front of her dress.

"At least you're out of the car." I dried my hands across the front of my shirt.

"For a moment, I was back in the car," Kate said. "Then I came back to you. I don't know how."

After drying my hands, I picked up the piece of car seat. I waved the flap of vinyl at Kate's reflection. "This probably has something to do with it. Men's room or not, you're out of the car now. It's a start."

"It's a start, but it's not enough." She sighed. "Thank you for getting me out, but I can't just follow you around forever. You have to help me or we'll both go crazy."

Kate's reflection consisted of blacks, whites, and various shades of gray. The bathroom mirror cast a better image than what we'd been using in the car. On this surface, she looked more solid. I studied her, from her slender figure to her uplifted chin. She was right. Pretty or not, I would go crazy if she were always there, visible every time I went to shave. Invisible every time I sat to take a shit. In the room with me, every time I went to masturbate.

"You're right," I said. "But what are we going to do? Even if we get the police involved, we're not going to be able to bring you back to life."

The temperature in the bathroom dropped noticeably. Kate took several long, steadying breaths. "Even if I don't get to go on to heaven afterwards, I'd feel better knowing that whoever did this to me was dead or in jail."

In that moment, I realized I still had a choice. I could choose to walk away from her. I could just drop the strip of vinyl, leave the store, and go home. My trailer stood within walking distance of the gas station. I'd miss out on the payday for bringing in the Nova, but there'd be other paydays. I didn't kill this girl. I didn't even know her. I didn't owe her anything.

Instead of dropping the bit of material, I gripped it in my left hand. "All right. I'll make the call. But after that, you and I are going to have to chat about our options."

I turned away from the mirror and stepped sideways to the door, hoping to avoid stepping through Kate. In addition to being cold, it just seemed rude to walk through another person. Eventually, she and I were going to need to figure out how to make this arrangement between us work.

Red and blue lights were the first thing I saw when I stepped out of the bathroom. They shone in through the front window. A New Orleans police officer stood near the clerk. Another stood near the door, one hand moving to the grip of his gun when the bathroom door closed noisily behind me.

"Don't move," the cop at the door said.

I didn't move.

3

THE INTERROGATION ROOM consisted of a plain table and a pair of unpadded chairs. I sat with my hands unbound, resting my elbows on the table. The room was well lit, with a mirror running along the wall across from me. A camera swiveled back and forth in a corner of the room, a red light above the lens like an angry eye. In the reflection of the mirror, Kate paced behind me.

"Okay, I'm sorry," she said.

"It's alright." I looked at the camera. I didn't want to say more. Thus far, no one else seemed to notice Kate, though I could see her reflection everywhere I went. In the car ride to the station, I shoved the bit of car seat down the front of my pants. The police had not found it yet. I wasn't sure what would happen if they did.

"Yes, it will be alright." Kate said, her voice firm. "When they question you, I'll be right here with you."

I rolled my eyes. I'd been in rooms like this before. Watching Kate walk back and forth as though psyching herself up for a big speech, I knew she would distract me when it came time to dance. I couldn't tell her that, of course. Instead, I looked at her reflection and nodded with a sly smile. If anyone watched me, I wanted them to think I was reassuring myself. It would be better if they thought I was scared, which was true, rather than crazy, which I hoped was not true.

The door opened and a slightly overweight man in a brown suit and tie walked in. His hair was light brown and thinning in the front, and he wore a woolly mustache. I'm not much of a judge of ages, but I guessed he was probably in his thirties. He wore his badge on a clip on his belt. His face looked long, as though constantly worried or disappointed.

"Mr. Walker?" he asked, dropping a file on the table. He took the seat across from me and squared the pages of the folder in front of him.

"Yes, sir."

"Can I get you some water before we begin?"

I licked my lips. After everything that had happened that evening, I felt parched. "Actually, yeah, if you wouldn't mind."

He smiled, the corners of his mustache flaring out like mandibles. His eyes remained mournful, like a basset hound. He stood and left, closing the door behind him.

"Your name is Mel Walker?" Kate asked.

I brought a hand up and coughed a "yes" into my fist. I rubbed my chin, looking back up at the camera. Kate wasn't going to make this easy for me.

Kate walked around the table. She looked at the folder the cop had left behind.

"This has your name on it. Mel is short for ... I don't know how to pronounce this."

"Melchizedek." I tried to keep my voice low. I reached across the table and tapped my name.

"The folder is almost as big as your name. I didn't think you were old enough to have a file this thick."

"This isn't my first time in a police station." My eyes flicked back and forth between the mirror and the camera.

The cop returned with two paper cups balanced in one hand. He set one in front of me before taking a seat. He sipped from his own cup, then looked at me with his disappointed eyes. "It seems you've had a bit of bad luck, Mr. Walker."

"It's all how you look at it, I guess."

"How do you look at it?"

"Just that it could be worse. I still have my health. And you seem like a nice enough guy. I'm sure it could be someone much more unpleasant questioning me."

The cop gave me another woolly smile. "Too true. Too true. Speaking of which, do you know why we've brought you here?"

"Be careful, Mel," Kate said.

I returned the cop's smile. "Well, I'm not too sure. When they told me that I had the right to remain silent, I didn't know they were going to exercise that right themselves."

The cop emitted a mirthless chuckle. "You're a clever man. I like you, Mr. Walker. That's why I'm going to suggest that you make it easy on yourself, and just come clean with whatever is on your mind. It will make you feel better. And, it will make your legal problems much easier. Just be cooperative, and everything will be okay."

"That's bullshit, Mel," Kate said.

I looked directly at Kate's reflection for a long moment. I knew she was trying to help, but she wasn't telling me anything I didn't already know. I liked having her in my corner, but I really needed her to be quiet for a while. I had been in this seat before, or a seat just like it. I needed to stay calm. I needed to stay positive, and not volunteer anything.

"I want to cooperate in any way I can," I said, looking back at the cop. "Maybe if you tell me what you think I did, I can help straighten out this misunderstanding."

The cop opened the folder on his desk and pulled out a five by seven photograph. He slid it across the table to me, his hand shaking. "Have you seen this girl before?"

A lump formed in my throat before I even saw the photo. I leaned forward to get a good look. My stomach clenched. The picture showed a girl from the chest up, wearing a blood-stained yellow dress. She had pale skin, blue lips. Her medium length blond hair spilled out wildly on the ground. Kate Lynnwood's corpse.

An intense chill filled the room. I wrapped my arms around my chest as the bitter cold cut through my t-shirt and pierced my flesh. Looking up at the mirrored glass, I saw Kate leaning over the picture, hand over her mouth and her eyes wide.

"No! No! No!" she kept repeating, her voice low but intense.

"What the hell?" the cop said. He thrust his hands in his jacket pockets and hugged himself, shivering in the cold. He craned his neck to look back at a ceiling vent.

19

I leaned forward and flipped the picture over on the table. Kate stepped back, looking at me with wild eyes. I expected her to be in tears, but her cheeks were dry. Her mouth hung open, and she held her hands out to her sides. She looked like she wanted to run.

"I've never seen her," I said. In my mind, I tacked on the word *alive*. When questioned by the police, it's important to stick to the truth as much as possible, even if it's only in your mind.

Kate lowered her hands and closed her mouth. She regained her composure, though she still shook. With the photo out of sight, the temperature in the room stopped plummeting. It remained chilly, even though warm air wafted in from the vent the cop faced.

"Are you sure?" the cop asked, turning back.

"Dead sure."

"I see." The cop picked up the picture and tucked it back in the folder. He drew out another page and stared at it. "It says here that you were brought in for marijuana possession, but didn't serve time. Were you Kate's dealer?"

"Oh shit," Kate said. "They found my pot."

I frowned at Kate's reflection. I turned back to the cop. "Is Kate the dead girl? I've never been anyone's dealer."

"But you have a history with marijuana. Several ounces were found in Kate's dorm room. It seems you have that in common."

"When I was brought in, it couldn't be proven that the pot was mine because there were other people in the van. I'm surprised it's on my record. I thought it was supposed to be expunged when I turned eighteen."

"When we're done here, I'll see what we can do about that," the cop said. He scanned down the list in front of him.

"He's fishing," Kate said.

I ignored her. "Was Kate murdered at that gas station?"

"Was she?" the cop asked.

"I don't know. I'm wondering why you're showing me pictures of her and asking me about her."

"Ah. The Chevy in the parking lot matched the description of a car that was phoned in anonymously, attached to Kate's disappearance."

I swallowed, trying not to look nervous. I cast my thoughts wide. I needed to think about something other than Kate or the stolen car. One trick to maintaining a good poker face is simply concentrating on some other memory. Like the first time I went to

Biloxi and gambled on the barges. I never won anything. I was terrible at craps and blackjack, but I could hold my own at poker. I have a decent poker face. I needed to keep cool and wear my best, unreadable expression.

Kate was right. This guy was fishing, and I wasn't going to bite.

"I don't own a car," I said.

"No, but that Chevy was reported stolen." The cop continued to look at the page in front of him. "According to this, you boosted a car when you were sixteen."

"That definitely shouldn't be on my record."

"I know, I know. You were a minor. It says here you wound up doing community service. The question right now isn't how this information wound up in front of me. The question is: what can you tell me that will make your life easier?"

Kate stood behind the cop, leaning forward to look at the paper. "I don't think they can use any of this."

"Sir, I really wish I could help you." I smiled an apologetic smile. "I never saw Kate before tonight, and that Nova isn't my car. I was in the bathroom washing my hands at the store when you picked me up. Now you're asking me about stuff that shouldn't even be on my record anymore. I don't know, but I think I should probably be quiet now. I don't want to get in trouble for something I didn't do."

In my head, I patted myself on the back. Everything I'd just said had been the truth, and the cop's frown told me that he didn't like where I'd taken the conversation. He put the page back in the folder and tapped the whole stack on the desk to straighten them. He stood up and looked at me, his bushy eyebrows drooping.

"Alright, Mr. Walker. You can go. But don't leave town. You're a person of interest in a murder case. I'm sure we'll be seeing you again."

4

THE COPS CALLED ME A CAB that I had to pay for. I had them drop me off at the gas station where I'd been picked up. The Nova was gone, of course. Not that I would have risked trying to take it after everything that happened that evening. I bought a can of coke and drank it while I walked home.

I lived in a silver bullet trailer just on the edge of the city. The trailer sat on cinder blocks on the unused border of someone's property. A dirty orange extension cable ran from a pole to my trailer, an umbilical cord feeding me power directly off the grid. No mailbox marked an address. Like my profession, my home functioned in a legally gray area.

The trailer creaked on its mounting when I stepped inside. I clicked on a standing lamp near the door and flopped onto a mattress heaped with wadded blankets. The bed consumed most of the floor in the trailer. Dirty clothes concealed most of the rest. I crumpled my empty soda can and chucked it towards a bin by the door. It bounced off the rim and clattered to the floor next to a few other missed shots.

I lay stretched out on the bed for several minutes, waiting for the world to feel normal again. This was my ritual after repossessing a car. I'd steal it, feeling the thrill and rush all the way to Marshal's lot. Then he'd pay me and either drive me home, or pay for a cab to drop me off. Once home, I'd lay on my bed and come back to reality.

Tonight, the rush refused to fade. I sat up, my heart still beating just a little too fast. I looked around the trailer, weighing my options. My fridge had a few beers. That might help. An Xbox controller sat invitingly on my beanbag chair. That might make for a good distraction.

I got up and pulled a bottle from the fridge. I popped the top using the edge of my tiny kitchen counter, then took a swallow. I waited a few moments, letting the taste of the beer go bitter in my mouth. Nothing. No amount of alcohol or video games would settle me down. As long as Kate floated around in my trailer, invisible and watching, I wouldn't find any peace.

At the other end of my trailer, I stooped down and opened a cupboard full of toiletries. Next to an unopened roll of toilet paper sat a can of shaving cream, and the thing I needed most: my shaving mirror. I pulled it out and hung it off one of the cupboards lining one wall of my trailer. When I took a step back, I could see Kate, looking around my home with a pinched expression. She held her hands close to her chest like she was afraid to touch anything.

"It's not much, but it's home," I said.

She looked down at a pair of boxers crumpled at the base of my flat screen. She wore an expression of pure revulsion, and a full-body shiver ran up her from her feet to her shoulders. She took a moment to compose herself, smoothing her dress and clasping her hands in front of her.

"This is smaller than my dorm room."

"I may not have running water, but I've got the necessities covered." I gestured towards the television.

Kate tsk-tsked and shook her head. She tried to wipe her finger through an impressive dust pile on one of my shelves, but her hand passed through the wood, and the temperature in the trailer dropped a degree.

I picked up the mirror and flopped into my bean bag chair. I took another sip of beer while shifting my seat so that I could see Kate. As I watched her in the small reflective surface, something occurred to me. The thought struck me so hard I nearly spilled my beer.

"Small as this place is," I said. "It's going to seem like a palace compared to a jail cell."

"It won't come to that."

"You don't think so? They're going to find my fingerprints in the car. They're going to find your blood in the car. Hell, they're going to find my fingerprints near your blood. When all this is through, you're going to be stuck in a car that gets impounded, and I'm going to be stuck in jail. Where I'll probably get 'impounded.'"

Kate opened her mouth to say something, but stopped. Her gaze dropped to the floor. She fidgeted with one foot.

"This isn't your fault," I said. "Don't feel bad."

She shook her head, then looked to meet my eyes. "You're going to have to leave town. Tonight."

I stared into her gray, unblinking eyes. "That's a terrible idea. I mean, they're going to find my fingerprints. Maybe it'll take them some time. But if I leave town now, that's as much as admitting that I killed you."

"But you didn't kill me. They'll have evidence that you were in the car, but nothing else. No motive. No murder weapon. Give them enough time, and they'll find other evidence. Maybe on my body. Other evidence will lead away from you. Then you'll be fine."

"They think I sold you drugs. You heard that cop. They'll twist that into some kind of motive."

"I got the pot from my ex-boyfriend. It wasn't that much, anyway. If that's the route they investigate, it's going to be a dead end."

"Okay, let's say you're right. Let's say that the best thing I can do is just go away for a while and wait for everything to blow over and go back to normal. Look around you. Do I look like the kind of guy that can just pick up and get out of town anytime I want? That Nova was supposed to score me a couple grand and keep me in ramen for a few weeks."

"You could steal a different car?" Kate suggested. She offered a weak smile.

"I could do that, sure. I mean, what's another ten or so years added onto a life sentence for murder? We both know that adding grand theft auto to my list of accomplishments isn't going to help. It's going to make things worse."

"Fine. Use my money. I've got some in savings. There should be enough for you to buy a ticket and fly somewhere."

I sat up straight and put down my beer. "That could work. How do we do it? The bank isn't open, and even if it was, they're not going to give me your money, no matter what I tell them."

"My ATM card should be in my dorm."

"I told the police that I didn't know you. I can't just go to your dorm. They'll probably be watching it by now."

Kate pursed her lips and started to pace. She wasn't paying attention to her movements, and wound up walking through a corner of the bed and part of the wall cupboards. After a few short laps around the trailer, she turned back to face me.

"You're like a thief, though, aren't you? You steal cars. Can't you sneak into my room? Pick the lock?"

I laughed, then took another swig from my bottle. "It'd probably be easier for me rob the bank."

"Alright. Fine. You can call my roommate. She's kind of a bitch, but I can tell you what to say, and she'll bring my stuff to you. Then we can go straight to the airport, and go wherever."

"Why would your roommate bring your stuff to someone she's never met?"

"I'll tell you what to say. Trust me, it'll work."

I couldn't think of any other arguments. It still sounded like a terrible plan, but it was the only one we had. If I didn't leave, I had maybe a day or two before the cops showed up to arrest me. If I did leave, then I had a chance to get away and start over somewhere else. The worst thing that could happen would be to get caught. But really, how much worse off would I be?

"I guess it's back to the gas station," I said. "Does your roommate have a car?"

5

BACK AT THE GAS STATION, I dropped some change into a payphone and dialed the number Kate provided. The booth had plenty of reflective surfaces, but all of the reflections were dim, making Kate's voice tinny and distant. She had to shout to be heard. I looked down the road in the direction of my trailer. I wished I brought my shaving mirror.

The handset rumbled in my ear and I turned my attention back to Kate. The cop had shown me the picture of her dead body, which provided proof of a sort that I wasn't crazy. I had plenty of reasons to believe Kate wasn't a figment of my imagination. This phone call took all of that a step further. I had dialed a number using information Kate provided, to call a person I'd never met. This was the difference between believing I could fly, and jumping off a tall building.

"Hello?" A girl's voice filled my ear from the receiver pressed against my face. The voice crackled with static, and I heard her stifle a yawn.

With all of the excitement and worry, I forgot how late it was. It must have been near four in the morning. I winced. "Hi, is this Jenny?"

"It's Jen." She paused long enough to yawn again, more loudly this time. "Or Jennifer. Jenny is a dog's name."

"Sorry, Jen. Listen, I need you to do something for me."

"Who is this?" She sounded more awake. Through the crackling static of the payphone, I heard growing impatience and anger.

"Uh ... Jim." I felt stupid. Why didn't I work out my story before picking up the phone? "Listen. Kate told me to call you, and tell you to bring me some of her things."

"You knew Kate?" Jen's voice hitched. Just as I'd forgotten how late it was, I hadn't considered that I was calling someone who just lost their roommate. Damn. I'm a real asshole.

"Yes." I looked at the best reflection I could find of Kate and covered the receiver with my hand. "Are you sure about this?"

"Just tell her!" Kate shouted. She sounded like she was hundreds of yards away.

I put the receiver back to my face. "Jen, Kate told me to tell you that there are some pictures of you that I can make go away. Or, I can make public, depending on if you do me this favor. Do you understand?"

The phone remained quiet for several moments. When Jen spoke, her voice sounded hesitant. "Pictures?"

I grimaced. "Dorm party. Two weeks ago. You were drunk, and Kate walked in on you with a guy that was giving you the-"

"Okay!" Jen cut in. "I get it. What do you need me to do?"

"I need you to bring me Kate's wallet. It should be in her closet, on the shelf near where she hangs her laundry bag." I glanced at Kate's reflection and saw her nodding.

"Where are you?" Jen asked.

I gave her directions to the gas station and we hung up. I put a hand on my stomach. I'd graduated from butterflies to a full sized marching band, parading all over my guts. I frowned at Kate. She shrugged.

"You said she was a bitch," I said. "But you took pictures of her banging some dude at a party, to use as blackmail?"

"It wasn't just 'some dude,'" The air in the booth became frosty. She took a deep breath. "Remember the ex-boyfriend I mentioned? The one that gave me some pot? But I didn't actually take a picture. I was too busy crying."

"Okay, so she is a bitch. Is there any chance she's going to call the police instead of doing what we asked?"

Kate shook her head. "She thinks she has a shot at becoming the next Ms. Louisiana. She'd do anything to keep her image clean."

"Oh, so she's hot?"

The phone booth chilled so violently that one of the windows cracked, lines spider webbing across the entire pane of glass. I pulled the door of the booth open and hopped out, teeth chattering.

Jen showed up about a half hour later. She drove a large black truck, an immaculate Ford with an extended cab. As soon as I saw the truck, I felt more sympathetic towards Kate. Jen drove over the curb and pulled into two parking spaces with a squeal of rubber. She didn't use turn signals. You can tell a lot about a person by the way they drive. In just a few, reckless maneuvers, I knew Jen was the kind of self-absorbed horror I hated to find on the road.

I opened the passenger side door and climbed in. When I saw Jen, I no longer cared how she drove. Her voluptuous figure strained the cotton of her white tee. Her tanned skin looked smooth and inviting. She wore her long, dark hair in a hurried pony tail. Patterned yoga pants covered her long, shapely legs. Her ankles and parts of her calves were exposed above expensive looking tennis shoes. I ran my eyes down the length of her body, then back up again, ending with the plain, delicate silver cross on a silver chain around her neck.

I licked my lips. I realized I was staring. I cleared my throat. "Jen?"

She let out an impatient sigh which made her breasts heave in an enticing fashion. "That's me. You're Jim?"

I blinked. Jim? Who was Jim? It took me a moment to remember the alias I'd given her on the phone. I cleared my throat again. "Yeah. Did you bring the wallet?"

"Did you bring the photo?"

"No, but it will be deleted as soon as you drop me off at the airport."

The truck grew colder. It wasn't the sudden frigidity of the phone booth, but it still felt colder than it should have been. Kate had joined us, and she was not happy to see her former roommate. I stole a glance down at Jen's breasts, wondering how her tee shirt was going to handle the extra chill.

If she noticed me checking her out, she didn't say anything. She flipped on the heater, then folded her arms across her chest, covering any show she might have given. "How do I know you're going to delete it when we're done?"

"I'm not lying to you." This felt like another gamble, but when you're already all-in, you don't have anything to lose. I couldn't back out now. "Look, you seem like a nice enough girl, and maybe you do have a shot at being the next Ms. Louisiana. Take me where I need to go. We'll go our separate ways, and you'll never hear from me again, and no one will ever see those pictures. Or, I can get out of the truck right now, and we'll see what happens when those pictures are posted online. What do you say?"

She narrowed her eyes at me, one eyebrow arched. She pushed her lips out like she was posing for a selfie. Then she turned towards the steering wheel. "Put your seatbelt on. And quit staring at my tits."

I did as she said. I tried to hide a smile by rubbing by chin. We rode in silence for most of an hour. Traffic was light, but the Louis Armstrong Airport had been built on the other side of the city. With the heater turned all the way up, it did a reasonable job cutting through Kate's chill. I tried to keep my eyes straight ahead and my mind on my predicament, but I'm only human. And Jen was hot.

Jen pulled up to a terminal drop-off. I opened the door. Before I got out, she handed me a tan leather wallet. "So we're done?"

I pulled the door, angling it so that the mirror showed me the rear of the cab. Kate sat on the backseat, her back straight and her posture stiff. I met her eyes and raised the wallet. She nodded.

"We're done," I said.

"Good. Now get out, you fucking creep."

I got out. When the door closed, Jen gunned the engine and pulled away with a squeal of tires and the smell of burning rubber. She forced an old Buick to skid to a stop, its horn blaring. Just like that, Jen went from some sort of supermodel goddess back to a bitch. I really hate it when people drive like that.

"All right," I said, hoping Kate could hear me. "Let's see what we can do."

The first order of business was finding an ATM. That wound up being simple. A pair of machines stood near the terminal door, silent and obvious. I unfolded Kate's wallet, slid out the ATM card, and then stopped where I stood. ATMs have hidden cameras, don't they? Sooner or later, someone would notice that Kate's account had activity after she died. If the cops watched a video of my smiling mug stealing Kate's life savings, they might see that as motivation. I couldn't have that.

I went into a men's room. In the still pre-dawn hours, the restroom stood empty. I parked myself in front of a long bank of sinks and looked in the mirror, waiting for Kate to materialize. I didn't have to wait long.

"I don't know if you're a creep," Kate said. She crossed her arms in front of her and tapped a foot on the floor. "But you are a dog."

I smiled. "I'm just a guy. Listen. Do you think you can do something to the camera on the ATM?"

"Like what?" Kate frowned. "I haven't been able to touch or affect anything since I met you."

"You don't have to touch it." I rubbed my arms. With Kate in a sour mood, the air in the bathroom took on the qualities of a walk-in freezer. "When you get upset, it gets cold around you. The more upset you are, the colder it is. Can you go stand next to the ATM and, you know, think of Jen or something?"

"You want me to go somewhere and get upset on demand?" Kate raised a slender eyebrow.

"Yes." I knew how silly that sounded, but a plan started to form in my mind. "But you need to focus on the camera, and not break the whole ATM."

"How do you propose I do that?"

"I don't know. Put your hand in there, or something."

I could tell by the crisp quality of the air what Kate thought of this plan. Her emotional aura of cold made the air in the bathroom chilly, but not so cold as to break glass as it had earlier. For this plan to work, I would need to help her.

"I can't get very far away from you," Kate said. "I'll need you to be near."

"Okay. I'll be close. Just not too close."

I offered Kate a toothy smile before leaving the bathroom. My footfalls echoed in the wide, empty terminal area. No one stood near the ATMs. I took a position near one of them, off to one side. I hoped the camera couldn't see me.

After a few moments, I began speaking with a soft voice. "Kate, I don't see anything happening. Make sure you don't break the whole thing. We need to be able to get that money that you never spent when you were alive."

Nothing happened. I continued speaking. "You know I still have some of your car seat stuffed in my underwear, right? It's kind of like having you in my pants, if you think about it."

I still couldn't see anything happening. I thought I could feel a slight chill coming from the direction of the ATMs. I felt like an asshole, but I kept talking. "Hey, you know, if this doesn't work, it's no sweat. Jen must have money, if she can drive around that big, dumb truck. I could just call her back and tell her I changed my mind, and that I need money instead. Heck, maybe I could talk her into doing some other stuff, too. She's got a fantastic body. Maybe we could use your old room to-"

The sound of glass cracking interrupted my speech. A thin sheen of frost covered the tiny display of the ATM. Above the display, the glass was completely white, with cracks and frost spider-webbing in all directions. I walked over and wiped the display with my forearm. The machine accepted Kate's card without a problem.

I shivered while conducting the business. Kate's savings had a little more than a thousand dollars. I tried to withdraw all of it, but got a prompt about exceeding a daily limit. It allowed me to withdraw five hundred.

"I'm sorry, Kate. Thank you for helping me."

I walked over to a monitor that showed a list of departures. The column beneath the monitor had a polished white and glossy finish. I could just make out Kate's reflection, standing behind me.

"Any suggestions?" I whispered.

Kate looked up at the monitor and pointed. I traced her finger to a United flight, departing within the hour to Sacramento.

"Really?" I asked.

"Take me home, Mel," Kate's voice came across too soft and distorted to understand, but I could read the words on her lips well enough.

I wandered off and found a sleepy airport clerk. I bought a single ticket, which took all of Kate's money and most of mine. As I walked towards the gate for departure, I thought about what this meant. I was taking Kate home, but I was also leaving mine behind. Perhaps forever.

There weren't going to be any more nights driving down a Louisiana highway with someone else's car. I would probably never see my silver bullet trailer again. I'd left everything behind. I hadn't even stopped to tell Marshal goodbye, or that I wouldn't be able to repo for him anymore.

Kate might have been the one to die, but it seemed that my life ended as well. A chill ran through me that had nothing to do with Kate's mood.

6

ONCE ON THE PLANE, exhaustion caught up to me and I passed out. The person sitting next to me nudged me awake somewhere over Texas. He was an average looking businessman with shiny shoes and a sports coat. He said, "I don't mind you using my shoulder as a pillow. I don't even mind your snoring. But I have to draw the line when it comes to drool."

The next time I woke up, the plane was pulling into the terminal. My neck ached from sleeping crooked, but I was warm. The man I'd drooled on had draped his jacket over me. I murmured a quiet thanks as I handed him his coat.

With a stiff neck and a sleep-weary brain, I shuffled off the plane with the other passengers. The businessman's unexpected, random act of kindness filled my thoughts. It distracted me so much that I forgot to worry over the kind of trouble I'd been running from, or what might be waiting for me on arrival. By the time it occurred to me that authorities might be waiting for me in Sacramento, I was already well past security, stepping onto a local bus.

I'd never been to Sacramento before. Looking through the tinted windows of the bus, I saw trees and gently rolling hills in the immediate area surrounding the airport. A short time later, we entered a highway and I could see a modest urban skyline obscured by light fog. The bus floated down the highway, moving through farmland on its way to the city. The rural colors melted into urban gray. The narrow highway broadened, crossing and splitting off with other freeways. Before I knew it, the bus crawled through a series of one way streets flanked by trees and tall buildings.

I'm not sure what I expected Sacramento to look like. Back home, whenever California crossed my mind, I imagined sun bronzed beach bodies. I imagined men strutting around with swollen pectorals and spiky hair. I imagined blond women with tiny waists, huge fake tits, and impossible puffed up lips. From the safety of my seat on the bus, everyone around me looked normal.

The bus stopped, and I walked off with my head down and my hands in my pockets. The November morning air, though not as cold as back home, still carried a chill that made me wish for a jacket. I walked a few blocks, hugging myself to hold in my body heat, before I stopped and really looked around.

I stood on a busy one-way street. Morning commuter traffic flowed around me, both on the sidewalk and on the pavement. A few buildings stood tall, their windows dark and reflective. Most were more modest. Trees, naked from the season, stood along the road in every direction, their bare branches reaching towards a cold, gray sky.

With very little money in my pocket and no living contact in the city, I wandered without purpose or direction. The pedestrians around me strode with their heads up. None of them made eye contact with me. They all had some place they were going, and presumably some place to return to. I teetered between envy for their jobs and joy for my absolute freedom.

Still trying to get a feel for the place, I began to pay attention to the street names. I turned down I Street, away from the freeway. Trees continued to flank the street between the sidewalk and the pavement. On the opposite side of the street loomed a stark white building with narrow windows and rough pillars. Probably a government building of some sort. On my side of the street, a darker, less imposing structure stretched the length of the block. Squares and rectangles made up its construction, and its windows were reflective black glass. I stepped closer to one and looked for Kate.

"This is the downtown library." Kate's voice sounded muffled, as if she were speaking to me from the other side of a sheet of drywall.

I grunted my response, more interested in looking at Kate than the building. She stood to my right, her reflection little more than a lens flare. While I continued to rub my arms and shift from foot to foot, she stood still, her arms at her side. She turned about in a circle, looking at the surrounding buildings.

"I'm going to need to find a place to stay," I said.

"I live in Orangevale." Kate turned back to face me. "It's a really long walk if it comes to that. But if we get on the light rail-"

"Kate, you don't live in Orangevale." A biting wind passed through the pores of my shirt, setting my teeth to chatter.

"You don't have to keep reminding me." Frost began to crawl up the window, lances of white crystal spreading in geometric patterns.

"I think I do. Your parents are not going to be able to see you, and they don't know me. I can't just go up to their house and knock on the door. Forget it, Kate. We're not going there."

•   •   •

We went to Kate's old home.

I'm not sure why I buckled. She didn't use tears against me. As far as I could tell, she never cried, though her wide eyes and turned down lips told me she wanted to. Maybe we went to her house because we had come so far already that it only made sense to go the rest of the way. Or maybe I knew that it would be torture for Kate to be this close to her family, yet unable to go the rest of the way to see them.

Following Kate's suggestion, I walked a few more blocks and hopped onto the light rail, a small train that connected the surrounding suburbs. I took a seat on a barely cushioned bench and glanced around at the other passengers. A few were teenage students wearing clean clothes and carrying heavy backpacks. Others looked like vagrants, with vacant, bloodshot eyes and dirt on their face and clothing. The scent of sweat, urine, and stale beer flavored the air, more subtle than an alley off of Bourbon Street, but just as nauseating and familiar. I turned my attention back to the window and watched the city move around me.

The changing landscape revealed different personalities of the city. I saw churches with elaborate, stained glass windows and Gothic fixtures. I saw office buildings stretching towards the sky, their faces thick with glass that glittered in the morning light. Some construction looked old, with worn brick and painted signs, their colors faded. Other places looked new, with improbable curves and large monitors displaying their name and logo.

For half an hour, the train slid from a cramped, urban environment to an open suburban backdrop. I got off at the station at Watt Avenue, a grimy platform next to a busy freeway, beneath an overpass. Car exhaust choked the air, and I climbed stairs to the upper station, just to get above the fumes.

After a brief consultation with Kate in a public bathroom that stunk of piss and beer, I started walking. I passed gas stations, fast food restaurants, and convenience stores. Then I found myself walking through modest neighborhoods. Yards were both smaller and cleaner than what I was used to seeing back home.

By late morning, I stood across the street from Kate's old home. I hunkered down next to an SUV and used the side mirror to see Kate.

"This is it," I said.

Kate didn't respond. She stood just behind me, staring towards her parents' house. Her arms were crossed in front of her chest. She chewed her bottom lip.

"We're here," I said.

Kate remained silent. The air around me did not feel supernaturally cold.

After a moment, I sighed. "Kate, I need you to pay attention. Do you have any nosy neighbors that will freak out if a stranger walks up to your front door?"

With a quick shake of her head, Kate turned to face me. "No. We don't even know our neighbors' names. Is that weird?"

"I wouldn't know. Wish me luck."

I straightened and looked around. No one appeared to be looking at me. I walked across the street, stooping to pick up a plastic wrapped newspaper. With a determined stride, I walked up the driveway, rounded the walkway, and stepped up to the front door. I gave it three quick knocks, my knuckles stinging against the cold wood.

With my heart beating like I'd just run a sprint, I thought about what I'd say when the door opened. I would tell whoever answered that I found their newspaper in the street, and then ask to use their bathroom. It worked when repo'ing cars. It could work here.

The moment stretched long enough for me to contemplate knocking again. I looked down at the newspaper. I turned it to over and smoothed the plastic bag until I found the date. Yesterday's. Of course no one would come to the door. No one would be home, because the Lynnwood's were probably in Louisiana, dealing with Kate's remains.

I tried the door. Locked. I looked around the front door. There wasn't really a porch, only a concrete step at the end of a walkway, leading to the front door. I checked under the doormat. No key. Just some dirt and a few wriggling insects. I lifted a potted plant near the step. Nothing. A decorative porcelain puppy sat to the side of the doorstep, a "Welcome" sign hanging from its mouth. I moved the statue. There in the concrete beneath sat a dull, gray key.

The key didn't enter the lock very easily, but after applying my weight and giving the key a few wiggles, the door opened. I slipped inside and closed the door behind me. For a moment, I leaned against the door, feeling relieved. Then I noticed the dull red glow of a motion sensor, hanging from the ceiling just ahead of me.

I hurried forward, rounded a corner and jogged down a hallway. The first door I tried led into a bedroom. The next belonged to a bathroom. I went in, flicked on the light, and stood in front of the mirror.

Kate entered the bathroom after me, her pace slow. She had a distant look in her eyes. She held her hands up in front of her, as if trying to avoid touching anything.

"Kate, is there an alarm on the house?"

"What?" Kate sounded distracted, but her voice reached me as clear as her reflection.

"The alarm code for the house?" I could hear panic creeping into my voice.

"Oh. Twenty-seven, twenty-seven."

I ran back into the hallway. The walls were covered with framed pictures, many of which featured Kate at different ages. I ignored them, looking for a keypad. Two panels stuck out on the nearest wall beneath portraits. I flipped open the lid of the first.

Thermostat. I flipped open the next. A number pad with some buttons that glowed green in the shadows of the hall. I punched in the code, thumbed the "Off" button, then let out a held breath.

Returning to the bathroom, I found Kate in the mirror. She stood near the door, looking out.

"Hey," I said.

"Hey."

"Which bedroom is yours?"

"First one to the right, down the hall."

I thought about saying something flirtatious. Something about taking her to her bedroom, going through her underwear drawer. Nothing seemed funny or appropriate. Though her eyes and cheeks were dry, there was something in the way she stood that spoke of despair. And yet, the temperature in the house remained a warm relief compared to the outside air.

"I'm sorry, Kate."

"I know." She turned to face me, and gave me a weak smile.

I stepped past her and found her bedroom where she said it would be. A well-made bed dominated the small space. A soft, brown and white blanket covered the bed, bearing the image of a rearing horse. Posters featuring boy bands covered one wall. Along another wall stood a writing desk. Everything in its place, neat and clean, with square corners and empty surfaces. It remained a girl's room even after the girl that lived there had moved out.

I rummaged through the drawers of the desk. In the second drawer, I found a compact mirror. I opened it and turned it about. Kate stood at the doorway, hugging herself.

"You were right, Mel. I don't live here anymore."

I shrugged. "We had to come, though. If we hadn't, you would have ... it's just better that we came."

"Yeah."

"Is there anything you want me to do while we're here?"

"No, Mel. Let's just go. Besides. I'm starting to wonder if I gave you the code for turning the alarm code off, or the code for turning on the silent alarm. I used to get them mixed up."

"Damn it, Kate!"

We left.

7

I LEFT AT A QUICK PACE. I focused on moving like a man in a hurry rather than a man trying to get away. It's a subtle difference, but an important one. A man in a hurry is ignored, while a man running, constantly looking back, with wide eyes and a worried face, attracts attention. The kind of attention that prompts neighbors to pick up their phone and call the police.

After a few blocks, I slowed and relaxed. I didn't hear any sirens. The long arm of the law had not extended in my direction, yet. I walked alone on the street feeling homeless and cold, but free.

A little bit after noon, I wandered into a Goodwill. The day had warmed considerably, but I still needed a change of clothes and a jacket. As I picked out a second-hand backpack to store all of my new worldly possessions, I spotted a ski mask. It hung out of place on a hook next to a pair of mismatched gloves.

I picked it up. While checking out, the clerk looked at the mask and asked with a grin, "Planning on robbing a bank?"

"You caught me." I smiled and winked as I scooped my stuff off the counter.

Outside the store, I pulled out the compact. I opened it and found Kate a few steps behind me, looking the other direction.

"Hey, if your parents were going to use an ATM, where would they go?"

"They'd probably stop at the bank on Madison, near San Juan. Why?"

"How far away is that?"

"A few miles, I guess. I've never walked around this much before. Do you think we'll steal a car pretty soon?"

I laughed. "I wasn't planning on it. How do I get to the ATM from here?"

Kate gave me directions, and I closed the compact. Then I walked some more. I'm not an athlete by any stretch of the imagination, but I've always walked a lot. As long as my belly is full, I can pretty much walk forever. I've never owned a car, and my feet have never let me down.

Even still, my dogs were barking by the time I reached the bank. I wanted to sit down or lean against a wall for a while and rub some life back into my limbs. But I controlled myself. For what I wanted to do next, I knew I couldn't be caught loitering any longer than I had to.

I ducked around the side of the bank and pulled out my ski mask. Then I let out a sigh of relief, relishing my first lucky break. The ATM sat on the back side of the bank, away from the busy street. With my face concealed, I pulled out Kate's ATM card and withdrew the rest of the money from her account. Almost five hundred dollars.

I felt wealthy enough to splurge on dinner. Further down Madison, I found a restaurant that looked like it wouldn't be too expensive. It stood not too far from a Denny's, and looked to be a little bit more upscale. I took a seat at the counter and looked at the menu.

That's when the reality of living in California hit me. Kate's money wouldn't last very long here. As hungry as I felt, I settled on a small chicken salad. I wanted a steak or a burger, but it was just too expensive. At the end of the evening, the restaurant lightened by wallet by ten dollars.

I splurged again on a hotel room. It was the cheapest I could find in the area, but it still put me out another thirty dollars. The walls were thin. The mattress sagged visibly in the center. A musty, mildew smell clung to the air. The door featured a sturdy lock, though, and the bathroom provided hot water. It felt safe enough, though I almost wished I had paid a little bit more.

I sat on the edge of the bed. A mirror sat on the wall in front of me, above the dresser. Within the reflection, I could see Kate inspecting the room, shaking her head.

"You always take me to the nicest places. You know, my dorm room was probably bigger than this."

"It was probably cleaner, too."

"What are you going to do tomorrow?"

"I don't know yet. Probably wander around some more. Find a cheaper place to stay."

Kate nodded. She walked over and stood next to me, looking in the mirror.

"Mel, you should leave me at my old house."

I pulled out the scrap of material I cut from the Nova's backseat. I held it in both hands, turning it slowly, feeling the rough underside of the fake leather with my fingertips.

"Are you tired of me already?" I asked.

"No, it's not that. Look, you're kind of a jerk sometimes, but you don't deserve to have a ... a ghost ... following you around all the time."

"But I saw you in that house. You were miserable."

"Maybe. But you'll be miserable with me around, eventually. I'm literally haunting you."

I folded the scrap in half and pushed it into my pocket. "If it comes to it, I'll leave you some place nice. But not your old house. And not yet."

Kate sighed. "Well, maybe it won't matter."

"Why?"

"In a few days, there will be a funeral. When that happens, maybe I'll just ... go away."

•   •   •

The next few days, I walked around Sacramento until I thought my feet were going to fall off. I explored the area and started to learn the place's secrets. For example, while places like Orangevale, Citrus Heights, and Carmichael contain vagrants, they do not necessarily embrace vagrants. Not all vagrants, anyway. If I was a woman, a number of facilities would have taken me in, offering shelter. If I was recovering from drugs, I could have entered one of several facilities and enjoyed a cot, coffee, and a place to detox. As a man in my early twenties, clean and healthy, my options were much more limited. Fair, I guess, but when you're hungry and tired and scared, social justice falls down the list of priorities.

Downtown Sacramento offered a few more choices. A handful of churches opened their doors to keep people like me from freezing on the street at night. The Greyhound station didn't kick people out if they fell asleep on their molded plastic benches. Best of all, there were a number of clubs open late, where a good looking guy like me might find someone to go home with.

Of course, I never got that lucky. I enjoyed the eye candy, but Kate's unseen presence served as the ultimate cock-block. Just when I'd start to make some progress with a girl, I'd catch sight of Kate's reflection and feel compelled to back off. Kate never voiced disapproval, but she didn't look happy, either. After the second night, I stopped trying to find a warm bed to share. Probably for the best. I'm not sure I would have been able to perform, knowing someone else stood by in the room with us, invisible and watching.

On the morning of my fourth day in Sacramento, I sat in a Starbucks. An empty cup I'd fished out of the garbage sat in front of me next to a day old newspaper someone left behind. Inside the newspaper, I found Kate's obituary. After reading it twice, I opened the compact mirror, set it on the table, and held my hand next to my cheek with my finger in my ear.

"Kate?"

She stooped behind me, her lips twisted into a smirk. "We're playing phone, now?"

"Yeah, I can hear you." I looked around the store. A few people sat with laptops. Baristas worked behind the counter, working and smiling with the fervor of the highly caffeinated. Everyone around me was too absorbed in their own world to give me a second glance. I turned my attention back to the mirror.

"Is today the day we turn to a life of crime?" Kate smiled. "There's a baby blue Mustang outside. We could steal it and be in Reno in just a couple of hours."

"Kate, stop. I'm not going to Thelma to your Louise today. It says here that your funeral is to be held at Pleasant Hills Cemetery. Do you know where that is?"

"I think so." She leaned past me and examined the newspaper herself. "Only two paragraphs. And it's not very personal. I was hoping it'd be longer."

I folded the paper and set it aside. "Let's focus. Kate, are you sure you want to go? We don't know what will happen. And, your family is going to be there. It's probably going to be really hard to see them like that."

"It will be hard." Kate stepped back and folded her arms across her chest. "But you only get one funeral, right? I think I need to go. I need to move on."

"We don't even know what that means."

Kate smiled. "I guess we'll find out soon enough."

8

I TOOK A BUS TO THE CEMETERY to make sure I'd get there on time. Like the rest of Sacramento, trees covered the burial grounds. A clean white building sat in the middle of the place surrounded by fields of grass. Headstones and memorials stood out in the carpet of green, a morbid bumper crop of the deceased. Most monuments were the same, a slab of cut marble etched with names and dates. A few stood out as large stone blocks or elaborate statues. Funeral processions filled a small portion of the circular driveway leading up to the main building.

I arrived early enough to wander around the grounds before the proceedings. Attending the funeral was going to be trickier than evading an ATM camera. An unwelcome stranger like me would stand out, especially if the funeral was a small, private affair. I needed to find a place close enough to hear, yet distant enough to respect the Lynnwoods' privacy.

Fortunately, another group of mourners were burying their dead not too far from Kate's grave. A large picture stood next to the flower arrangements depicting a white-haired grandmother with a warm smile. In the picture, she sat in a wheelchair. In the

47

distance between the old woman's grave and Kate's stood a massive oak. I took a position beneath the branches and faced the older woman's funeral.

With a shaky hand, I opened the compact and looked for Kate. She stood behind me, her eyes wide and her mouth agape. When she noticed me looking at her, she pointed towards the older woman's funeral.

"Mel, look!"

I frowned in the direction Kate indicated, but didn't see anything out of place. Then I turned, directing the mirror towards the funeral. A short distance apart from the men and women in black stood a woman in a hospital gown. Like Kate's reflection, she appeared devoid of color and slightly transparent. I recognized her as the grandmother from the picture, no longer confined to a wheelchair.

I watched, fascinated. A bald man stood in front of a podium, speaking to the attendees with a voice too quiet for me to hear from my position under the tree. The elderly ghost did not appear to be paying attention to him. Her gaze remained steady on a woman sitting in a chair in the front row.

A few other people took a turn at the podium. The ghost continued to look at the woman in the front. Every once in a while, she'd smile. After a few minutes, the woman in the front row stood and strode to the podium. Once she faced me, I could see a resemblance between her and the ghost. The old woman's daughter, I guessed.

I still couldn't hear the words. I counted myself lucky. Whatever she said had an impact on the crowd. More people dabbed at their eyes. They put their arms around their loved ones.

The ghost approached her daughter. She stopped a pace or two away from the podium and dabbed at her cheeks with a corner of her hospital gown. Then she began to glow. Golden light spilled out of her skin and her hair. I squinted against the light, but tried not to look away. The ghost took the last two steps to reach her daughter. Then, she disappeared.

The woman behind the podium finished her speech and returned to her seat. Another man stepped up to the podium. No one gave any hint or sign of seeing what I witnessed. I blinked, and felt a tear roll down my cheek. I wiped it away and looked at my hand, dumbstruck.

Turning around, I used the mirror to find Kate again. She stood smiling, her hands together in front of her, as though praying.

We both spoke at the same time. "Did you see that?"

I laughed and rubbed my eyes again.

"Are you crying?" Kate asked.

"A little, I guess."

"Did you know her?"

"No. I'm not even sad. That was just ... beautiful."

"I think I'm ready." Kate stood taller and straightened her dress. "I'm not as scared as I had been."

"I'm not, either."

The procession for the older woman began to break up and leave. At the same time, another group emerged from the central building. Time had slipped by. Kate's funeral would begin soon.

"Mel, before I forget, I just want to say thank you. You've been a real friend to me. You came all the way out here. I don't think anyone else has been there for me the way you have these last few days."

"Well, it was your money we spent to get out here. And it was your idea to leave New Orleans. If I'd stayed, I'd probably be in a cell right now instead of-"

"Mel? Shut up and say 'you're welcome.' I'm trying to say goodbye before it's too late."

"Okay, which do you want me to do? Do you want me to shut up, or do you want me to say you're welcome?"

"God, you can be so annoying sometimes."

I opened my mouth to say something annoying and playful, but before I could get the words out, Kate took several steps forward.

"There's my dad. Oh God, there's my mom! Look at them! I've never seen them so sad!"

I turned around and looked. An older man with a neatly trimmed beard and a long coat walked with his head down and his arm around an older woman. The woman looked like Kate. She wore her hair shorter, and the shape of her chin was different, but she looked to be the same height and held herself with the same unimposing dignity. Dark, puffy circles underscored her eyes. She clung to her husband, and every step looked heavy.

Another couple walked a short distance behind the Lynnwoods. They held hands, and while they looked sad, they were nowhere near as despondent as the pair that preceded them. I guessed they were family friends.

The air around me became frigid once again. I spun around, trying to find Kate. She stood half a dozen steps away, reaching in the direction of her parents. As she leaned forward, her reflection in the mirror flickered. Another step and she'd be back in the Nova.

I cradled the compact mirror low and close to my body. As casually as I could, I sidestepped away from the tree, moving towards Kate's grave. Though cold air surrounded me, I felt sweat beading on my brow and forming between my shoulder blades. I did not want Kate's parents to notice me or pay me any attention.

Facing away from the grave, trying to keep the compact inconspicuous, I did not see Kate's father approach me. "Are you one of Kathryn's friends?"

I clicked the compact shut and stuck my hands in my pockets. I turned to face Mr. Lynnwood. Behind him, I saw that Mrs. Lynnwood and the other couple had taken seats. Another man in a suit stood in front of Mrs. Lynnwood, speaking to her in quiet tones.

When I spoke, my voice cracked. "Yes, sir."

"The high school will be having a service tomorrow."

"Ah, I didn't know Kate from high school, Mr. Lynnwood."

"I see." He turned and gestured towards the seats. "Feel free to join us. Most of Kathryn's friends went out of state when she did. We're not expecting many people. There's plenty of room."

I could not see a way to refuse. I wanted to stand apart, with my back to the whole thing so that I could watch Kate with the mirror. At the same time, I needed to be close enough so that Kate could be an unseen participant in her own funeral. More importantly, I wanted to avoid drawing unnecessary attention to myself.

I wound up sitting in the second row, behind the Lynnwoods. The minister that spoke to Mrs. Lynnwood took a position at the head of the grave, which was roped off and covered with a red cloth. With wide eyes and a stomach roiling with acid, I attended Kate's funeral.

It amounted to a short sermon, pretty much. The minister reminded me of the pastor in my mother's church, the one that spent so much energy trying to "save" me. Just like in church, I sat still and quiet, the minister's words rolling by without penetrating me. I resented the minister, trying to feed me a lesson I did not want while I sat there as a captive audience. Then I looked at the Lynnwoods in front of me. Perhaps the minister's words comforted them. For all I knew, it could have been a comfort to Kate. With the mirror closed in my pocket, I had no way to know.

The minister began to wind down. "...we commend this daughter of God in His holy name. We commit her body to the ground. Earth to earth. Ashes to ashes. Dust to dust."

I had to see her go. I lowered my head as if in prayer. Without making any sudden moves, I slipped the compact from my pocket and opened it. It took me a moment, but I managed to turn it at an angle in my lap so that I could see Kate. She stood a short distance from her parents, looking at them. She kept her back to the minister.

"May the Lord bless her and keep her in peace," the minister finished. "Amen."

Kate closed her eyes. She wrapped her arms around her body. Her brow furrowed, and she began to shake. Then, like a match's flame in a gust of wind, she disappeared.

I let out a long sigh. I closed the mirror and put it back in my pocket. It was over. I was alone again. Kate had moved on, and I needed to do the same.

The Lynnwoods stood and I rose with them. I shook Mr. Lynnwood's hand and murmured condolences to them both. I walked away, leaving the same way I arrived.

Once away from the cemetery, I walked towards the bus stop. A few blocks away, I stopped at another Starbucks. I ducked into the men's room to splash water on my face.

After drying my cheeks, I reached into my pocket and pulled the triangle of material from the Nova's backseat. I stared at it for a long moment. I didn't need it anymore. While it made for an interesting souvenir, it also physically tied me to the scene of a murder. I held it over the garbage can. Before I could let it go, I felt the temperature in the bathroom drop enough that I could see my breath form mist.

"You have got to be shitting me," I said, turning to face the mirror.

"The men's room? Really?" Kate scowled at me, her hands on her hips.

"What happened? I thought you were gone."

"I tried to go. I wound up back in that damned car."

I stuffed the material back in my pocket. "Well, it's nice to see you again, anyway."

Kate took a deep breath. "Now do we steal a car and go to Reno?"

"No. Now, I need to find a job."

9

T HE NEXT COUPLE OF WEEKS went rough. The money disappeared at a steady rate and I didn't always find a warm place to sleep at night. I panhandled a little, but some people were turned off as soon as they heard the twang in my voice. Most murmured an apology while trying to avoid eye contact. I became acquainted with some of the destitute of Sacramento, which came in all shapes and sizes. That's something that impressed me. The poor people in the South mostly looked like me, but those in Sacramento came in all shades. The place supported equal opportunity suffering.

I eventually found myself hanging my proverbial hat at a shelter not too far from the downtown area. As long as it wasn't too crowded, I could take a bunk. In the mornings, I did chores and enjoyed bagels for breakfast. Coffee was available all the time, though sometimes it bore the look and consistency of motor oil, long past the need for changing. It warmed the hands and belly, which was all I cared about. November nights could get mighty cold, regardless of whatever mood Kate might be feeling.

I spent my days trying to find unconventional work. A normal job was out of the question. For one thing, I didn't want to fill out any forms with my name and social security number. For another, I wasn't qualified to do much that wasn't repo work. Maybe I could work in a garage but without references, finding an under-the-table job as a mechanic or assistant would be like finding the Golden Ticket. And I don't eat chocolate.

I needed to find a specific kind of repo man. Marshal, the man I'd worked for in Louisiana, had been in business a dozen years before I'd been a twinkle in my mother's eye. That was the kind of man I needed to find. Someone a little bit older, a little bit wiser, and a little less greedy.

At one point, Kate asked me why I didn't just repossess cars on my own. Most people don't realize that to work those kind of jobs, you have to get a license through the state. You have to register with the Department of Motor Vehicles. Lots of paperwork involved. The people you're repossessing from have certain rights that must be honored, and you're supposed to be familiar with those rights. In Louisiana, if I wasn't hiding from the law, I might be able to do it. In California, I'd have as much chance getting a repo license as I would have passing the state bar exam.

If I'm being completely honest, I could have lied on an application and flipped burgers. Instead, I hit the streets and held out for the job I wanted. Call it pride or foolishness. I like cars. I like the thrill of stealing them. I like feeling like I got away with something. Repo work is a little like being a bounty hunter, but with less chance of dying.

Like I said, I wasn't having any luck finding someone I could work with. One man laughed in my face when he heard my offer. A few days later, another went so far as to pull a knife. I met one at a park off J Street that thought I was an undercover cop.

A few days after that prospect ran off, I sat on a bench in the park and reconsidered my options. Sunset painted thick clouds in orange and red. The shadow of a bronze statue reached along the ground towards my feet. I took my mirror out and found Kate standing behind me with her hands clasped in front of her. She wore a long-suffering look, with her lips tight and her brow furrowed.

"I wish you would reconsider talking to my parents. The funeral was weeks ago, but my Dad will remember you. I think he liked you. He could find you a job."

"Kate, you know that's a bad idea." This was an argument we'd had often enough that we could recite the other's position verbatim.

"Even if the police are done with them, it's still a bad idea for me to associate with your parents. Besides, they don't know me. They'd ask questions about you that I couldn't answer. And I'd feel like a jerk, taking advantage of them while they're suffering."

"I can tell you what to say."

"No, Kate!" My voice carried further than I'd intended, drawing the attention of a passing jogger. I gave the jogger a quick nod and a smile before turning back to my mirror. "Look, we both know what this is really about. You want me to find a way to tell them that you're okay, and that you're still here. But I'm not Whoopi Goldberg."

I saw something out of the corner of my eye and turned to look before Kate could offer a rebuttal. A man and a woman approached along one of the narrow walkways that meandered around the perimeter of the park. The man wore black from head to toe. Black slacks, shirt, and a flat brimmed hat. The woman wore a dress that would fit right in at a Renaissance fair. Lace and cream colored frilly bits covered her arms and legs, while a bodice worked overtime to hold in her midsection and prop up her bosom. She held the man's hand, leading him in my direction.

Kate noticed the pair as well, and her eyes went wide. "One of them is glowing, Mel."

I sat up straight and looked at them more carefully. The man was carrying a book. The only thing missing from marking him as a priest was a white collar. The woman's free hand held something small and glass. As I watched, the glass caught what little sunlight remained and cast dozens of tiny rainbows all around her.

"Which one?" I asked.

"The woman." Kate backed away. I had to turn the mirror to keep her in view. She held her hands out to each side, and she moved in quick, jerky motions. She looked on the verge of panic.

"It's close," the Ren fair woman said when they were only a few feet away.

"Heavenly Father," the man said, raising his book. He opened it and began to read, but I couldn't understand the words. It sounded like Latin.

"Mel, they're both glowing now!" Kate screamed. The immediate area became as frigid as the depths of winter. "I don't like this, Mel! Make them stop!"

55

I crammed my free hand into my arm pit and clenched my teeth to keep them from chattering. The Ren fair woman and the priest were right in front of me and I froze, in every sense of the word.

The woman shivered. Her dress left the skin of her shoulders and her cleavage exposed, which quickly turned to goose flesh. She held her glowing crystal ball high and yelled, "It's here, Mark! Keep going!"

Mark shook with the cold, but his voice boomed, loud and steady. He took a few steps forward. Though I'd been sitting directly in front of them, they ignored me. Then the realization hit me: they were there for Kate.

I've never been a violent man. I've never been in a fight in my life, though it came close once when I was repo'ing a car from a guy that was more observant than he looked. Usually, I can avoid conflict by cracking a joke, or simply listening and agreeing with whoever is trying to get in my face. I'm laid back and easy going most of the time.

It's hard to stay calm and easy when your friend is screaming like she's being murdered. The ones responsible for her pain stood right in front of me. I didn't know what the man was saying, but I knew it needed to stop. I jumped to my feet. Then I ducked my head down, charged, and tackled him.

We went down in a heap, arms and legs tangled. The woman yelled something at us, but I couldn't make out her words. I was too busy rolling on the ground with the priest. His book flew from his hands and landed open a few feet behind us. He brought a knee up. Tried to kick me in the groin. I turned, catching the blow on my thigh.

He twisted out from under me and reached for his book. I dragged him back, then lunged for the book myself. He hadn't been a threat until he'd started reading from it. If I could keep it away from him, maybe it would buy Kate and me enough time to figure out what to do next. The woman continued yelling something at me, but I ignored it.

My hand closed on the book. Light blazed in my mind, a bonfire of warmth and brilliance that burned away all thought and emotion. I gasped. My eyes opened wide. I could still see the browning grass of the park. I could still feel the dirt beneath me, cold and covered with a thin layer of frost created by Kate's emotional outburst. All of that was secondary. At the forefront of my mind, a vision overwhelmed me.

Mark stood in the bedroom, his vestments as clean as his soul. A girl thrashed in the bed. Her arms and legs strained against the heavy rope that bound her to the bed frame. Sweat drenched her dirty bedclothes and the dingy bed sheet beneath her. Father Philip, Mark's mentor, stood on the other side of the bed, praying with a voice that shook the walls.

"Lord, free this girl from the chains that bind her," Philip was saying. "In Jesus' name, let this child be cleansed of the foul spirit that touches her!"

Mark felt numb with fear and shame. The church sent him with Philip to try and ease the minds of the girl's family. He had not expected their visit to turn into a true exorcism. Before this evening, he had not truly believed in the power of demons and spirits. But now he saw things he could not unsee.

Philip continued praying and Mark fumbled his Bible open. The younger priest was out of his element. He didn't know what to say or do. He looked to The Word to find some answer.

He found himself looking in the book of Acts, reading about the day of Pentecost. He felt something inside him open. Something deep in his chest that he'd never felt before. He felt light well up from his heart, pouring through his veins. Words welled up, spilling from his mouth. He recognized it as Latin, but the words passed his lips too quickly for him to discern.

His fear melted, replaced with awe. His shame faded, turning into humble acceptance. He channeled the Spirit of the Lord. The words rolled out of him, his voice louder and stronger than he had ever spoken. The Word of God bore into the possessed girl. It pressed her against the mattress, filling her the way a wind fills a sail.

The girl convulsed. A final spasm arched her back so high that Mark feared she would snap in half. She screamed. Her cry, wordless anger and defiance, stretched an impossibly long time. Her eyes bulged, and the veins on her neck stood prominent from the effort. When the scream ended, she collapsed, her breathing ragged. The torrent of words running out of Mark ceased. He stood gasping and shaking, fearful and elated.

As Philip bent to tend to the girl, Mark's thoughts turned prophetic. This was the last evening he would wear the collar. This was the last time he would stand as a man of the church. Like the apostle Paul falling blind along the road to Damascus, this was the end of his old life. But it was the first night of his true calling.

I let out a ragged breath. The vision lasted only a moment, but it felt much longer. It disoriented me. While I came back to the present, Mark pushed me down. He stretched to reach the Bible still in my right hand. I pitched it away from both of us. It landed on the grass and slid a short distance away.

"Stop!" I yelled.

"You don't know what you're doing!" Mark yelled back.

I realized Mark was no longer trying to fight me. I twisted and pulled away from him. Looking back on our scuffle, I started to think he might not have been trying to fight me at all. He'd just been trying to get his Bible. He might not have meant to kick me, either, though the charlie horse on my thigh suggested otherwise.

Ren fair woman stood a short distance away. She clutched a small glass sphere in both hands. Sun blond hair framed a round face, etched lightly with lines around the corners of her hazel eyes. I guessed her age to be in her early thirties. With her head cocked to one side and her mouth slightly agape, she studied me.

"He has The Sight," she said.

"Are you sure?" Mark asked. "Maybe the demon went into him, and that's what you're seeing."

The woman didn't say anything to this, but she rolled her eyes so hard she could have strained her neck. Then she smirked at Mark.

"We have to be certain, Bella. We've been fooled before."

"If he was possessed, he wouldn't have been able to pick up the book."

"He didn't hold it for long."

"I held it long enough." I climbed to my feet and brushed dirt and grass off my jeans. "And you weren't chasing a demon, either. She's a ghost, and her name is Kate."

Mark and Bella exchanged shocked looks. They both turned back to me, but Mark was the first to speak. "You've had fellowship with the dead?"

"That's one way to put it, I guess. She's my friend. And you were scaring her."

"Is she still here?" Mark asked.

I started back towards the bench where I'd dropped the mirror. Before I'd gone three steps, Bella raised her sphere. Golden light filled it, growing brighter as she directed it towards me.

"She's with him," Bella said. "Do you have her anchor?"

I knew what she meant, but her choice of words still made me think of a boat. "What do you want with her? We haven't done anything wrong."

I picked up the mirror, opened it, and panned it around. Kate crouched low, keeping the bench between her and the two strangers.

"She's still glowing, Mel." Kate's eyes locked with mine before she gestured towards the strange woman.

I considered this. If Bella had the means to hurt Kate, she could have done so while Mark and I were on the ground. These strangers worried Kate, but I didn't think they posed a danger unless Mark held his Bible.

"It'll be okay." I tried to make my voice sound reassuring. I shook from the lingering cold and the after effects of adrenaline. I drew a deep, steadying breath. Then I gave Bella and Mark a firm look. "It'll be okay, Kate. I won't let them hurt you."

"You can hear her now?" Bella asked.

"Yes, I can hear her." I cast a quick glance at the mirror, making sure Kate remained in my peripheral vision. "She says that you're glowing. Do you know anything about that?"

"Many creatures of the supernatural can see auras," Bella said. "The auras of practitioners are usually quite brilliant."

Mark regained his feet. He took the few steps necessary to kneel down and reclaim his Bible. Returning to Bella's side, he put an arm around her. "I think it best if we get back to the office. You should come with us."

I looked at Kate. She rose from where she hid behind the bench. She still looked hesitant, but not as scared as she had a moment ago.

"What do you think?" I asked her.

"It's up to you. If they try something like that again, though, I'm going to the car."

"Okay," I said. "We'll come with you. But you have to promise not to do anything that's going to hurt Kate again. She's had a really rough couple of weeks."

"Agreed," said Mark.

And that was how I met The Society of Supernatural Investigations.

10

T HE SOCIETY BASED THEMSELVES out of a narrow office just off of K Street. It nestled between an old garage and an even older bookstore, all three buildings looking like they'd be at home in a war zone. No signage hung over The Society's door, and the windows were painted black. The Society did not offer an impressive first impression.

Inside, things were different. Where the outer face stood in nondescript gray, the inside glowed with warm, dark wood and soft lighting. Stairs and hallways led to rooms and offices I couldn't see. Mark and Bella led me past all that to a cavernous room dominated by a large, black conference table. Mahogany bookshelves concealed three of the four walls. Books old enough and thick enough to be called tomes filled the shelves. Some of the books were bound in leather or wood. In contrast to the ancient books, a computer desk stood out from the fourth wall, along with another table holding a printer and scanner.

"Wow," I said. "It looks like your club is doing alright for itself."

"Please, have a seat," Mark said. He gestured to one of the chairs at the table. "Can I get you something to drink? Mr. Ortega should be with us soon, and then we can talk about what happened in the park."

I stiffened. I felt like they were corralling me, leading me further away from any exits. "Is Mr. Ortega your club leader?"

"We're not a club," Bella said. "We're more like private investigators."

"We aren't going to ask anything of you," Mark said. He gave me a reassuring smile, which did little to ease my apprehension. "We just want to talk. People with gifts like ours are very rare. We might be able to help each other."

I took a steadying breath and tried to relax. I still had a bad feeling about being confined in a strange place, but it was hard to feel too worried when the guards were a priest and a tavern wench. I sat down. "Do you have any beer?"

"I'll see what we've got," Bella said. She departed through a hall leading deeper into the office.

Mark took a seat across from me. He set his Bible in front of him without opening it. I looked at the book and pulled my hands closer to my body.

"I saw what happened with you and the girl." I kept my voice low. I looked over my shoulder. I had no intention of sharing this man's secrets if he didn't want them shared.

It was Mark's turn to stiffen. "Which girl?"

"The one you and Father Philip exorcised."

A pained expression washed over Mark's face. He squared the book in front of him. He kept his eyes there as he spoke. "That was a long time ago. How do you know about that?"

"I saw it when I picked up your book."

"Ah." Mark nodded, without looking up.

An awkward silence grew between us. It felt like I caught him doing something embarrassing that neither one of us wanted to talk about. I knew things about him that I shouldn't be able to know. For a moment, I'd felt what he felt in that room. It was a sudden intimacy thrust upon us that neither one of us welcomed. Mark clasped his hands in front of him on the table. I cleared my throat and let my gaze roam around the various books that surrounded us.

Bella returned with a brown, unlabeled bottle and a tall glass. The bottle had a wire top, which Bella opened with a flourish.

Maybe she really was some sort of tavern wench, right out of some strange fantasy story.

"This is some that Mr. Ortega brews himself," Bella said. She filled my glass with a rich, amber beverage with a thin head of foam.

I muttered my thanks and took a sip. Room temperature and a little bitter, it tasted fine. I might have enjoyed it more if it had been served cold. When it comes to beer, I'm pretty easy. She could have brought me a Coors and I would have been just as happy.

"I caught the name of your companion," Bella said. She took a seat next to Mark. "But I don't think you gave us your name."

"Oh, I'm Mel." I raised my glass to her and smiled.

I'd sipped about a quarter of my beer before Mr. Ortega arrived. We hadn't sat in complete silence, but it was close enough. They'd asked me where I was from, and I told them Louisiana, without elaboration. They didn't volunteer information, and I didn't, either.

We may have been on the verge of chatting about the weather when the exterior door opened with a chime of bells. A man with a dark complexion, immaculate gray suit, and eyes that looked like they were always squinting, entered. He looked like new money. The kind of guy that grew up with dirt under his nails, but now gets a manicure every other week.

"Good evening, Mark. Isabella," Ortega said. He had a thick Hispanic accent and a deep voice. In addition to a priest and a tavern wench, I was now in the company of a Mexican cartel boss.

"Good evening," Mark said. He stood and clasped hands with Ortega. Mark waited for Ortega to take a chair before returning to his seat. "Where's Bobby?"

"He has a show tonight in Rancho. Now. Who have we here?"

Ortega had the body of someone that enjoyed quite a bit of his home-brewed beer over the years. His tailored suit couldn't hide his pronounced belly and weak shoulders. He had a round face, wings of gray in his black hair, and deep crow's feet flanking his perpetually squinting brown eyes. Yet when he turned those dark eyes on me, I saw an intensity that was more than a little bit unsettling.

I stood up and offered Ortega my hand. "Mel Walker."

Ortega's handshake was firm. "Pedro Ortega. Welcome to our office, Mr. Walker. Has Mr. McAdams or Ms. Theroux filled you in on what our organization is about?"

"Not yet, sir. I think they were waiting for you."

"I see. If it pleases you, you may call me Pedro."

We exchanged smiles. I felt uncomfortable and out of place. I had maybe twenty bucks to my name. The last few weeks, I slept in a place that smelled of vomit and urine more often than Clorox and Pledge. These weren't my people, and I wondered what would happen when they realized that.

"I'm a student of archeology," Ortega said. "I've been lucky in some of my digs in Central and South America, and I've been lucky in my investments. But in my studies, I've seen things that could not be explained. Things that defy traditional scientific approaches.

"I founded this organization several years ago, after I met a few individuals that shared certain other, unexplainable experiences. Mr. McAdams is one of the first permanent members of The Society. Ms. Theroux joined us last year.

"Ms. Theroux texted me this evening. She said that you, Mr. Walker, have something in common with us. That you may be special. We would like to talk to you about sharing your gift with us. Maybe even joining us."

I took a long drink from my glass to give myself time to consider. What did these people want from me? What was their angle? Whatever differences there may be between Sacramento and New Orleans, you don't take someone in off the street, give them a beer, and expect nothing in return.

I licked my lips clean and set my glass on the table. "The last person I talked to like this, wanting me to volunteer information, was looking to throw me in jail for something I didn't do. What are you really after, Mr. Ortega?"

Ortega frowned and looked towards one of the bookshelves. "Isabella, would you bring me the Werner Record, volume 2?"

Bella retrieved the book and set it in front of Ortega.

Ortega opened the book, but didn't look at it. "An old Teutonic Knight named Johan Werner wrote about a text he'd acquired shortly after conquering Old Prussia. The text was an account of an older record, which may be an account of something older still. Werner's original text is lost forever, but what we have talks about a cycle, going all the way back to the Great Flood."

Ortega paused. He looked down at the pages, then pushed it in front of me. "At the end of each cycle, there is pestilence. There are storms. And the dead are unable to rest. Does any of that sound familiar?"

I looked at the book, and my stomach twisted in knots. I couldn't read the text, but there were pictures. In one, a tidal wave rolled into a city on the sea. It made me think of New Orleans, and all of the flooding and devastation that came from Hurricane Katrina. I had been one of the lucky ones, but the memories of that storm still hurt.

It took me a moment to find my voice. When I did, it had a harder edge than I intended. "You're talking about the end times."

"The Werner Record doesn't give us a timeline. It doesn't tell us how long the cycle lasts. It just tells us what to expect to see when the bad times start."

I turned to Mark. "I can't see you going along with and accepting all this. Don't you have rules against prophecy and this sort of thing?"

Mark's eyes widened, surprised he'd been brought into the conversation. "I believe that the end will come like a thief in the night. But I think what we're doing here is good work. It's God's work, whatever my friends believe."

"And what work is that, exactly? What does all of this have to do with me? Or Kate?"

At the mention of Kate, Ortega shot Mark a questioning look. Bella leaned forward and said, "A ghost. He has her anchor."

Ortega nodded and turned back to me. "We're trying to minimize the damage. If we are coming to the end of the cycle, we will need to gather information. We'll need to provide proof to the right people that measures need to be taken so mankind will survive. We need to gather together people equipped to battle the rising tide of supernatural agencies. People like Mark and Isabella. People like you, Mr. Walker."

And there it was. The hook I'd been watching for. Ortega had laid out the bait and spun a strange tail as a lure, drawing me in. The problem was I still didn't see why they were fishing for me in the first place.

I turned the question around on them. "What do I get out of joining your club?"

Ortega let out a relieved sigh. He shared a smile with Mark before saying, "We can offer you a modest retainer, and lodging, if you require it. Before we get to that, though, I'd like to know more of what you'll be bringing to The Society. I've gathered that you can communicate with spirits."

"He also may possess psychometry," Mark said.

"Really?" Ortega said, sounding impressed.

"He has The Sight," Bella said. "Though I can't tell to what degree."

"Interesting." Ortega rubbed his chin as he studied me.

"I don't know what this psycho thing is, or The Sight," I said. I glared at Mark and Bella. "But so far, there's only one ghost I've talked to. And she's my friend."

"Can we see the anchor?" Ortega asked.

I hesitated. I didn't know if there would be any harm revealing the vinyl scrap, but I also couldn't shake the feeling they were trying to play me. I reached into my jeans pocket and pulled out the ragged triangle of coal gray material. The limp, slightly damp triangle smelled from traveling across the country stuffed down the front of my pants. I never washed it, too afraid that messing with it would send Kate back to the car.

Ortega drew a pen from an inside pocket of his suit jacket and poked the vinyl. Mark and Bella leaned forward, staring at the material as though I had put something rare and magical in front of them. The level of interest these sophisticated strangers gave my pocket trash struck me as humorous. I covered my mouth and suppressed the urge to laugh.

Bella drew her crystal ball out of a pouch on her belt and held it near the vinyl. The smooth glass caught the light of the office, but did not light up as it had in the park. Bella frowned and gave me an accusing look.

"This isn't an anchor," she said.

"What? No, it has to be. When I took this, Kate was able to follow me."

Bella brought her crystal ball near me and a golden light filled the center. The light started small, but then kept growing brighter and brighter. Before long, a sliver of noonday sunlight rested in the palm of her hand and I had to look away. I shielded my eyes until she withdrew the crystal and put it back in her bag.

"That smelly rag is garbage," Bella said. "If you don't want to trust us, that's fine. But please don't lie to us."

"I'm telling you, that's a piece of the car where she died. I'm not lying to you. I don't have anything else."

Ortega studied me for a moment, rubbing his chin. "Did you make a sacrifice for Kate?"

"What, like killing a chicken or something? No, sir. Never."

Ortega shook his head. "A sacrifice doesn't need to be so literal. It can be any selfless act, where you give up something for the good of another."

I thought back to the gas station, at the outskirts of New Orleans. I thought of the Nova. I remembered the sound of the tool blade cutting into the car seat. It hadn't been like cutting my own flesh, but I remembered feeling like I was giving up more than just a bit of the payday. I said, my voice quiet, "Yeah. I guess I might have made a sacrifice."

Ortega smiled and turned to Bella. "He is the anchor. He's bound her to himself. It's a simple, old magic. Love and sacrifice are the forces that change the world, even if only a little bit at a time. When someone with a gift makes a sacrifice, the effect can be even more dramatic."

I looked at the car seat material, still sitting on the table. I started to feel foolish for carrying the thing around for so long. Then I thought about the park and how Bella and Mark had been gunning for Kate. I didn't even exist in their world until I got in their way. Was this their attempt to separate Kate from me, by getting me to discard the thing that held her to me?

I picked up the vinyl and stuffed it back in my pocket. "Maybe I'm her anchor. Maybe I'm not. I think I'll just go ahead and hold onto this a little longer, if it's all the same to you guys."

A corner of Ortega's mouth quirked up in an amused smile. "Suit yourself. If you're worried about our interest in the ghost of your friend, let me set your mind at ease. We have reason to believe that there is something dangerous moving through downtown Sacramento. Something spiritual in nature, like a ghost or a demon. All we want to do is stop it, putting it to rest before too many people are hurt."

I finished the beer and felt a low buzz. I'm not a lightweight when it comes to alcohol, but it'd been a while since I'd indulged, and I was drinking on an empty stomach. I wasn't drunk, but I was relaxed and pliable. "Alright. I believe you. How can I help? How much is the retainer?"

Ortega smiled and offered to shake my hand. "We'll work out those details tomorrow. Welcome to The Society."

11

T HE RETAINER TURNED OUT to be two hundred fifty a week, and the lodging was an upstairs room in The Society's office. It exceeded my expectations and significantly improved my quality of life. The room contained an old bed made of heavy wood and squeaky springs. A small writing desk stood across from the bed, making the tiny room feel a bit cramped. A private bathroom more than made up for the cozy quarters. I hadn't had my own bathroom since I lived with my parents. Back in Louisiana, my "toilet" involved a shovel, and I took my showers at the gym.

Ortega himself showed me to the room that evening as part of his welcoming tour of the organization. He clapped me on the shoulder and directed my attention to a full length floor mirror, which stood just inside the door. After Ortega left, I adjusted the position of the mirror and sat on the corner of the bed.

"What do you think?" I asked, once I was able to see Kate again.

"I don't know. They make me nervous, but I don't know why. Mr. Ortega seems like a nice fellow, and they seem to have noble intentions."

"Yeah, about that." I shook my head. "I have a hard time believing they're hunting demons out of the goodness of their heart."

"Why?"

"Because that's not what people do. People don't help other people for nothing."

Kate studied me a long moment. "It's what you did. You could have ditched me anywhere along this road, but you didn't."

"That's different."

"To me, it's not."

"Well, I appreciate your high opinion of me. But if they're right, I couldn't have left you if I wanted to. You're stuck with me."

I drew out the wad of gray vinyl and looked at it in my hands. Whether or not it was an anchor holding Kate to me, it connected me to the night my life changed forever. It was the frayed end of a thread leading back to my old life, before ghosts or magic or psychic visions were real. I pulled open the desk drawer and placed the material inside, smoothing it gently.

"Good idea," Kate said. "If you leave that here and I'm bound to this room, we'll know for sure. And maybe it's not too late for you to sneak it back into my parents' house. Not that I mind your company. I just don't want to be a bother to you anymore."

"You're not a bother. Except when you get upset. But imagine how nice that will be in the summer?"

·　　　·　　　·

I slept late the next morning. When I woke, I felt refreshed in a way I hadn't felt since I'd left New Orleans. I showered, shaved, and dressed in fresh jeans and a clean tee shirt. Clean enough, anyway. It smelled vaguely of flowery detergent.

Downstairs, I found Bella sitting in the library conference room. She sat at the massive table, bent over a thick, musty book. A red velvet cloth held her crystal ball like a beer coaster. Her lips moved as she read quietly to herself. The crystal ball pulsed like a heartbeat.

"Good morning," I said. I scrubbed a hand through my hair.

She finished the sentence she was reading before looking up. "Actually, I think it's afternoon, now."

"Oh. What are you reading?"

"It's a copy of a book written by someone that worked with the Knights Templar." She looked up and met my eyes. When she failed to find comprehension there, she continued, "It's a book on magic."

"Ah. So you're some kind of witch?"

She drew in a deep breath and let it out through her nose. "I guess you could say that."

Wearing a red blouse and black pleated skirt, she no longer looked like she belonged to the Ren Faire. She wore her long hair up in an elaborate braid, with rods and clips and other feminine contraptions holding it together. She might have been stunning ten or twenty years ago, but now I found her just vaguely pretty. As I studied her, she looked back at me, tapping her foot silently.

"I'll just go out and see about lunch," I said.

I turned around and started for the front door. Before I had taken two steps, she pushed her chair back and stood.

"Wait up. Let me get my jacket."

•   •   •

We wound up going to a small sandwich shop with outdoor seating. The November day felt warmer than it had the last few weeks, so we took one of the outside tables. It made for a great place to do some people watching.

"I could get used to this," I said after we'd taken our seats.

"The diner?"

"No, California. The weather. The people."

"What is New Orleans like this time of year?"

"Oh. Well, the thing about the weather there is that if you don't like it, just wait a few minutes. It'll change."

Bella smiled and shook her head. "Are we really talking about the weather?"

"I guess? What would you rather talk about?"

"Your ghost." Bella frowned, then said quickly, "The one that's bound to you, I mean. You're not dead yet, so ... ugh. Never mind."

"What do you want to know about Kate?" I pulled out my mirror, unfolded it, and set it on the table. My heart skipped a beat when I didn't immediately find her. I'd left the strip of vinyl back in my room. What did that mean if The Society had been lying about the anchor?

Then Kate appeared behind me. She stood behind me to the left, frowning. I sighed in relief.

"I've fought a few ghosts, but I've never had a chance to ask any of them questions," Bella said. "Let's start with the big one. What's the afterlife like?"

"Boring," Kate said.

I started to laugh, but thought better of it and tried to cover it with a cough. I wiped the smile from my mouth and said, "Kate says it's not quite what she expected it to be."

"Don't start putting words into my mouth!" Kate yelled. Though her voice rose in volume, I felt none of the usual accompanying chill.

"What did she expect it to be?" Bella asked.

I looked into the mirror and met Kate's eyes. She looked away, turning towards the street. The temperature started to drop. I rubbed the goose flesh on my arms before saying, "Maybe we should talk about something else."

"No, it's okay," Kate said. "I guess I thought I was going to go to heaven."

"Is something the matter?" Bella asked. She felt the cold in the air as well, and hugged herself.

"This just hasn't been easy for her. For either of us. How would you feel if you were stuck following someone you didn't really know, all of your dreams and hopes gone? I can't imagine how it must feel to be in Kate's shoes."

Out of the corner of my eye I saw Kate move, lifting her head and reaching a hand out to touch my shoulder. She caught herself and stopped. She gave me a sad smile, which I returned.

"Maybe we can help her find peace," Bella said.

I shook my head. "Whatever Mark was doing to her yesterday was not peaceful."

"No, not like that. Maybe there's some unfinished business that we can help her take care of."

I looked back into the mirror. "What do you think? Is there something you'd like us to do for you?"

"I'd like you two to change the subject."

I grinned. "Let's talk about you instead, Ms. Theroux."

Bella laughed. "Only Mr. Ortega is so formal with me, Mel. Mark calls me Bella. Bobby calls me Izzy. You can call me whatever you like, but you don't strike me as the formal type."

"Alright, Bella it is. How did you come to join The Society of Supernatural Investigators?"

Bella turned away with an expression I couldn't quite read. Was it embarrassment? Pain? She took hold of herself and made her face neutral before turning back to me. "That's a complicated story."

Before I could inquire further, our overly friendly waiter rescued her. He placed plates of sandwiches in front of us, smiling and schmoozing for a future tip. Once he left, I dug in greedily, filling my mouth with salami and provolone. Bella took a more delicate approach, plucking bits off her eggplant and spinach abomination.

After a few bites, I didn't feel quite so ravenous. "So what happened? Did Mr. Ortega put out an ad on Craig's List? 'Secret society seeks sorceress for serious success?'"

As impressive as my alliteration had been, Bella did not look amused. She swallowed her bite, then dabbed at her lips with her napkin. "Mr. Ortega rescued me. I wouldn't be here if he hadn't saved my life."

I glanced at Kate's reflection and bit my tongue. It didn't seem polite to either lady to mention something that struck me as obvious. Whether or not Ortega saved her, she could have been here. Just less corporeal.

"So ... you got lucky?" I asked.

"Something like that."

We ate the rest of our lunch in silence. Bella nibbled at her sandwich, her expression thoughtful, while my meal vanished more quickly. After I made my sandwich disappear, Bella offered me half of hers. It was some sort of organic or free range thing, but I accepted it and ate it without complaint. I didn't want to be rude, after all.

On the way back to the office, Bella said, "I'm going to try and find that demon again. Would you like to try and help me?"

I stopped picking food from my teeth. "How do you know there's a demon?"

"I don't, for sure. There isn't much hard evidence. Homeless people have been disappearing off the streets. In one case, a witness said he saw his friend pulled straight into the air and dropped in the American River. Another witness said an unnatural cold came over them before her friend disappeared. None of these witnesses are particularly reliable. But the spell I cast to detect spirits is never wrong."

"That's how you found Kate?"

"Yes." She sounded embarrassed.

"Can you teach me magic?"

Bella gave me an appraising look as we walked. "Hmm. I'm not sure. You might be able to learn."

"You seem a little doubtful."

"You're not the first person to ask me to try and teach them what I do. I tried showing Bobby, but it didn't work for him. Maybe it will for you."

"Who is Bobby?"

"His stage name is Robert Greenwood. He's sort of our marketing director. He's really good at cold reading people, and he does this show on stage where he puts people in contact with their dead relatives. Only, it's all an act. There isn't anything supernatural about him at all."

"You're saying that Robert Greenwood pretends to do what I started doing by accident?"

"That's one way of putting it. You and he ought to get along smashingly."

For some reason, I had my doubts about that.

12

BACK AT THE OFFICE, Bella led me to a mid-sized kitchen at the back of the building. I thought it was a kitchen, anyway. A stove and range lined one wall, two refrigerators along another. A microwave occupied a counter beneath a set of cupboards. If you needed to throw the kitchen sink at someone, this was the room to come for ammo. It had three, one set against the far wall, another pair in an island counter.

A second look around the room revealed it to be some sort of lab. Next to the refrigerators stood glass shelves full of beakers and glassware, the envy of chemists or would-be Heisenbergs. Racks of shelves contained items dry and wet, living and dead, colorful and drab, with labels and dates marking each specimen. Subtle arcane symbols decorated each wall, etched into the brick and sheet rock with what I guessed was a Dremel tool. In an open cabinet next to the oven sat a heavy, iron cauldron. A heavy metal grate supported the large pot. Beneath the grate, a shallow pit lined with stones waited for logs or coal, or whatever other fuel they used.

Bella must have seen the questioning look on my face. "If you get hungry, the black fridge is the one with food. The silver one is for other stuff."

I nodded. "So are we going to brew a potion or something?"

"We're going to heat one up. There's something called the Third Eye, or The Mind's Eye, or sixth sense. It goes by many names. Eventually, I should be able to open my Third Eye on my own, but I haven't figured it out yet. For now, I use a concoction I got out of one of the books in the library."

"What's in it?"

Bella gave me another appraising look. "Do you have a queasy stomach?"

"Sometimes."

"Then you don't want to know."

Bella opened the silver fridge and picked up a pitcher filled with thick, gray liquid. She poured some in a glass. It ran with the consistency of lumpy pancake batter. She started to pour some in a second glass, then stopped. "Do you even need this stuff?"

"I don't know. What's it like for you, when you open your Third Eye?"

Bella lowered the pitcher and rubbed her chin with her free hand. "You know those hidden image pictures that are made of a bunch of dots, but if you stare long enough and let your eyes cross, you see a dolphin or a horse or something? It's like that, only it's not just a little picture, it's everything. And instead of a dolphin, you see auras and spirits and things that people think are impossible."

I thought about my experience in the Nova, when I was able to see Kate without a mirror. "If I can already open my mind's eye, will this stuff hurt me?"

"I don't think so. It didn't do anything at all for Bobby. I don't recommend drinking lots of it, but that's just because it can damage your kidneys. A little shouldn't hurt you, though."

Bella's words did not reassure me, but I've always been more curious than cautious. "Alright, bartender. Give me a shot."

She poured a second glass. After putting the pitcher away, she set both glasses in the microwave. She tapped in thirty seconds, and the microwave began to whir.

"This *is* magic, right?" I watched the pair of glasses do little pirouettes through the microwave door.

"It is. Specifically alchemy, but still magic."

"I just wouldn't expect a microwave to be part of the spell."

"Technically, it isn't. I just find it's a little easier to chug down when it's warm."

We took our magic-nogs back to the library. Bella set her glass on a coaster and began going through a short cupboard next to the computer desk. She set out a crystal on a long string, some incense, and a lighter. Then she went to a bookshelf, pulling off a couple of books, one old and brittle looking, the other glossy and colorful.

She scooped up her glass and raised it in a toast. "Here's to the other side."

I clinked mine to hers. "Livers that we're about to destroy, we salute you."

We chugged our drinks in unison. It tasted worse than I expected, worse than I could imagine. I nearly choked as the concoction tried to turn around and come back up. It didn't smell like anything, but it felt oily, and had a strong, sour and salty aftertaste. It made me think of chewing raw grass or tin foil, and it clung to the back of my mouth. I swallowed several times, and my throat started to hurt with the effort.

I looked at Bella. Aside from wrinkling her nose, she didn't look upset.

"I guess you get used to it," I said.

She shrugged and smiled. "It helps if you don't fight it. I just put it my mouth and try to imagine something else. Kind of like ..." She trailed off, a wistful look on her face. It took me a moment to catch the innuendo, but when I did, I laughed.

It didn't take long for the magic-nog to start working. Warmth spread from my belly, radiating out from my center. My hands felt cold and tingly, like they'd gone to sleep. The shadows in the back of my mind melted, and a soft, gentle illumination crystallized my thoughts and memory. I didn't feel high or drunk. I felt different. Open.

I turned around in a slow circle. Books stood out that I hadn't noticed before. They didn't glow, exactly. I can't say how they were different, but looking at them with the Third Eye, I knew they were special. Magical. Other items I'd ignored as decoration stood out in a similar way. A candle holder sitting next to the computer. A letter opener. A figurine depicting a ballerina caught in mid spin, poised on the tips of her toes.

Before I could complete the circle, I saw Kate. She stood near the entrance to the library, her yellow dress bright, her skin healthy and vibrant. She regarded me with bright blue eyes, one slender eyebrow arched. She no longer looked like a figure ripped out of an old photograph. In that moment, she looked more real and more beautiful than anything else in the library.

"Mel, are you okay?" Kate asked. Her voice sounded clear and musical.

"Yeah." The word came out as a croak. I cleared my throat. "You look real enough to touch."

"It's better if you don't," Bella said from behind me. "Doing things that defy your senses has a tendency to ground you and close you off. If you pass your hands through her with the elixir in your system, it might make you sick."

"Can you see her?" I asked.

"No." Bella sounded disappointed. "That's your gift, not mine."

"Stop staring," Kate said, smiling. She waved her hands at me in a shooing motion. "Get back to your magic lesson."

I turned, but it was difficult to look away. I couldn't get over how radiant Kate looked, with her hair made of sunlight. Once again, I wished that I'd met her when she was still alive.

"Alright." I focused on Bella. To my surprise, I noticed a subtle aura surrounding Bella's head, like a silver halo. "You're glowing, a little bit."

"You are, too," Bella said. "Now let's see what you can do."

The glossy book on the table turned out to be full of street maps for the Sacramento area. A thin line along its spine marked where it had been opened until it broke. Bella flipped to a page showing the downtown area and the book remained where she opened it. I looked at the crystal on the string, still untouched on the table. I saw where this was going. I picked up the crystal to hand it to Bella, but a shock of energy raced into me. It passed through the skin of my hand, up along the bones of my arm, raced past my neck, and into my brain. As had happened with Mark's bible, a vision overwhelmed me.

Bella stood on the other side of the table from Mark, the dowsing crystal and string in her hand. Mark paced the length of the room, his lips moving in silent prayer. From time to time, Bella wondered how Mark was able to reconcile what they were doing with the whole "suffer not a witch to live." If she wanted to, she could borrow Mark's Bible and find the passage. She wondered what he'd do if she showed it to him. Perhaps the importance of what they were doing transcended religion and philosophy.

Bella opened her notebook and read the pseudo-Latin phrase she'd marked out earlier in the day. Her mind conjured up the memory of her first lesson in magic. Spells were a matter of intention and will; the words helped to focus both into action.

"Videre praeterita umbras," Bella said. A surge of energy welled up from her belly. From her womb. The energy rose slowly, flowing along her veins and her bones to her extremities and towards her eyes. As the sense of energy and purpose reached her outstretched hand, she let the dowsing crystal drop towards the map.

The vision ended as abruptly as it began. I gasped.

"Whoa. That was-" I started to say something else, but another vision pulsed out of the crystal, overwhelming me.

"I can't believe you hid my keys," Bobby said. He gritted his teeth and stared daggers at Izzy. She sat at the head of the conference table, smiling and tapping one of her teeth with a long, lacquered nail. Bobby leaned forward, his fists on the surface of the table. It was past time he put an end to this little charade.

"There has to be real need for the spell to work," Izzy said, taking on that lecturing tone that Bobby hated. "The greater the need, the more likely the spell will work."

Bobby scowled and tried to picture his keys in his mind. He'd envisioned this day unfolding differently. First, she'd teach him a little bit of magic. Maybe they would need to strip off all of their clothes for the magic to work properly. Her cheeks would flush, but then she would guide him. Then they would go up the stairs, and he'd teach her his own kind of magic. They would ...

"Need helps us tap into our primal selves," Izzy said, drawing him back to reality. She still spoke with the deliberation of a kindergarten teacher. "It helps us get back to our instincts."

Bobby shook his head and tried to focus again. It proved challenging, with the taste of the foul concoction still curdling in the back of his throat. Why couldn't it have been a nice red wine? And why hadn't she taken any for herself? This had to be some kind of joke at his expense. He knew it.

He cleared his throat and spoke the words from the notebook. "Vie dear pray tear it a umber ass."

Izzy opened her mouth to say something. Before she could voice her protest, Bobby let the crystal drop.

I dropped the crystal back to the table before it could grab me again. Bella looked at me with her eyes narrowed and her head cocked to one side.

"Do that again," she said.

"No. I don't want to."

"You saw something, didn't you?"

I drew in a deep breath and tried to center myself. I lowered my voice and recited what I'd heard twice, once in each vision. "Videre Praeterita Umbras."

Bella's eyes widened. She picked up the crystal. "I've been studying magic for a little over a year now, and I still get excited when stuff like this happens."

"You get visions, too?"

"I wouldn't call them visions, exactly. I get feelings. My intuition becomes stronger and more specific. I couldn't snatch words out of the past like you just did. If I could, that would make some of what I do much easier."

"Your intuitions weren't too sharp when you tried to get Bobby to do this." I leaned against the table, imitating what I'd seen Bobby do. I straightened and said, "He was really upset with you."

"Oh, you saw that?"

"And I saw you with Mark. Last night, if I had to guess. You were wondering how you and Mark were able to get along as well as you do."

"Marvelous!" Bella hopped up and down, clapping her hands. Then she slid the map book in my direction and gestured towards the crystal. "So you know what I felt and what I was thinking? Can you do the spell?"

I reached for the crystal again, but stopped just short of taking it. "You said that need makes us tap into our primal instincts, or something like that. What is it I'm looking for?"

"The demon or spirit that's been abducting the homeless."

I hesitated again before taking the crystal, but not for fear of another vision. I was afraid of succeeding. If something supernatural hunted and killed people for sport, did I really want to have anything to do with it?

"You can do it, Mel," Kate said.

I swallowed down the bile that had risen to the back of my throat. With a shaking hand, I took up the dowsing crystal. A surge of visions pressed against my palm, and my knees buckled. I put my free hand on the table and steadied myself. The visions surged against my skin. I felt their potential, like standing near a high-voltage line. They wanted to be seen, to drive into my brain like electricity going to ground, but I held them at bay.

I breathed a sigh of relief. I could hold back the visions and retain my own senses. Now that I'd done it once, I felt like I could keep doing it. It felt natural, like breathing or blinking. How do I describe what it's like to do something so automatic? Once you're aware of what you're doing, you just do it.

"You've used the hell out of this thing, haven't you?" I asked.

"I've tried to." Bella shrugged.

I shook my head. For a moment, I forgot my fear. Some sort of spectral monster waited out there in the shadows. I was about to shine a light on it. I took a deep breath and steadied myself. "Okay. Let's try this."

"It helps if you close your eyes."

I closed my eyes, but I could still see the room. I shut my eyelids more tightly and felt a brief, dizzying panic when the room around me refused to darken. If anything, it seemed brighter. Luminescent, and hyper-real, like Kate.

"Wow, that's weird. That stuff I drank is really fucking with me, Bella."

"Why, what do you see?"

"You. The table. The room. Everything. I can see with my eyes closed."

I tried to turn to towards Kate, but something else happened. I felt a sensation of turning, of corkscrewing in one direction without physically moving. Like that first night with the Nova, when I first met Kate. The sense of moving without moving confused me and made me unsteady, disrupting my balance like a spun coin wobbling on its side.

Bella's lips moved, but I couldn't hear her voice. She shrugged. Then I saw my hand place the crystal on the table, the string winding itself into a curl to one side. My hand hovered over the crystal a moment, until Bella gestured towards the crystal. Bella placed the tips of her fingers against the map book, and it slid back towards her. She straightened and hopped up and down, smiling and clapping. Her lips moved again, but I still couldn't hear her.

"What?" I asked.

"I didn't say anything," Bella said. Bella's words were out of synch with her lips.

Even though I watched myself put the crystal down, I could still feel it in my hand. Then I realized what was happening and gave the crystal a gentle squeeze.

"I'm seeing the immediate past. Like someone just hit the rewind button."

The sensation of turning persisted. My stomach flopped and writhed while the sense of twisting to my right continued. My life played itself out backwards. Instincts took over. By force of will, I made what I was seeing slow down and stop. Bella stood in the middle of turning towards the drawer that held the crystal and lighter. Her image faced me, slightly stooped over, offering a generous view down her shirt. I put my hand over my mouth to suppress a laugh.

"What's so funny?" Bella asked.

I opened my eyes. I saw two Bellas. The one from the past stood superimposed over the living, breathing woman of the present. I concentrated on dismissing the vision of the past, pushing it away the same way I'd kept the visions from entering me from the crystal. The vision resisted at first, but then faded like a memory. I looked around the room with my eyes open. Magical books and knickknacks still stood out from the mundane, but the room looked pretty much as it had before I drank the magic-nog. Perhaps a little darker.

I looked at Bella and saw that she still had a questioning look on her face. I wiped my face with my hands, feeling weirded out and just a touch nauseous. "It was nothing."

Bella pointed at the crystal in my hands. "Are you ready to try the spell?"

I closed my eyes again. The world around me brightened, the shadows of reality disappeared. I could feel how I might turn, rewinding time to replay the past around me. I resisted the urge.

My breathing slowed, and I tried to feel that sense of energy that I'd felt when the vision showed me the world through Bella's eyes. My stomach churned. My nausea intensified. I wondered if the elixir in my stomach was getting ready to make another escape attempt. I continued to try and feel what Bella had felt.

When Bella performed the spell, the desire to find the thing hurting people had been clear in her mind. I focused my thoughts and feelings. I couldn't quite match what I remembered from her perspective. My thoughts churned, as sluggish and roiling as the feeling building in my stomach.

Bella had felt something radiating out from her belly. I felt something rising from my stomach. Sweat beaded my brow, and I concentrated. I leaned forward and said through clenched teeth, "Videre! Praeterita! Umbra-"

The last word turned into a protracted retching. Magic-nog, stomach acid, and partially digested sandwiches came up in a rush. The former contents of my stomach flooded the streets contained in the maps of Sacramento. The crystal slipped from my hands and landed in a shallow puddle with a small splash.

"Okay," Bella said, wincing. She turned away, pinching the bridge of her nose. "I think that's enough magic for you today."

13

S TILL FEELING QUEASY, I prepared myself to clean up the mess
I made. Bella pointed me towards the broom closet. I pulled out
a mop and bucket, then dragged them to the kitchen for water. By
the time I wheeled the bucket back to the conference room, Bella
had acquired a stack of towels. As I mopped and scrubbed, with my
stomach performing Olympic level acrobatics, I considered the lack
of practical magic. We had no enchanted brooms or magical elves
ready to help with the hard work. Apparently, real magic doesn't
resemble anything out of a Disney cartoon. I wished it did. If a wish
was a dream your heart makes, then my heart dreamed of nose
plugs and a powerful wet vac with every stomach spasm and wave
of dizziness.

When I threw up, my mind's eye closed. The world cracked back
into normalcy with the same sting as a snapped rubber band, and my
head throbbed to the rhythm of my heartbeat. Through the
discomfort, I remembered Kate laughing just before my supernatural
senses shut down. I thought about that laugh while I mopped, and I
smiled. I had never heard her laugh like that before.

Once we cleaned the room, Bella replaced the books and the crystal on the table. She lit incense, closed her eyes, and began to meditate with the crystal in her hand. I sat in one of the chairs and rubbed my temples while I watched her. The headache felt sharpest just behind my eyes, like a hangover after drinking too much wine.

Bella spoke the phrase of the spell I witnessed during the vision. She opened her hand and let the crystal drop over the map. The cut stone dropped faster than it should have, and the cord went taut, humming like a plucked guitar string. In her other hand, Bella held her crystal ball. Light inside it flared in rhythmic pulses.

Bella opened her eyes. We both looked down at the book. The crystal pulled towards the map like iron towards a magnet. The tip veered away from downtown proper, and quivered between 22nd and 23rd, on one of the upper letter streets.

"There's some older townhouses in that area." Bella passed her orb beneath the dowsing crystal, and the string went slack. "Once Mark gets here, we'll go investigate."

"Wait. I don't know if I'm ready for this. I agreed to join your club, but I don't know about ghost busting yet."

Bella started to put the crystal ball away, then stopped. She frowned at me like I was a difficult math problem that needed to be solved.

"I need to tell you something that Kate may not want to hear," Bella said. "Would you ask her to leave for a few minutes, so we can have some privacy?"

I pulled out the mirror and found Kate within it.

"It's not like I have much choice," Kate said. "I'm stuck here, or has she forgotten?"

I opened my mouth to repeat Kate's words, but before I could say anything, Bella's crystal ball flashed with a cold blue light.

"Spiritus et abierant," Bella said. The air whipped around us, stirring pages. The sudden wind picked up smoke from the incense, stinging my eyes. I squeezed them shut, wincing away from the blast. When the air stilled, I opened my eyes and looked in the mirror. Kate was gone.

"What did you do?" I said, my voice a rough whisper.

"I just sent her away for a little bit. She's fine. Don't worry, she'll be able to come back in a few minutes. It really is better if she doesn't hear what I have to tell you."

I took several deep breaths, trying to calm down. It bothered me that Bella could send Kate away like that. Kate deserved sympathy and respect, and Bella just discarded her like an empty beer can.

"We may not find a ghost when we go to investigate the town house," Bella said. "But if we do, you're going to get a chance to see what will eventually happen to Kate."

"I'm listening."

"Eventually, Kate is going to become a monster. The further she gets from the time of her death, the more out of touch with humanity she'll become. If she's lucky, she'll find peace and move on before it gets too bad. But because she's anchored to you, it is much more likely she'll grow angrier and colder until there isn't anything left but pain."

I stared at Bella, unable to speak. What do you say when the doctor tells you your friend has cancer? Kate died once already. If Bella were to be believed, she was going to die a second time, only worse.

"What can we do?"

"Help her find peace. There is probably some issue holding her here, and she may not even know what it is. If we can help her find closure, she'll be ready to say goodbye to this world and move on to the next. That's the best we can hope for her."

"And if we can't help her go peacefully?"

"Then we'll put her down before she hurts anyone."

"You seem pretty calm for talking about destroying a human being. It really doesn't bother you?"

Bella frowned and looked away. "She died before I met you, Mel. People die all the time. We can't afford to get too attached to the dead. We have to do what we can for the living."

I looked down at the mirror. Still empty. "I'm not sure I can go with you to the haunted house now. I'm not ready for this."

Bella picked up her crystal ball and slipped it into a velvet-lined bag. "We're just going to look around. I understand if you're scared, but it's never going to get less strange, and it's never going to get any easier. The best way to handle this is to just jump in with both feet."

"Maybe." I remained unconvinced. A pit widened in the core of my stomach that had nothing to do with the foul drink from earlier. Fear clawed at my insides. I tried to clamp it down and focus on practical matters. "At the haunted house. What about Kate? If Mark has to go Holier than Thou again to destroy the spirit there, how do we know Kate will be okay?"

"If Kate is in any danger, you'll know, and you'll be able to stop us." Bella sounded confident. "If the spell is pointing us towards something else, something supernatural that doesn't mean anyone harm, then we'll need you to stop us then, too. But that is very unlikely."

"I just don't understand. You say Kate is going to go bad eventually, but why? Why can't there be friendly ghosts, just hanging out?"

"Because being alone with nothing but unresolved issues will drive anyone mad after enough time. Being in the world, unable to touch it? You have no idea how terrible that is. Unable to eat, or touch, or be with the ones you love in any real sense. It's a prison sentence with no hope of release."

"Okay, I get it. It's really bad. Worse than anything I can imagine. Like waiting in line at the DMV forever. I hear the words you're saying. I just don't believe it."

I shivered, then rubbed my arms with my hands. I didn't have to look into the mirror to know that Kate returned and was pissed. Frost painted the insides of the blacked out windows, and the walls groaned from the sudden drop in temperature.

"She put me back in the car," Kate said through clenched teeth.

"Oh? Where is it now?" I asked. Maybe I could distract her with questions before she started to ask some of her own.

"I couldn't tell," Kate said. "It looked like a parking lot. Lots of other cars all around."

"We're getting ready to go to check out a haunted house. You ready to go?"

I met Kate's eyes in the mirror and saw fire. She looked ready to claw someone's eyes out. Whatever we were about to face, one truth became clear to me: I better grab a jacket.

14

WRAPPED IN MY FADED denim jacket, I looked towards the mid-day sun. Mark and Bella stood to my left and right, the three of us making a small mob on the sidewalk in front of the haunted house. We'd walked from The Society office, the wind whipping and biting at us the entire way and spreading loose autumn leaves across our path. Though the sun still shone brightly, the shadows of nearly naked trees blanketed us, granting a taste of the approaching winter.

Bella's orb led us to a faded white townhouse. Broad steps reached up to a shallow porch on the second floor. The shuttered upstairs windows frowned down at us as we looked at the property. A sign in front indicated the place was for sale. Ragged clumps of brown grass and broken weeds told me it had been empty for some time.

"What now?" I asked.

Mark extended his hands towards me and Bella. "Now, we pray."

I rolled my eyes, but accepted the outstretched hand. Once Bella clasped Mark's other hand, the priest closed his eyes. She studied the former priest, her lips tight and her eyes narrowed.

From the vision earlier, I knew how she felt about Mark's faith. She respected it, but she didn't share it. I kept my mouth shut and tried to emulate Bella.

"Lord," Mark said. "We thank You for the gifts You've bestowed us, and we ask for the strength of heart to see Your will be done. Give us the wisdom to know when to act in Your name, and when to remain still. We walk in the shadow of the valley of death, but we will not be afraid, for You are with us. Thank You for Your goodness and Your mercy, and Your grace, until the day we dwell in Your house forever and ever. In Jesus' name, amen."

I mumbled something that could be construed as "amen" and my thoughts ran back to my childhood and all the times my mother dragged me to church. Momma would have appreciated Mark's prayer. In the rustic, ramshackle church of my youth, the congregation roiled with praying and singing and falling on the floor. The words Mark used matched those of my old pastor, but Mark's carried something different, and his face held something I never saw before. A kind of certainty, as solid and unflinching as old stone.

"We might as well go in," Bella said.

I looked at the house again and shuddered. It looked the same as before, but it had changed in my mind. The building ceased being a vacant house for sale and became an occupied lair, home to some malevolent spirit or demon that made a habit of taking people off the street. An actual haunted house, and we stood on the verge of entering.

We ascended the stairs, the wooden planks creaking their disapproval. A gust of wind slipped a finger down the collar of my jacket, raising goose flesh and making me shiver. I let out a nervous laugh, feeling the first hints of hysteria beginning to take root. I dug into my pocket and fished out my mirror.

Bella held her crystal ball in her left hand and opened the door with her right. The doorknob refused to turn, but the door hadn't been latched. It swung open with a gentle push. The light of Bella's orb filled the front room, revealing wadded newspaper, fast food wrappers, and nests of tattered blankets.

"Squatters," I said. "That's not so bad."

"Maybe they're the ones that have been disappearing," Mark said.

We crossed the threshold, Bella and Mark in front of me. Bella held her crystal ball high and walked slowly, turning her head left and right. Mark held his Bible open in both hands, alternating between scanning the room and scanning the page. I felt like I should have some sort of talisman, too, so I held up my mirror. I saw Kate following behind me, tiptoeing and looking as nervous as I felt.

Behind Kate, I saw the front door slam behind us. Even though I watched it happen, I still let out a startled scream and jumped, turning to face the door. To my surprise, Bella also squealed. Her eyes were as big around as mine. Seeing my fear reflected in her face made me feel a little bit less alone. It did nothing to reassure me, but it helped, knowing that we were in this together.

"That happens, sometimes," Mark said. He hadn't jumped, and he spoke with the same certainty and confidence he'd shown when he prayed. "It just means we're in the right place."

I scanned around with my mirror, looking for Kate. I found her standing deeper in the room, putting Mark between her and the door.

"Did you see anything?" I asked.

"No," Kate said. "If I wasn't a ghost, I think I would have peed a little."

I walked over to the door and tried to open it. Having seen enough scary movies, I expected to find the door locked, trapping us inside and sealing our doom. It opened easily. It didn't even squeak.

"Okay, so we can leave if we want to," I said.

"Our work is not yet done," Mark said.

We searched through the piles of blankets and trash. Each blanket I touched came with visions, which I held off. As nervous as I felt, I didn't want my senses swept away, even if it was only for a moment.

"Let's try some other rooms," Bella said.

The floorboards creaked as we moved through dark hallways. In the next room, we found two more blankets and a frequently patched rain coat. When I touched the coat, a strong vision pressed against me. I strained to keep it from taking over before dropping the coat back to the floor.

Bella frowned at me. "Did you see something?"

"Almost." I pushed the coat towards her with the toe of my shoe. "I think I'm getting the hang of keeping the visions out of my head."

"Mel, we need you to look."

"Why? All I'm going to see is someone sad and down on his luck. I've seen enough of that myself already."

Bella placed a hand on my shoulder and gave it a gentle squeeze. "I know you're nervous. It's okay. We're here with you. We'll keep you safe."

"The Lord is with us," Mark said.

I rubbed my face with both hands. Through the cracks in my fingers, I looked down at the coat. The lumpy brown and gray garment didn't appear menacing in any way. Just a bit of clothing left on the floor. With a groan, I bent to pick it up.

The vision began as soon as I touched it.

The nice weather held out longer than most years, but the cold and wet couldn't stay away forever. Nikolay walked along the street, huddled into his coat as the first of the fall rains poured down upon him. The coat didn't do much to keep the rain from getting in, but it beat facing the weather in just his street clothes. Maybe this year, he wouldn't get sick.

He needed to find a different place to hang his hat for a while. The shelter he liked best started to fill with strangers claiming more and more space. He could count on one hand the people at the shelter he actually knew. Walter, the heavy Samoan that had been a doctor in his previous life. Juan and Carla, the couple that drifted up from Los Angeles. The new kid, Mel, that talked to himself when he didn't think anyone was looking. And Janet, the woman that shared Nikolay's blanket on more than one occasion.

Janet might still share a bed if he asked, but he knew he wouldn't. She ran with a different crowd these days. With her teeth turning black and her preference for long sleeves, even during the hottest days of summer, Nikolay knew better than to warm himself by her fire.

Of course, others in the shelter shared Janet's habit of seeking escape. Juan had long been a fan of weed and always seemed able to keep a stash. According to the grapevine, Walter somehow managed to keep his fill of the same prescription meds that ended his career. If Mel's secret conversations weren't the product of hallucinogens ... it didn't take a genius to see the writing on the wall. Nikolay planned on being somewhere else when the shelter popped like an overinflated balloon.

The rumor mill whispered about something going on at a house on O Street. If true, an abandoned house stood with its doors open. Either the neighbors were away or they were turning a blind eye towards people crashing at the house. It sounded like a good place to get in out of the rain and wind and wait out the storms, both literal and figurative.

Standing on the sidewalk, shrouded in the dark of night, Nikolay looked up at the house. All of its empty windows reflected street lights, the blackness inside making them perfect mirrors. A "For Sale" sign stood in the front yard next to the narrow driveway. Nikolay crept up the stairs, head down. He pulled his coat tighter around him. The locked-but-unlatched door opened with a gentle shove. He let himself in, closing the door behind him.

The rumors were true. Two others claimed the front room ahead of him. Empty blankets along one wall made up a hard bed. In a corner near the front window, a man lay curled into a ball, snuggled into a bed of his own. The smell of cheap beer wafted off him, filling Nikolay's nostrils. The sleeping man continued to snore, undisturbed by Nikolay's entry.

Tiptoeing, Nikolay moved slowly down the hall and turned into the first room on the right. The only light in the house came from the street lights outside. The light streamed in through the uncovered window, pooling in a yellow rectangle on the floorboards. The patter of rain on the roof sounded distant. Nikolay let out a sigh and relaxed his shoulders.

"This will do for now," he said.

"Where is she!?" The woman's voice came as a rasp from behind him.

Nikolay's heart lurched. He turned to face the woman. Something flashed out of the corner of his eye. Something heavy and hard struck Nikolay in the head. Pain chased away all other thought, and blackness consumed him.

I dropped the jacket and ducked. The vision receded, but Nikolay's fear and pain still gripped me. I turned in place, looking for the person that struck Nikolay from behind. The only people I could see in the room were Bella and Mark.

"Are you okay?" Bella asked. She grabbed my shoulders and stopped my frantic turning.

"I'm okay." My heartbeat slowed back to a normal pace. I took several deep breaths. After a few moments of steady breathing, I knelt down and looked closely at the floor. I traced my finger along a brown spot on the hardwood. "I'm okay, but Nikolay isn't."

Bella and Mark knelt with me. Bella's orb illuminated the blood stain, making it more obvious.

"What did you see?" Mark asked, his voice deep, steady, and calm.

I explained it as best I could. I felt guilty as I described Nikolay's thoughts, like I was revealing someone's trusted secrets. I described how Nikolay had known who I was with shame and disbelief. I couldn't help but wonder if Nikolay would still be alive if I hadn't been staying at the shelter.

Bella must have read some of what I was feeling. Once I finished describing the vision, she said, "It's not your fault. You had nothing to do with him leaving the shelter."

"Maybe." I rubbed unshed tears from my eyes with my palms. Some of the tears had been from the pain at the end of the vision. That's what I told myself, though I knew there were other reasons I wanted to cry.

We looked through the rest of the room and found other spots on the floor that could have been blood. It may have been Nikolay's, or it could have been from someone else. It could have been evidence of a tomato soup spill. None of us were forensic specialists, and none of the splatters invoked a psychic vision.

"Let's try downstairs," Mark said.

15

WE DESCENDED TO THE COLDER, lower floor, leaving behind the light from the windows above. Bella's orb provided sufficient illumination, but the chill cut through everything, seeping through my jacket to prickle my skin. Bella shivered next to me, our shadows quivering and shaking as though afraid. Mark appeared unaffected by the cold, as resolute and imperturbable as ever.

"If this was a movie," I said, "this is where we'd split up and one of us would get killed."

"It's a good thing we're not that stupid," Bella said. She did not sound amused.

"Let's check the kitchen," Mark said.

A cramped hallway with creaky wooden flooring led to the kitchen at the back of the house, which the owners had adorned with white tiles and brass fixtures. Cupboards lined the walls, the well-used doors revealing old wood beneath flaking paint. A battered faucet craned its swan's neck over a chipped sink. It dribbled slow, heavy droplets, plunking away the silence. An open area between the counter and one wall yawned mildew and dust, a hungry mouth waiting to be filled with a refrigerator.

I started for the drawers next to the range. A scratching sound from behind us stopped me before I could pull the drawer handle. Not scratching. More like something heavy dragged across the wooden floor. I turned to look. Not fast enough. A strange man lurched towards Mark.

"Where is she?" The stranger swung a heavy length of pipe. It whistled through the air before smashing into the side of Mark's head. The hollow pipe rang like an aluminum bat crashing into a fastball. Mark fell in a limp heap, his Bible falling open next to him.

"Mark!" Bella yelled.

Our attacker, a tall man dressed for hard life on the street, smelled of urine and alcohol. A scraggly black beard covered the lower half of his face and part of his neck. His bloodshot eyes looked at us without emotion from the shadows of his dirty face. A thin line of drool hung from the corner of his mouth, which hung open, his jaw slack. In the bright light of Bella's crystal ball, he looked like a zombie. He wasted no time raising his weapon again, swinging it at Bella with both arms.

Bella recoiled. I moved on instinct. I pulled the nearest drawer out and swung it in a high arc. It met the attacker's pipe. The drawer exploded in a shower of splinters and wood fragments. The pipe deflected, whirring over Bella's head and missing her by inches.

The light in the crystal ball changed from amber to crimson. Bella's face twisted in rage. She slammed an open hand into the man's chest.

"*Apage!*" she shouted.

The headache I'd felt earlier came back, sudden and sharp. It felt like knives driven into my temples. I staggered to one knee. In the span of a heartbeat, the pain broke, my mind's eye snapping open. The silver halo circling Bella's head rolled down her arm, moving past her outstretched hand. The light struck the attacker's chest, penetrating it. A silhouette of a woman flew out from the man's back.

The man collapsed, rag-dolling next to where Mark lay on the ground. The apparition floated beyond him, her narrowed eyes fixed on Bella. Stringy black hair swirled around her head as though she were under water. Rags covered her body. Gore covered her hands up to her elbows. Her mouth turned into a snarl before she fled from the kitchen, a swift black shadow stretching long and thin.

"She ran," I said.

Bella ignored me. She dropped to her knees next to Mark and checked for a pulse. From where I stood, I could see his chest rise and fall. Blood ran from a gash on his head, pooling on the floor around him.

"Bella." I kept my voice low and quiet. "The man that attacked us was possessed."

"I know." Bella picked up the Bible, closed it, and set it gently on Mark's chest. She folded his hands over the book. Her voice became steady and even, as if trying to match the priest's unflappable calm. "You said it was a woman?"

"Yeah. She looked like one of the homeless. Her hands were covered in blood."

"I could see her, too," Kate said, startling me.

"Holy shit, Kate."

"Sorry." Kate stepped around from behind me to stand next to Bella.

"So what's the plan now?" I asked, looking at Bella. "We can't just leave Mark here."

"No. You need to go find some help."

"Split up? I thought we weren't that stupid."

"Things have changed. Mark is the only one of the three of us that can destroy a ghost. I can chase it away, but that's only while it possesses someone."

I looked at the stranger passed out next to Mark. "What about that guy? Is it safe to leave you with him alone?"

"I don't know." Bella shook her head. "When he wakes up, he probably won't remember anything he did while possessed. If he wakes up."

I noticed Kate chewing her lower lip, frowning in the direction of the hallway. "What's the matter?"

"I don't know. There was something really wrong about her."

I turned back to Bella. "If she comes back, will she be able to possess you?"

Bella shook her head. "No. And from what I read, she shouldn't be able to possess you, either."

"Shouldn't?"

"Look, this isn't science." The fake calm broke and Bella raised her voice. "There aren't many rules set in stone. It's more chaos than order. We should be safe from possession but we won't really know until she tries."

I didn't have a response to that. I looked down at Mark and felt my stomach writhe. So much blood covered the floor. It surrounded him. I turned my gaze back towards the hallway, in the direction the possessing spirit had gone.

"I'll be safe," Bella said. "And I'll keep Mark safe."

I shook my head. I didn't like this, but I didn't see any other choice. I didn't know much about medicine or first aid, but I knew you weren't supposed to move someone with a head injury like Mark's. One of us needed to leave and get help. It had to be me.

"Any advice before I go?"

"Move quickly," Bella said.

I hurried from the kitchen. Kate fell in beside me. We stepped out of the warm, comforting light of Bella's crystal ball. Cold darkness surrounded us.

"Mel?" Kate asked.

"Yeah?"

"It's going to be okay. Mark's going to be okay."

I shook my head and focused on putting one foot in front of the other, retracing our steps to the stairs. I tried to count my blessings. Kate stood with me so I wasn't alone. We crept through wintry darkness, but with the house devoid of furniture and my mind's eye open, I didn't have to worry about tripping or banging my shins. And, as monstrous as it made me feel, I counted myself lucky that I hadn't been the one smacked with a metal pipe.

I rounded a corner and started up the stairs. Then stopped. I could hear sounds from the floor above me. The wooden floor creaked with slow, deliberate footsteps.

"Shit. Kate, can you scout ahead and see if that's our ghost in another body?"

"I don't think so. It's like this place doesn't like me being here. If I get much further away from you, I'll be back in the car."

"Damn it. Okay, stay close, then."

I moved as quietly as I could up the stairs. Every other step creaked, the traitorous stairs calling out my position. I gritted my teeth and kept moving. I could still hear sounds of movement coming from the upper floor. I hoped that it was just the sounds an old house made when the wind blew, but I knew better.

I poked my head above the highest step and looked ahead of me. I held my breath. Another vagrant moved down the hallway in front of me. He hunched over as he walked, poking his head into each room, wringing his hands.

"Where is she?" he asked, his voice low and desperate.

He slipped into the room where we found Nikolay's jacket. An opportunity. I could sprint up the last of the stairs, round the corner, and bolt out the door. As long as I could outrun a possessed vagrant, I would be fine.

But that would leave Bella alone in the dark. I'd watched her knock the ghost out of the pipe wielding attacker, but she had to get really close to him to do it. If the ghost walked downstairs with a fresh body and a new weapon, would Bella really be able to protect herself and Mark?

I backed down the stairs more slowly than I'd ascended. I kept watch of the floor above me. The stairs were more agreeable, only squeaking every third step.

"What are you doing?" Kate asked. "Why aren't you going?"

"I don't know," I said, once I reached the bottom of the stairs. "I can't just leave Mark and Bella behind."

"Mel, please don't do anything foolish. Bella says she can defend herself. You should go. Get the police. Get Mr. Ortega. Get some help! There's nothing we can do here but get hurt."

"I hear what you're saying, but I just don't know. I think if we leave, that possessed guy is going to come down here and kill both Bella and Mark. That's what my gut is telling me, and my gut is usually smarter than I am."

Kate sighed. "This is stupid ... but fine. What is your gut telling you to do? Hopefully something that isn't going to get *you* killed."

"The ghost is looking for someone. She keeps asking 'where is she?' Maybe if we find whoever she's looking for, this whole problem will go away."

Kate looked up the stairs but said nothing. I turned and moved towards one of the rooms at the front of the house. With the windows covered, my physical eyes were useless. I closed them and allowed my mind's eye to eliminate the shadows and darkness.

"Kate, give me a warning if anyone creeps up behind me."

"Okay."

I got on my hands and knees and crawled across the floor, feeling with my hands for loose boards. The room stood as empty as the rest of the house. All I found were splinters and dust bunnies.

As I stood upright, I heard the stairs creaking. I froze in place and listened. My heart pounded in my ears. I didn't hear any more footsteps. After several moments, I let out a sigh and moved to find another room.

I stepped into the hallway.

"Duck!" Kate shouted.

I ducked. A board whistled over my head and struck the wall behind me with a splintering crack. I dove into the next room. I heard another crack, the vagrant's board striking the floor where I'd been standing.

The floor in the next room rushed up to meet me. I tried to get my feet under me, but tripped. I caught myself on my hands, rolled onto my back. Crab walking backwards, I pushed myself away from my attacker. The vagrant's slack features stood out to me, my mind's eye seeing him clearly. His cold, dead eyes regarded me.

"Where is she?" the vagrant bellowed. He stomped after me, brandishing his broken plank.

My back struck a wall. I slid up it, bringing in my feet. I reached out to each side, looking for something I could use to defend myself. My right hand brushed across a vent and suddenly, the possessed vagrant was the least of my worries.

16

A VISION PRESSED INTO ME. With my attacker bearing down on me and my heart trying to crack my ribs, I didn't have the willpower to resist it. The vision absorbed through the skin of my fingers, raced up my arm, then burrowed straight into my brain. It overwhelmed my senses and I became lost in it.

James staggered into the house, dragging his lame foot behind him and leaving a trail of blood. The wide, heavy bag in his right hand made for an awkward carry, but he managed it. His fingers encircled the handle with an iron grip. It slowed him, but he wouldn't leave it behind. He knew he didn't have much time. He needed to find a safe place.

He took a few steps into the living room, stumbled, then sat down hard. His back thumped against a wall. In spite of the weariness and clumsiness that came from the wound in his chest, he managed to set the bag down gently.

He still couldn't believe she'd stabbed him. He'd known for years Mary was crazy, but he never thought her homicidal.

A woman's voice pierced the night from the street just outside. "James! Where is she, James?" No time to rest, now. Mary had found him.

James used the wall to push himself back to his feet. Sweat slicked his face from the effort. Nausea twisted his guts. A wave of dizziness threatened to bring him back to the floor. He took several steadying breaths. He needed to stay calm and focused. He didn't have much time. He had something to do before he bled out.

Very carefully, he picked up the heavy bag. The weight and bulk of it nearly pulled him back to the floor. He shuffled deeper into the house, pushing past a decorative table supporting a vase and fresh flowers. He staggered again. His elbow went out, knocking the vase to the floor. The shattering crash echoed through the hall.

He limped down stairs, holding the bag in front of him with both hands. At the bottom of the steps, his knees buckled. He managed not to fall. No time left. His strength ran out of him, like the blood seeping from the knife wound.

He shambled into a modestly decorated office and set the bag down. Something stirred from within the bag, but it remained quiet. He let himself fall against the heavy desk that dominated the far wall. It moved under his weight, sliding a few inches to his left. As he held himself up, breath coming in shallow, burning gasps, he saw a wide air vent just behind the desk. He shifted his weight, shoving the desk enough to reveal the rest of the vent. Though his fingers were slippery with blood, he managed to get a fingernail under the bottom of the grate. He lifted it up to expose the dark shaft beyond.

A baby's sleepy cry came from the bag. He crawled over to it, opened it, and looked down at his daughter, still buckled into a car seat.

"Shh, sweety," James said. "Shh."

James pulled his daughter out of the car seat. He noticed his own blood marring her green and white sleeper, and his vision blurred. With a shaky hand, he pulled a short bottle of formula out of the bag. He set his daughter in the exposed duct. He propped the bottle in her mouth, then lowered the grating back over the vent.

"I love you, sweety," James said. "I love you so much."

He pulled the desk back into place, then fell to the floor. He panted and bled, knowing he couldn't stay there. If Mary found him, she'd find the baby.

"Where is she?" Mary's voice echoed down from the top of the stairs.

James crawled out of the room, dragging the bag behind him. He could hear the stairs creak behind him. He managed to crawl most of the way to the kitchen before Mary was upon him.

"What did you do with my daughter?" Mary cried. Blood covered her hands and arms up to her elbows. She still held the long knife she'd used on him before. She raised it high and brought it down hard.

James fell flat on his back and caught Mary's wrist with both hands. The tip of the blade bit into his shoulder, tearing a new hole in his flesh. New pain drew a cry from his lips. He shoved her away. Mary's wrist twisted and turned.

Mary gasped. She convulsed and fell off Jeff, clutching at the knife. Jeff's eyes dropped to the blade, driven into her chest up to the handle. He tried to get up, but his strength left him. His vision narrowed into a long, dark hallway. Somewhere else, he could hear a baby crying.

I regained my senses just in time to see a chunk of wood whistling through the air towards my head. I ducked. The end of the plank shattered against the wall behind me, dropping splinters into my hair and down my shirt. I swept my leg out, catching the vagrant in the back of the knee. He collapsed. The chuck of floorboard he'd been wielding clattered on the floor next to me.

I scrambled on top of the vagrant and pressed his shoulders against the floor. He thrashed and tried to throw me off, but I managed to hold him down.

"Mary!" I yelled. "Your daughter was here! Stop fighting me!"

The vagrant quit struggling. He raised his head and looked at me. Muscles in his cheek stood out, his jaw clenched. The taut muscles of his face and neck contrasted his eyes, which remained dull and blank.

"Where?" the man said, his voice quiet and strained.

"She was in the vent." I jerked my head towards the wall. I didn't trust the ghost enough to raise my hands. "I saw James put her in there with a bottle of formula."

Whatever advantage of position I thought I had disappeared when the possessed vagrant turned his attention towards the vent. He threw me off of him as though I were a child. I landed on my side and skidded across the floor. The vagrant rose to his hands and knees. He crawled to the vent and ripped the grating off the wall. The duct was empty.

"Where?" the vagrant yelled, his voice echoing through the empty house.

"James put her in there, just before you both died! I saw it!"

The vagrant dropped low and put his head and a hand into the vent. With his back to me, I saw another opportunity to escape. The ghost paid me no attention, focused completely on searching for the lost child. I could slip out and try to get help.

The situation hadn't changed, though. I knew something more about the ghost, and what she searched for, but the danger to my friends hadn't changed. If I left now, the ghost might get even more pissed, thinking I'd tricked her. What would she do then?

I climbed to my feet and waited. My body shook from fear and adrenaline.

After a moment searching, the vagrant went as still as a statue. He withdrew from the vent, his hand clutching a tiny bib. Though dark and dusty, I could see the bib's faded green and white colors. The vagrant's hand trembled, his dull, bloodshot eyes directed at the tiny fabric in his hand.

"This was Emily's," the vagrant said.

I started to reach a hand for it, but hesitated. I knew there would be another vision wrapped inside the bib, but I didn't think I wanted to see it. Obviously the girl had been found, but what if they found her too late? I didn't want to see that. And if I did, I knew I wouldn't be able to hide that truth from Mary's ghost.

With a sigh, I stepped forward. "Let me see it. I can tell you what happened to Emily, if you let me touch it."

The vagrant's face remained strained and unreadable. Slowly, he stretched his hand out, offering me the bib. I drew in another deep breath and touched it. The vision hit me as soon as my fingers touched the cloth.

Darkness filled Emily's world. Beneath her, she felt something cold and hard. She didn't have a bottle in her mouth anymore. Something cold and heavy rested on her arm and her shoulder. Somewhere far away, there were sounds. They were not nice sounds.

They sounded like The Nice Ones, the Soft One that brought the food, and the Hard One that made it safe.

Emily did not like this at all. She wanted food and warmth. She wanted someone to hold her. She wanted something soft beneath her or around her. Emily opened her mouth and cried, giving voice to the wordless, raw needs that filled her.

Time passed, though Emily did not understand the concept of time. The sounds that were not nice had stopped. The cold hardness beneath her felt colder than ever. The need increased, and Emily filled her lungs and cried out louder and stronger than before.

Emily lost herself in the wailing. Her face felt hot and wet from the effort. The hard thing on her shoulder shifted and rolled off. It felt better, but she still had need. Emily's voice warbled, and her throat hurt. The crying continued.

The darkness broke. Light came from somewhere else, along with other sounds. Emily heard voices. None of them were The Nice Ones, and Emily didn't know the words, but she felt the emotions. Fear. Anger. Frustration. The need inside changed, and her crying changed.

A heavy sound filled Emily's ears, close enough to shake the cold hardness beneath. More light filled Emily's world. Deep voices said something, and the emotions changed from fear to surprise and tenderness. The cold underneath went away. Emily felt herself moving up, lifted towards the light. The need diminished. The crying stopped.

The face of one like The Hard One filled her vision. The face had eyes behind glass and hair above lips. Emily felt afraid of this new face, but the face was better than the cold and the darkness. Arms surrounded Emily. She felt safe and warm. Emily relaxed. Sleep took her.

I let go the bib and staggered back. For a moment, I struggled with the concept of words. Everything from Emily's perspective had been emotions and senses. I couldn't tell how long the vision had lasted, because Emily had no concept of time.

"She was found," I said, once I was able to speak. "Someone found her, and she was okay."

The vagrant took a step towards me, and crumpled, a graceless flop just like when Bella forced Mary out of the other vagrant.

Mary's ghost stood before me, her hands raised in a pleading gesture.

"My baby," she said, her voice pleading and mournful.

"Emily's gone, Mary," I said. "She's safe. You're not going to find her here."

Mary fell to her knees, just in front of the collapsed vagrant. She covered her eyes with her hands and began to cry. Her shoulders shook with each sob. As she cried, she began to lose color, becoming more and more transparent. Her voice thinned and grew distant. I watched her, unable to offer any comfort. She cried, and her tears washed her away, out of existence.

17

I WAITED TO BE MAKE SURE that Mary was gone, and then waited some more. When it seemed certain that Mary would not come back, I checked in with Bella. A few minutes after I left the kitchen, she had the presence of mind to use her cell phone and call Ortega. By the time I returned to the kitchen, Ortega ascended the outside stairs with a private physician and a trauma kit.

It turned out Mark's injuries looked worse than they were. In spite of the severity of the blow and all the blood, his skull remained intact. He started regaining consciousness while the doctor examined him. When it came time to leave, he walked out with some assistance, which Bella and I eagerly provided.

The doctor examined the two homeless men that Mary had possessed. After he gave them a fair assessment — they were as healthy as anyone living hard on the street could be — I thought we might take them with us. Instead, we moved them to the front rooms and covered them with the blankets we found there. After that, we rode back to the office in Ortega's SUV.

We sat in the library, the air still flavored with the incense Bella burned during the earlier spell. I described the visions I experienced in the haunted house. It took a while. Ortega and Mark kept interrupting me to ask questions. By the time I finished, my mouth felt dry and my voice cracked.

"If the ghost of Mary was mad with grief for the loss of her child," Mark said, "then it's hard to believe that your explanation was enough to put her at rest."

Before I could respond, Ortega said, "I don't think that's what happened."

I frowned. "Sir, I'm not lying or exaggerating."

"No, that's not what I meant." Ortega gestured for me to settle down. "I meant it wasn't your explanation alone that did it. You said she was holding the cloth when you had the vision of Emily?"

I nodded. "I think so. It was all very confusing."

"It's possible you could have shared the vision with her. I've read cases where psychics can pass on what they see with their gift through physical contact. If you allowed her to see for herself that Emily was rescued, safe and secure, it could have been enough."

"The Lord works in mysterious ways." Mark nodded slowly, his fingers folded in front of him and his eyes narrowed.

"Right," I said. "So are we done with that case?"

"For now," Ortega said.

"I'll need to do some more scrying," Bella said.

"Mary is at rest, but the man you saw in your vision may still be out there," Mark said. "We should stay vigilant."

"And," Ortega said, "That wasn't the only haunted house in Sacramento. There is no shortage of supernatural phenomena for us to investigate. We have plenty of work ahead of us, Mr. Walker. It is only going to get busier, the closer we get to the end of the cycle."

I concentrated, remembering what it felt like in the haunted house when my mind's eye opened. With an effort and a moment of pain at my temples, my mind's eye opened again. It seemed to be getting easier. Looking over my shoulder, I met Kate's eyes. She smirked and gave me a shrug.

"If you ask me," she said, "You ought to take a break."

I turned back to Ortega. "We don't have any present leads or anything now, right?"

Ortega shook his head. "Not yet."

"So you all wouldn't mind if I took some time off, right? Maybe go out and stretch my legs?"

Ortega exchanged looks with Mark, then with Bella. He turned back to me and said, "Mr. Walker, I hope we didn't give you the wrong impression. You're not a prisoner here. You're a guest. As long as you wish to stay with us and work with us, the room and the stipend are yours. But if you wish to go and do other things, we won't stop you."

"It's not that I want to leave. I just need to take a break. As dangerous as repo work can be, I don't remember anyone ever trying to kill me before. I kind of want to maybe go somewhere and do shots until I forget."

Ortega nodded. He reached into a pocket and pulled out a cell phone and slid it across the table to me. "Take this. Our numbers are in there. Call if you need a ride."

I picked up the phone and stuffed it into my front pocket without looking at it. "Thanks. You guys are alright."

•   •   •

In New Orleans, there's this little place called Bourbon Street. It's pretty rowdy most nights and it gets downright crazy during Mardi Gras. After repoing a car, I used to spend some time there. I'd get wasted, dance with some girls in the clubs, kiss a few that I knew I would never see again, and basically get stupid and have fun. The first time I did it, I learned the hard way not to take all of my money with me when partying. It was an expensive lesson, but a good one.

Ortega gave me my first week's allowance before I left, and I wanted to find a place like Bourbon Street. Unfortunately, New Orleans is a one-of-a-kind place, and Sacramento didn't have anything that could compare. Clubs could be found, both straight and otherwise, and neon beer lights marked bars for what they were all over the city. But these places were too spread out and too civilized. Nowhere in Sacramento had the feel of a continuous party. I wanted to get lost in a crowd, but the kind of crowd I needed was nowhere to be found.

I walked the streets through a chilly evening, and even through the glare of the city lights, I could see a dark and angry sky above. I stopped a few blocks from the downtown mall, contemplating which direction to walk. I opened my mind's eye and saw Kate a little ways ahead of me, looking into the window of a dusty old antique store.

"Kate, your town sucks," I said.

Kate turned her head slowly and glared at me. "My town isn't interested in putting you in jail for my murder."

"Okay, your town rules. But it's still boring as hell. There's nothing to do here."

"What? Sure there is."

"Like what?"

"Whatever you want," Kate said. "When I lived her before, my friends and I would go out and do whatever."

"Friends." I looked down at the sidewalk. "That's what I'm missing. I don't really have any friends to hang out with here."

"You've got me."

I looked back up at her and saw her smiling.

"I bet I'm the first girl you've ever met that wouldn't think you were cheap for trying to sneak her into a movie."

I grinned back at her. "You're probably right. Fine, let's see what's playing. Oh, do any of the theaters around here sell beer?"

•   •   •

I wanted to go to the IMAX, but the cost of the ticket would have taken a much larger bite out of my allowance than I liked. The money may have been burning a hole in my pocket, but I liked the warmth. Besides, I needed to save enough for beer later. Maybe even a steak.

We wound up going to the Plaza where I bought tickets for a chick flick. I could have picked an action movie or one of the horror movies left-over from Halloween, but after the ordeal at the haunted house, I needed to settle down and relax. I didn't think Kate would appreciate the guns or explosions, either. A nice, soft, predictable romantic comedy seemed like a good change of pace.

I fell asleep ten minutes into the film. Just as the quirky redheaded protagonist opened her bedroom door to find her boyfriend cheating on her with her roommate, my lids grew heavy, my head fell back, and sweet oblivion consumed my world. I probably snored.

Some time later, a gruff, masculine voice whispered loud in my ear, "Mr. Walker?"

I snapped awake with a snort and a gasp, like I was coming up for air. I flailed and two sets of hands grabbed my arms and held me down.

"Sorry to wake you, Mr. Walker," the voice said again. I turned to the speaker and saw a clean-shaven white man with dark hair. He wore a business suit and smelled vaguely of Old Spice and gun oil. He said in a louder voice, "I'm Special Agent Tim Bennett. We're going to need you to come with us."

18

THE TWO AGENTS ESCORTED ME out of the theater like a couple of overdressed ushers. They hustled me into a black van with tinted windows. Agent Bennett slipped into the back seat beside me and strapped on his seatbelt. The other agent rode in the front with the driver. As the van pulled away from the theater, I watched The Plaza disappear behind us. I wondered if I'd ever see anyone from The Society again.

A short time later, they pulled me out of the van and hauled me into an office building. They took me to a room and sat me on a plain chair next to an empty table. One-way glass covered the wall I faced. My stupefied expression stared back at me.

Again, this was not my first time in a room like this. Sometimes the authorities offer water or coffee. Sometimes they make their suspect go thirsty. Sometimes they make their captive sit for a long period of time alone, letting all the fear and doubt take root and grow. Fortunately, Agent Bennett decided to get right to business.

"This is Special Agent Walters," Bennett said, gesturing to his partner. Walters, a clean-shaven black man with short hair and a receding hairline, nodded to me. He wore a gray suit slightly darker than Bennett's. Neither of the agents shook my hand. Bennett placed a file folder on the table in front of him.

"You're probably wondering why we've brought you here," Bennett said.

"I am a bit curious," I said, smiling.

"You are a person of interest in a murder investigation," Bennett said.

I blinked. "The FBI is investigating Kate's murder?"

"Not exactly," Walters said.

"You went under the radar for several weeks after you skipped out of New Orleans," Bennett said. "At this time, a warrant has not been issued for your arrest, but the investigation is ongoing."

"Wait, hold on," I said. "You were involved before I came to Sacramento, weren't you? The New Orleans cops had a file on me that was full of information they shouldn't have had."

Bennett and Walters exchanged looks. Walters said, "We didn't bring you in specifically about Kate Lynnwood's murder."

"However," Bennett said. "If subject material becomes available that implicates you in her murder, we have the authority to take you into custody and bring you back to Louisiana, where you will stand trial and in all likelihood go to jail for a very long time."

"Wait," I said. "Agent Bennett? I thought you were going to play the good cop, and Agent Walters was going to play the bad cop."

"This isn't a game, Walker." Bennett clenched his teeth, and a muscle in his cheek spasmed.

"Then quit playing around with me!" My pulse raced and my own voice sounded loud to my ears. I could see my face flushed in the mirrored glass. Kate fretted, her monochrome reflection pacing silently behind my chair.

"This is about your new friends," Walters said. Walters made a contrast to Bennett, his features controlled, his voice slow and calm. I began to think that the good cop/bad cop routine wasn't something these two needed to rehearse. Bennett made a very convincing hothead while Walters appeared to be unflappable.

Bennett opened the folder and drew out a series of pictures. With the way he spread them in front of me, I wondered if he ever worked in a casino. "Look. You know these people."

I looked. All of the pictures were black and white, and most were grainy from being taken at long range. The one on the far left

114

showed Ortega sitting at an outdoor restaurant, leaning forward to talk to another man that I didn't recognize. The next picture showed Mark descending the steps of a church next to a priest I did recognize. Father Philips, from the vision I received when I touched Mark's Bible. A wave of emotions flooded over me when I saw Father Philips' face. It took an effort to keep my expression calm.

Another picture depicted Bella walking next to some cars with an older man I did not recognize. The last picture featured another white man that seemed familiar. He wore jeans and a button up shirt while standing on a stage surrounded by a crowd sitting on bleachers. The corners of his mouth turned down in a pitiful frown. His sorrowful eyes pleaded as he looked to his audience.

"I recognize some of the people in these pictures," I said. "Bella, Mark, and Mr. Ortega. I assume that last one's Bobby Greenwood. I don't know any of the people that are with them."

Bennett picked up the picture of Mark. "This is Father McAdams and Father Philips, formerly of Saint Mary's. Philips worked with McAdams before McAdams parted with the church on bad terms. Shortly after their falling out, Father Philips' body was found in his home. He'd been stabbed and bled out."

A lump rose up in my throat. I felt my eyes begin to tear up. I never met Father Philips personally, but some part of Mark's love and appreciation for the man stayed with me after the vision. The news of his death struck me unexpectedly. I tried to get a hold of myself by focusing on the present. I sat in a chair, federal agents questioning me. I could not afford to let another man's emotions get the best of me. I placed my hands flat on the table, and kept my expression blank. I hoped whatever emotions bled through came across as nervousness and not grief.

Bennett picked up the pictures of Bella and Ortega and held them out together. "The man next to Isabella Theroux is the late Sebastian Theroux, Isabella's husband. Financial records tie Mr. Theroux and Ortega back several years. We dragged Mr. Theroux's body out of Lake Natomas a little more than a year ago. Financial records indicate Mrs. Theroux started working for Mr. Ortega shortly after her husband died."

"Be careful, Mel," Kate said.

Bennett didn't pick up the last picture. Instead, he slid it forward on the table and tapped it with two fingers. "And then there is Mr. Robert Greenwood. Greenwood's become quite the celebrity. He's been helping the bereaved find reconciliation with those that they've lost. He's even started doing one on one consultations with celebrities. We became interested in his stage show after we found financial ties between Greenwood and Ortega. It's interesting how accurately Greenwood is able to describe the deceased, even going so far as to describe the manner in which they died."

"You're right," I said. "That's interesting. I had no idea his show was so good that it would fool the FBI. I'll have to check it out sometime."

"It sounds like you're missing the point," Walters said. He leaned forward, resting his arms on the table. "All of these people have circumstantial evidence tying them to unexplained deaths. And now here you are, flown all the way from Louisiana to join their company. And you're tied to an unexplained death."

My stomach churned white hot lava. For a moment, I found it difficult to breathe. The jaws of some terrible trap just clamped down on me, and I hadn't seen it coming. I tried to keep my expression neutral, and I tried to stay calm and relaxed, but it was like trying to hold back flood waters with your hands. There's only so much you can do when the levies break.

"Listen." My voice quavered. "I didn't know any of those people before yesterday. This is all a big misunderstanding."

"Relax," Walters said. "You're not in trouble yet, Mr. Walker."

"Yet," Bennett repeated.

"Personally, I think you've just had some bad luck, and you've wound up in the wrong place at the wrong time," Walters said. "But maybe we can turn your luck around."

"I'm listening." I did not find Walters' words or tone reassuring. A headache began forming at my temples. I felt uncomfortable, and it was all by their design. Walters and Bennett crafted this conversation to put me off balance so they could offer me some sort of life line when I was most vulnerable. They executed their plan perfectly.

"You're inside," Walters said. "Pedro Ortega appears to have taken an interest in you and has invited you into his company. We've tried to get an agent where you are for months but we haven't had any luck. This is an opportunity for you to help yourself while helping us out."

"You want me to spy on them for you?"

"We don't want you to do anything out of the ordinary," Walters said. "Just stay with them. Participate however you were going to participate. And then, sometime down the road, be ready to answer a few questions for us."

"So … spying."

"Look at it this way," Bennett said. "You can do this for us, or we can extradite you back to Louisiana, where you will be held and scrutinized until the Kate Lynnwood murder is resolved."

I looked down at the surface of the table. My cheeks felt hot, my hands felt cold. They laid out my options very neatly. I didn't see any way out.

"You think this is a group of murderers and you want me to go back to them, alone, and spy on them." I paused to lock eyes with Bennett and Walters in turn. "If they are murderers and I'm caught, then I'm dead."

"We're not entirely sure you're not a murderer yourself, Mr. Walker," Bennett said.

"Like I said," Walters said. "Don't do anything you wouldn't normally do. Don't ask questions you wouldn't normally ask. Just be yourself, keep your eyes and ears open, and maybe you'll see or hear something useful. We don't want you looking for trouble."

"These days, I don't have to look for it," I said. "Trouble has a way of finding me."

I looked between Walters and Bennett again. What choice did I have? I sighed. "Looks like I'm your man."

19

I FOUND TWO KEY DIFFERENCES between the FBI and the New Orleans police. First, the FBI proved to be much more effective at getting under my skin and forcing me to dance to their tune. Second, the FBI were not as cheap as the New Orleans cops. Instead of sticking me in a cab and making me eat the fare, the FBI drove me back to the theater where they picked me up.

I pulled out the phone Ortega gave me and checked the time. Nearly midnight, and the theater's lights were dim. Sacramento lights fought back the darkness, but it didn't compare to the nightlife of New Orleans. Sacramento streets held more shadows than people. Back home, the streets would still be full of music and bodies roaming around, looking for the next party to land on.

A light, misting rain plastered my hair down and made my shirt cling to my body. California rain. Maybe that had something to do with the streets being so empty.

As I walked down the street in the direction of The Society's office, I opened my mind's eye. I found Kate walking beside me, hugging herself, with her head down.

"Are you cold?" I asked.

"No. I don't feel cold, anymore. I feel worried. For you."

"That's sweet, but really, I don't know that there's much to worry about."

"You seemed pretty worried back in the questioning room."

"I was. But there's no sense in worrying now. Worry isn't going to change anything."

"Not going to change anything? Mel, they think Bella and Mark murdered people. How can you be so blasé about this?"

"You don't believe them, do you?"

Kate frowned. She hesitated before saying, "I don't know. There is something about them that scares me."

"Well I don't believe it. I know how Mark felt about Philips. I felt it. For God's sake, when they mentioned that Father Philips was dead, I almost started crying, because that's how Mark would feel."

"And Bella?"

I opened my mouth to come to Bella's defense, but stopped. Earlier that day, in the haunted house, I watched the light in Bella's crystal ball change color. I remembered the look on her face when she cast Mary out of the man that attacked Mark. In that moment, she certainly looked capable of killing someone.

I shook my head. "No. I still don't believe it. They're trying to save the world. They're not murderers."

A headache began to grow beneath my temples again, pounding into my brain with each step. I closed my physical eyes and pressed my hands to the side of my face, trying to hold my head together. I could still see where I walked, and the strangeness seemed to make the pain worse.

I opened my eyes and turned to Kate. "I need to close my mind's eye for a bit. This headache is killing me. Sorry."

With my mind's eye closed, I walked the rest of the way in silence. By the time I got to my new home, rain soaked me from my head to toe. I kicked off my shoes, toweled off in the bathroom, and unceremoniously flopped onto my bed. I felt so exhausted, I might have been asleep before my body hit the mattress.

•   •   •

I woke a little earlier the next day. Early enough to find Bella and Bobby Greenwood downstairs. They sat at the table in the kitchen over a breakfast of bagels and coffee.

"Good morning!" Bella raised her cup to me and smiled.

"Ah, you must be the psychic everyone is talking about." Bobby stood and extended a hand to me. "Izzy was just telling me about how you pulled her and Marky's fat out of the fire yesterday. It's good to meet you."

Bobby's handshake was firm but not bone crushing. I gave him my best smile and said, "It's nice to meet you, Mr. Greenwood."

"Please, call me Bob. Or Bobby."

Bobby sat back down and I took the chair across from him. Bella smiled and reached for the coffee.

"How are you feeling this morning, Mel?" Bella tilted the carafe into a fresh cup before sliding it towards me. "Not still shaken up from yesterday, I hope."

I thought of my unexpected visit with the feds and felt my face flush. "No, my wanderlust is cured. I'm convinced I'm right where I'm supposed to be, for now."

"Good," Bella said. "After my first experience with the occult, I didn't sleep well for a week."

I snagged a bagel from the box and spun it slowly in my hands. "So. What do you two have planned for the day? Anything I can help with?"

"I'm probably going to spend most of the day in the library," Bella said. "If you want to help me there, that's fine. Just ... you know. Bring a bucket this time."

"You can tag along with me if you want," Bobby said. "I'm going to check with some folks on the street. Pedro wants me to make sure that people aren't still going missing."

"How will you do that?" I asked.

"The same way I do my show," Bobby said. "I'll just talk to people. Read them. People always say more than they know, as long as you know what to look for."

I took a bite of my bagel. As I chewed, I felt Bobby's gaze weighing and measuring me. I swallowed too soon and it hurt my throat going down. How much could this man see? I tried not to think of my meeting with the feds. When that didn't work, I cleared my throat.

"I'll help," I said. "No problem. Sounds like a good time. When do we start?"

"Great!" Bobby showed me a smile which featured an abundance of straight, white teeth.

I turned my attention back to Bella. "How is Mark doing? Is he going to be okay?"

"Oh, he's fine," Bella said. "Mr. Ortega had him taken to the hospital for a more thorough checkup. They gave him fresh stitches, and he'll probably have an amazing scar. But they said he didn't have a concussion."

"Good. I was worried about him."

I took another bite from my bagel and chewed thoughtfully. I imagined Mark sitting in a hospital bed, his head wrapped in too many bandages. I remembered the ringing sound of the metal pipe striking his head, and the pool of blood that surrounded him like a crimson halo while he lay unconscious. It nearly made me believe in a higher power, looking out for and protecting children and fools and people of faith.

"When you're done, meet me outside and we'll head out." Bobby drained the rest of his cup and left.

"He seems nice," I said.

"He does seem so, yes," Bella said through a forced smile.

"And he's good enough at reading people that he passes himself off as psychic?"

"He's good at reading most people." Bella's smile faded and she shook her head. "He's good enough that Mr. Ortega had me check to see if he had any psychic or magical talent. If supernatural gifts were water, Robert Greenwood would be the Sahara Desert. But he definitely has some kind of gift. If someone is hiding something, Mr. Greenwood will read it."

"Oh, great." I sipped my coffee, trying not to think of my burden of fresh secrets.

I found Bobby around the corner sitting in a Ford F-150. The truck had more than its fair share of miles on it. Its dull, rust red exterior would never shine again. By contrast, it sat high above the concrete on new tires, its suspension lifted and caked with clumps of mud. I felt like a little kid when I pulled myself up through the passenger side door. When Bobby pulled onto the street, his truck growled and shuddered, like an old man woken too soon from his nap.

Normally, I can't stand it when people take large vehicles on city roads. They can't turn worth a damn, they are a nightmare in parking lots, and they make it harder for people in more reasonable cars to see what they're doing. Whenever I repo'd an SUV, I considered it an act of justice. But Bobby appeared to know how to drive his truck, and he maneuvered it through the Sacramento streets as nimbly as anyone else on the road. If I led the coupe and sedan revolution, I would allow Bobby Greenwood to keep his truck.

"So," Bobby said. "What's bothering you?"

"Who says anything is bothering me?" I said, a little too quickly.

"You did, back in the kitchen. Not in so many words, but I could tell you were holding something back."

I studied Bobby as he drove. He had dark skin for a white man and short black hair with wings of silver at the sides. He wore jeans, work boots, and a button-up shirt. Every line of him screamed confidence. He smirked as I studied him but remained silent as he waited for me to answer his question.

"I might have gotten into some trouble before I left Louisiana." I decided to treat this conversation the same way I treat police interrogations. Stick to the truth, but don't volunteer more than necessary.

"Yeah. That makes sense. But that's not what's bothering you."

"It's the root of what's bothering me."

Bobby stopped at a red light. He turned and looked me up and down. "That may be, but you're still hiding something. The pitch of your voice dropped when you mentioned Louisiana, and you rubbed your thigh with your right hand. You're being careful and deflecting, just so you can hold something back."

"So what if I am?" I said, a little more angrily than I intended. "Do you divulge everything to people you've just met?"

"Nope." Bobby shot me a friendly smile. The light changed, and he pulled the truck forward. "I'm only asking because whatever it is, you're bothered by it. If it's none of my business, then it's none of my business. But you're working with Izzy to put down ghosts and monsters and things that go bump in the night. If you're distracted, you might put my friends in danger. Maybe you should find someone to talk to about whatever is on your mind, before someone I care about gets hurt."

I sighed and looked out my window. Office buildings and store fronts passed by in a multicolored blur. "Bella told me you're not a real psychic. That you don't have a supernatural bone in your body. I'm starting to think she made a mistake."

20

OUR FIRST STOP TURNED OUT to be my old shelter. I didn't want to go in and see those people again. Thanks to the visions from the haunted house, I knew things about some of the regulars that I shouldn't know. Things I didn't want to know. How would I react if I ran into any of them? I thought I'd flown under the radar while I'd been staying at the shelter. I was wrong. I always thought I could hide my thoughts and feelings and just blend in, but recent events made me feel like an open book.

"You can wait in the truck if you want," Bobby said. He shook his head, and laughed. "I'm sorry. I should stop doing that. I assume from the way you're rubbing your chin and looking at the homeless shelter that you're familiar with the place. You've reached for the door and stopped, which tells me that you aren't sure about going in. You don't have to. I don't expect to find anything here."

"No, I'll go." I pushed open the heavy door and slid down to the concrete.

In the weeks that I'd been staying at the shelter, I never went out of my way to get to know the staff. To my surprise, I recognized the young man behind check-in desk. He wore thick glasses, a white button up shirt and dark slacks that didn't quite reach the tops of his shiny loafers. I always assumed him a missionary of some sort. I couldn't recall his name, but he remembered mine.

"Oh hey, Mel." He adjusted his glasses and hitched a thumb towards the bunks. "I'm sorry man, but we gave out your cot last night. We can set you up with another one in the same room if you want."

"That's okay," I said. "I've got a new place I'll be staying at for a while."

"Mel and I are here to help with the kitchen for lunch," Bobby said. "Unless you're full up on volunteers?"

The missionary laughed. "There's never enough volunteers. Just sign in and we'll put you to work."

I've been on both sides of a soup kitchen counter. It's just a facet of the luxurious life style I've lived. Up to that point, my reasons for volunteering had always been personal. When I volunteered, I squared up the tab. This time, my reasons for volunteering were not so noble, and I felt like a real dirt bag. First the feds set me up to spy on The Society. Now Bobby set me up to spy on the homeless.

By the end of the lunch shift, I didn't feel so bad. The people I served accepted their food with genuine gratitude. They didn't have to go hungry, and neither Bobby nor I asked any invasive questions. As far as I could tell, Bobby didn't ask anything, other than how many scoops of mac and cheese someone might want.

I didn't recognize anyone that passed through my line, though a couple of people gave me a familiar nod. I didn't see any of the people from Nikolay's vision.

We signed out, made our goodbyes with the missionary, and left. I couldn't decide how I felt about the experience. On the one hand, it seemed like we'd wasted our time. On the other, how can I be such an asshole to consider helping the homeless a waste of time?

Back in the truck, Bobby said, "No one in there was missing anyone."

"You're sure?"

"Yeah. There were a few guys in there worried about drugs, and there were a few women worried about losing their children, but I didn't get the sense that anyone was actually missing."

"How can you be so sure?"

Bobby shrugged. "I just am."

Downtown Sacramento can be a labyrinth of one way streets. We moved through traffic more smoothly than during rush hour gridlock, but we still trailed behind a cluster of tail lights gliding over rain slicked concrete. After hitting a series of red lights, Bobby turned the truck down one of the narrower side streets.

"Short cut," Bobby said with a grin.

A block and a half later, a silver sedan and a burgundy SUV whipped passed us. They pulled in front of us single-file and stopped abruptly. Bobby stomped on his brakes. His heavy truck skidded across the wet concrete. It slammed into the back of the sedan with a bone-jarring crunch. I caught myself on the dashboard. The palms of both my hands stung. Bobby let the truck roll back away from the sedan. The smaller car in front of us looked crumpled, its bumper hanging askew.

The other vehicles opened. Several large men poured out like ants attacking a picnic. They scowled at us through the windshield. One of the men wore a black leather jacket, his hair in a crew cut. He carried a tire iron. The others wore jeans and winter coats. They looked unarmed, and they walked with a bulldog's swagger. They all looked ready to fight.

"Shit," Bobby said. He shifted the F-150 into reverse. Before he could go anywhere, another truck pulled in behind us, blocking us in.

"Do you know these people?" I asked.

"Not personally."

The man with the tire iron raised his weapon and threatened to smash Bobby's window. "Get out! Now!"

I looked past the thugs outside the truck, hoping to see bystanders breaking out their phones. We were surrounded by the backs and sides of buildings. I couldn't find any rubberneckers. Any hope of the Sacramento police showing up washed away like the rain filling the gutters.

Bobby showed his empty hands before opening his door. The man with the tire iron grabbed the door with his free hand and pulled it wide. One of the other thugs reached in, grabbed Bobby by the throat, and pulled him out of the truck.

I sat in shock, my mouth hanging open. It all happened so fast. Before I knew how to react, one of the other thugs came to my door and jerked it open. Rough hands grabbed me and tried to pull me out, but I still had my seat belt on. The restraint bit into my chest and waist. I thumbed open the clasp on the next pull. The thug pulling me tripped backwards, and I fell out onto the ground.

I didn't spend much time on the concrete. Two of the thugs hauled me up and dragged me around to the front of the truck. I flinched and tried to pull myself free, but they held me easily. They dragged me to the driver's side and pressed me against the front quarter. One of the thugs held Bobby in a full nelson. The one with the tire iron stood in front of him, tapping his weapon into his open palm. He took one look at me, then gave a nod to the thug that dragged me. The thug responded by punching me hard in the stomach.

I folded like a wallet. Tears blurred my vision. I retched, and vomit burned the back of my throat. I would have curled into the fetal position on the ground, but someone pulled me back up and pressed me back against the truck. I sucked in air, and wondered if they were going to kill me.

"Do I have your attention now, Mr. Greenwood?" the man with the tire iron said.

"Damn it, Kyle, leave him out of this!" Bobby said.

"Hit him again," Kyle said.

This time, they punched me in the face. My vision flashed white. I rocked back. Time slipped forward without me for a few seconds. I found myself sagging, held up between two thugs. I took a moment to really feel the rotational velocity of the Earth. When the world's spinning seemed to lessen, I lifted my head and looked at Kyle. I felt more curious than angry. I wondered what the hell I'd done to deserve this.

"Until I get my fifty thousand," Kyle was saying to Bobby, "you'll think twice about telling me what to do. Now. Do I have your attention?"

"Yes," Bobby said. He sounded defeated.

"Good," Kyle said. "Now. Where's the money, Robby?"

"I don't have it yet."

Kyle turned to the man that beat me. "Harry. Hit him again."

Harry raised his fist. Before he could sucker punch me again, Bobby yelled, "I can get it! I just need another couple of days."

"Hold on, Harry," Kyle said. "Another couple of days?"

Harry lowered his fist. His shoulders slumped and his eyebrows lowered in disappointment. This man's job involved beating up perfect strangers. He clearly loved his work.

"I have a client set up," Bobby said. "Personal consultation. Very rich. I'll get you the money, I swear."

"In two days, it'll be sixty thousand," Kyle said.

Bobby sighed and lowered his head. Kyle apparently took that as acceptance. "Let them go. We'll see you in a couple of days, Robby."

The thugs holding me let go. I fell to my hands and knees. I stayed there several moments, still feeling nauseous from the punch to the stomach. Bobby knelt next to me and put an arm on my shoulder. I heard car doors close. The thugs were gone.

"Sorry about that, Mel," Bobby said. "I'm real sorry."

21

BOBBY SLIPPED AN ARM around me and pulled me to my feet. The world wobbled, threatening to pull me back down. I leaned against the truck for support. After a moment, I twisted the driver's side mirror around so I could see where they punched me. Bobby walked to the front of the truck and examined the front bumper. With both my face and the truck, the damage appeared to be fairly minor. Just a little bruising.

We climbed back into the truck. Bobby hesitated before restarting the vehicle. He watched his hands, waiting for the shaking to stop.

"Drugs? Gambling?" I asked.

"Gambling." Bobby sighed. "Thundervalley is close. Reno isn't that far away, either."

"How'd Kyle the Tire Iron get involved?"

"They work for someone else with money. A former client of mine."

"Are you going to have their money in a couple of days?"

Bobby smirked. "What do you think?"

"What's going to happen when you don't have the money?"

"You're the psychic. You tell me."

"I think they're going to start cutting pieces off of you." I shuddered. "Or me, if I happen to be with you at the wrong time."

"Well, you're not wrong."

"So what are you going to do? I just got beat up because of your stupid gambling debts. I think you owe me some answers."

"I'll figure something out." Bobby's shaking stopped, and his usual facade of arrogance and confidence snapped back into place. But, like one of those 3D pictures where you have to unfocus your eyes to see the picture, I couldn't look at Bobby without seeing the man behind the illusion. A man out of control, scared, hiding behind a mask.

"Mr. Ortega has money," I said.

"I couldn't ask that of him. I couldn't ask that of anyone."

"Have you even talked with him about it? The way I see it, you can fuck around and have your knees broken, or you can get down on your knees in front of someone like Ortega. If you ask me, it's an easy choice."

Bobby frowned. "Mel, I'm sorry they hit you. But to be frank, it's really none of your business how I handle this. I'll find a way out of this. I always do."

Instead of taking me with him to the next shelter, Bobby pulled in front of The Society's office and dropped me off. I watched the F-150 merge into traffic, one more drop in a river of vehicles. Before the truck was out of sight, a fat droplet of rain splattered on top of my head. I ducked and hurried into the building.

Bella sat in the library. Several stacked books surrounded her on the conference table like a fort made of words and paper. Others lay open in front of her, their secrets exposed. Her crystal ball sat on top of its velvet bag nearby, pulsing occasionally with an amber light. Bella wore reading glasses, her head down as she pored over the books. When I walked in, she looked at me over the rims of her glasses. After a moment, she smiled.

"You pissed off the homeless?"

I reached up and touched my bruised cheek. "I ran into a door. I fell down some stairs. Whatever. What are you doing? I thought you were going to be scrying."

"Oh." Bella looked at all the books around her as if just noticing them. "I was looking for a better spell. The one I've been

132

using is too general and I keep zoning in on Kate. Are you really not going to tell me who hurt you?"

I had been hoping to avoid the topic. As embarrassing as it may be to get beat down so handily, I felt no shame on that front. No one would have fared much better, aside from a few professional fighters. I didn't want to talk about my bruises because I didn't want to divulge Bobby's secret. He never told me I needed to keep it for him, but he didn't need to. When it came time to reveal his gambling debts, it would be from Bobby's lips, not mine.

I gave Bella a sheepish smile and shrugged. "It's like you said. Someone got pissed off, and I didn't duck."

Bella nodded and glanced down at her books. "I guess if I was homeless, I'd have a short temper, too. Oh! That reminds me." She gestured to one of the books on the stack nearest her. "I found something in one of the compendiums on ghosts that will probably interest you. Or more specifically, it will interest Kate."

I walked around the table and shifted the stack around until I could get to the book she'd indicated. "What did you find?"

"A spell for creating ectoplasm."

I flipped open the book to a random page and saw a very detailed drawing of a man getting vivisected. Askew text crawled on the opposite page in a language I didn't recognize. I turned the page to hide the image. The next section contained more unintelligible text.

"That's nice." I closed the book and examined its binding. The cover offered no hint of its author or its contents, and I didn't know anything about ghosts beyond what I learned in my time with Kate. I cleared my throat, then repeated the word Bella had used. "Ectoplasm."

Bella sighed and rolled her eyes. She reached over and turned to a different section of the book in my hands. "Ectoplasm is a malleable material that spirits and ghosts can use to form temporary constructs. Kate could have a body. For a short while, anyway."

That got my attention. I still couldn't read the language on the page, or even identify the language, but I looked at the strange scrawl with great interest. "That sounds interesting."

My thoughts crystallized into a fantasy. I imagined Kate grateful for all that I'd done for her. She would touch me with her hands and kiss me, eager to show her appreciation. I imagined Kate slipping out of her yellow dress. Several scenes of a pornographic nature played out in my head. I didn't think of Kate as a dead woman, so it didn't occur to me that my spontaneous carnal fantasy might be considered necrophilia.

Meanwhile, my hands fidgeted. While I stared at the page, holding the book with my left hand, I reached over and picked up Bella's crystal ball with my right. I don't know why. Maybe the pulsing light had attracted my attention. Maybe some unspoken curiosity inspired me to reach for it. All I know is that as soon as I picked up the orb, my mind's eye snapped wide open, and a vision gripped me more strongly than any other I'd experienced up to that point.

22

P INE TREES LINED THE ROAD *on both sides. Isabella wanted to roll down the car window to breathe in the scent of the forest around them, but the dust kicked up by the tires made that a bad idea. She pressed her forehead against the window and peered up, looking with wide eyes and a wide smile at the sliver of cerulean sky above them. A perfect day beckoned them to frolic in the country, and neither Isabella nor her husband could resist.*

"We should have done this a long time ago," Isabella said.

"I couldn't agree more, dear," Sebastian said.

Isabella turned and regarded her husband. His white hair still carried patches of brown, hinting at the coloring of his youth. Lines next to his eyes stood out, much more pronounced than they were when they married. In spite of their age difference, she still felt the same unyielding strength from him that she felt when they first met. She still felt safe and protected and loved in his presence.

Isabella looked out the window at the trees again. "How did you find this spot, anyway? This is way off the highway."

"I found it online." Sebastian pointed a finger towards the road ahead of the them. "In about half a mile, there's a place for us to

park. Then there's a little hike along a trail, until we get to an old cabin next to a waterfall. It's supposed to be very beautiful."

Isabella gave Sebastian's arm a squeeze. She settled back into the car seat and enjoyed the sound of the tires crunching over the road. "You can be such a romantic."

A small dent in the surrounding tree line made for a shallow turnout, just large enough for three cars if they parked bumper to bumper. Sebastian maneuvered their Buick into the turnout and killed the engine. He leaned over and shared a kiss with Isabella before they both opened their doors and stepped out of the car.

Sebastian reached into the backseat and took up the picnic basket, leaving the blanket for Isabella to carry. Sebastian led them to the trail. Enough bushes and weeds grew over the trail such that Isabella wondered if it was a path at all. Sebastian proceeded with confidence. Isabella followed.

There were more than just pine smells to delight Isabella as they pushed into the wild. Spring took hold of the area and in her fullness, the scents of wild flowers and new growth filled the air. Though the rain from the previous night softened the ground, Isabella strayed from the path to approach a patch of wildflowers in full bloom. After taking her fill of the sweet scent they offered, Isabella hurried back to her husband. She walked next to him, her hand under his arm.

They didn't have far to hike. They came into an open area full of tall grass and twisted weeds. Isabella could hear the babble and splash of a small stream somewhere up ahead. An old abandoned cottage sat at the other end of the glade, its walls tilting away from them lazily. Weathered and worn out; Isabella would have called it rickety and dangerous on any other day. Today, intoxicated by the fragrances of Spring, she considered the old house quaint.

"The grass is a bit wet for a picnic," Isabella said.

"We can set up our things in the cottage," Sebastian said.

Isabella gave her husband a curious look but said nothing. As part of the scenery, the old home made for a fine contrast to the wall of trees beyond it. Going inside was a different matter. It did not look the ideal setting for a romantic picnic. Quaint as it may be, there were sure to be insects and small creatures nesting inside. A strong wind would likely topple it over. On the other hand, paneless windows faced them, meaning the musty smell of mold and mildew would be minimal. Unless something had crawled in there to die.

Sebastian opened the door for Isabella and she stepped inside. She expected to step onto soft dirt or moldy wood, but instead found the cottage floored with concrete. Strange symbols were set into the hard floor. Unlit candles of various sizes filled the room along the walls, but seeing them did not inspire feelings of romance. The room looked macabre, pulled right out of a horror movie.

"Sebastian, what are—"

"Rapio!" Sebastian's voice boomed, echoing off the inner walls.

Isabella felt something tighten around her hands and feet, seizing her and holding her in place. The blanket fell from her grip. She screamed. The invisible force binding her wrists and ankles pulled her into the room, lifting her off the ground. It turned her, holding her horizontal a few inches above the floor.

"Sebastian! What's happening?"

"I'm sorry, dear." He set the picnic basket down near the door before bending to pick up the blanket Isabella dropped. He began folding it back into a neat square. "I'm so, so sorry, Isabella. I've looked and I've looked. I've tried everything. There's just no other way."

"What are you talking about?" Isabella struggled against the bonds that held her. They didn't bite into her flesh like rope or chains, but they didn't yield, either. "Sebastian, let me go!"

"Isabella," Sebastian said her name slowly, savoring it. "Please don't make this any harder than it already is."

"What are doing? Please, let me go!"

"I have to give you up." Sebastian's voice hitched. Sunlight from an open window made his eyes sparkle. He blinked, and a tear made a jagged rivulet down his cheek. He scrubbed it away with the back of his hand. "The cycle is ending. We need more power if we're to stand against it."

"What cycle? Sebastian, you don't have to do this. Let me go. Let's talk about this."

Sebastian placed the folded blanket on top of the picnic basket. He fished a lighter from his pants pocket and turned to the nearest candle. His hand shook as he snapped the lighter into flame and lit the wick.

"Sebastian, look at me! I'm your wife! This is insane!"

He refused to look at her. He walked counterclockwise around the room, lighting candles as he went. Isabella shook and sobbed, but her husband would not turn his eyes to meet hers. When he completed his circuit around the room and all the candles were lit, he dropped the lighter back in his pocket. He scrubbed at his eyes and cheeks with his palms.

"I love you, Sebastian," Isabella said through her tears. "Please let me go."

"I love you." He knelt and pulled a long knife from the picnic basket. It glimmered black and silver in the candlelight. Sebastian straightened to his feet and considered the knife. "It has to be someone I love, otherwise it is not a sacrifice. You're the only one it could be. If I could do this any other way, I would. But I can't. Isabella, you're the only one I love enough to make the magic work."

He turned and gazed at a space in the air above Isabella. He began to chant something in a language she didn't recognize. She thought it might be Latin, but there were too many guttural sounds involved. She cried and struggled against the bonds again, still unable to move.

The air above Isabella shimmered like hot air in the desert. The shimmering intensified, and Isabella froze in fear. An image of a face took shape. The face, with its writhing flesh the color of burning coals, regarded Isabella with five eyes of different shapes and colors. The eyes were unevenly arranged beneath a thickly furrowed brow. One eye, slitted like a cat's, stared at Isabella unblinking. Another, distinguished by a strange barbell shaped pupil, wandered around the room, the candlelight reflecting in its moist iris. Blood ran from the corners of all of the eyes like tears. A golden ring set in the middle of a monstrous nose glowed dimly. An asymmetrical mouth hung open, revealing sharp, triangular teeth.

"Azslav," Sebastian said, addressing the face.

"Sebastian Theroux. I see you." The apparition spoke with many voices at once, like a chorus of screams.

"Will this subject satisfy our arrangement?" Sebastian pointed at Isabella with the knife.

Azslav turned two more of its mismatched eyes to regard Isabella. She felt cold where the gaze lingered on her.

"Remove her clothing. Let me see her."

Sebastian hesitated before going to one knee. He set the knife down and began to unbutton Isabella's blouse. During the drive out of the city, Isabella imagined and planned for Sebastian to remove her clothes. Not like this. They were supposed to enjoy their meal.

138

They would drink the wine they brought. Then, feeling young and tipsy, they would have made love out in the open, like they had when they first married.

Sebastian's hands shook, but they were gentle. He removed each article of clothing, folding each piece and setting the clothing in a pile. Her blouse and her pants went through the invisible bonds as if they weren't there. He stripped her naked. She screamed again, and tears obscured her vision.

The invisible bonds remained firm, holding her in the air over the strange markings in the concrete she'd witnessed when they first entered. Sebastian's magic held her in place, but it did not prevent her from shaking with fear and shame.

"This subject will serve," Azslav said. He regarded her, his gaze impressing a physical sensation of cold wherever his eyes roamed. "Bathe in the subject's life blood, and the power will be yours."

Sebastian knelt again. He placed a tender kiss on Isabella's forehead. With his free hand, he cupped one of her breasts. He moved to kiss Isabella's lips, but she turned her head away. He laid his cheek against hers, his tears mixing with hers.

After a long moment, he straightened. Still resting his weight on one knee, he raised the knife high. Isabella turned to look at her husband, her murderer, one last time. Sebastian's face become stony, his eyes emotionless.

"Sebastian!" yelled a male voice from the door.

Sebastian brought the knife down. The knife bit into Isabella's flesh just above her right breast. She screamed. A gun fired, the thunderous sound filling the tiny cabin with its rumble. The scent of gunpowder filled the air, mixed with the sweet spice of the candles. Sebastian's chest exploded. Blood and bone rained onto Isabella. She screamed again. The gun blasted again. Sebastian twitched a moment before slumping over Isabella. The bonds disappeared, and they both fell to the cold concrete, their blood mixing and pooling in the gutters of the inscriptions.

"The sacrifice is made," said Azslav. The rumbling chorus of voices rivaled that of the gunfire. "The power is yours."

Fire burned through Isabella's veins, starting from the place where the knife pierced her flesh. She howled and writhed, trying to beat out the flames with her hands. With the intensity of the heat, she felt as if her flesh should be twisting and crisping like bacon in a

139

fire. Where she beat at the flames, her hands only found warm flesh, slick with blood, both hers and Sebastian's.

"I've got you." The man that shot her husband was suddenly there, wrapping her in the picnic blanket. His hands shook, but they were strong.

Isabella blinked at him. She pushed through the fog of shock and revulsion and pain. She knew this man. "Pedro?"

"It's okay, Mrs ... Bella. You're safe now."

Pedro Ortega helped Isabella away from the corpse of her husband. He kept pressure on the stab wound. The blanket soaked through with blood, but to Isabella's surprise, the pain faded. She sat with her back against one of the walls of the cabin, her eyes fixed on Sebastian. Pedro continued to hold the blanket against the wound. He said things that were meant to be reassuring, but Isabella didn't listen.

She lost track of time. She blinked, and when she opened her eyes, Pedro stood over Sebastian's corpse. She didn't remember Pedro leaving her side. During the lost moments, Pedro had rolled Sebastian onto his back. He knelt down next to the corpse, scrutinizing the wound in Sebastian's chest.

"Why did he do it?" Isabella's voice came out as a croak, hoarse and shallow from screaming.

Pedro looked up at Isabella and frowned. He reached into a suit pocket and pulled out a handkerchief. Using the cloth, he reached down and pulled something out of Sebastian's chest cavity. Isabella's stomach turned, but she watched without flinching. Pedro shuffled back to Isabella and offered her the cloth wrapped object.

"Take this." He kept his voice low. It sounded raspy. "A terrible price has been paid for this. Take it."

Isabella accepted the object. She shifted it in her hand, letting the handkerchief fall away. It was a perfectly round crystal ball, a little bit smaller than a baseball. Ortega pulled it from the corpse of her husband, yet the ball remained unblemished and clean. She touched it lightly, and the center filled with a warm, golden light. It pulsed in time with her heartbeat.

23

T HE CRYSTAL BALL SLIPPED from my hand and fell back onto its velvet pouch. My knees buckled and I stumbled backwards. Bella and Kate were both looking at me with the same worried expression. A silvery brilliance surrounded Bella. It made me think of the moon trying to outshine the sun on a cloudless night. A subtle yet dangerous-looking aura surrounded Kate as well. I'd never seen it before. It seemed to consume light rather than exude it. With my supernatural senses opened as they were, I saw the constant winter Kate carried with her in death.

I tried to close my mind's eye. It would not shut. Some pressure point inside me had been pressed, but instead of making me open my hand or flinch my knee, the lid of my mind's eye retracted. I could see more than I had ever seen before. Stabbing pain began to press in at my temples.

"Isabella," I said. I blinked and tried again. "Bella. I saw how you. I saw ..."

"Mel, calm down," Bella said. "Sit down. Just breathe."

I dragged out one of the chairs and fell into it. My eyes found the crystal ball and I couldn't look away. It blazed with light, the hues shifting and pulsing rhythmically. I stared at it, the memory of the vision haunting me. The ball came from inside Sebastian's chest, where his heart should have been. The light inside the crystal ball pulsed, like a heartbeat. My stomach twisted and I thought I might throw up.

"I saw the demon." I looked at Bella, and my natural vision blurred with tears. "I was you, in the cabin. We were stabbed."

"The blade didn't make it past my ribs," Bella picked up the crystal ball and slid it into the bag. "I think at the very end, Sebastian hesitated. He couldn't quite do it."

With the ball no longer visible, my nausea subsided. I tried again to close my mind's eye, but it would not shut. The pressure at my temples intensified. Tears welled up and ran down my cheeks. I wept not just from the physical pain, but from the memory of pain felt during the vision. I never knew such betrayal before. I never felt so powerless, so certain that I would die.

Kate walked around the table to kneel next to my chair. She reached out a hand to touch me before remembering that she could not. "You don't look well."

The pressure at my temples continued to intensify. It felt like my head had been caught between two giant gears, turning and milling my brain into jelly. I felt sick to my stomach again. When Bella warned me to bring a bucket to the library earlier, it seemed more like a lame joke than a prophecy. The thought brought a bitter smile to my lips.

Once more, I tried to close my mind's eye. Had I forgotten how? Panic crept into my voice. "I can't make it stop."

"Take a deep breath," Bella said. She put a hand on my shoulder and gave it a firm squeeze.

I closed my natural eyes and filled my lungs. My vision remained clear, unhindered by my eyelids. I saw my surroundings in colors that were impossibly crisp. The world my physical eyes presented to me seemed cheap and fake by comparison. With my mind's eye flared open and my eyelids closed, it felt less like seeing the world, and more like the world forcing itself into my mind.

"It hurts." I pushed myself out of the chair, stumbled, and fell to one knee. The nausea worsened, and I tasted bile. By will alone, I kept myself from getting sick in the library again. I scrambled out, rounded a corner in the hall, and dove into the bathroom. Stomach acid and the mostly digested bagel from breakfast splashed into the toilet. I flushed and held myself above the bowl. Throwing up did not bring any relief, and my head still felt like it would crack open.

Bella's hand felt cool against the back of my neck. I turned and sat with my back against the bathroom sink, my left arm propped against the side of the toilet. Sweat slicked my skin, and I felt dizzy. None of that mattered. The pain drilling into my temples held most of my attention.

"I can't make it stop." Despair, fear, pain ... I couldn't stop crying and shaking, but I didn't care. When you're pinned down by pain, you don't have time for pride or shame.

Bella took my head in her hands. Tears filled my eyes, but my supernatural sight made every detail of her face clear and magnificent in my mind. Her skin had not always been perfect. She regarded me with a young woman's eyes, though I could see where the wrinkles would become more prominent in a few years. Her genuine concern for my wellbeing drew her brow down into a maternal frown.

She pulled my head to her shoulder and held me, making soothing, shushing sounds. I surrendered to the pain and wept into her shoulder. During the vision, I felt Bella's certainty that her time had come. Sitting on the bathroom floor, with my head squeezed slowly in an invisible vise, I knew I'd reached the end of my mortality. Bella held me and I took small comfort in knowing that I would not die alone.

We stayed there an indeterminate amount of time. With normal, physical pain, the body's natural defense is to release endorphins to keep the pain from getting out of hand. Pain centers in the brain simply stop receiving signals. After a while, you become relatively immune to the pain. At least, that's what they taught me in health class back in high school. Burn victims went through a different kind of hell, but I didn't want to think about that.

Relentless, supernatural pain overwhelmed me. It did not diminish in intensity or in clarity, much like the vision of my mind's eye. My heart raced, and I had trouble catching my breath. It stretched out time, making each second a distinct event which could not be ignored.

I must have passed out, though I don't remember any interruption in the agony. One moment, I sat on the floor in the bathroom. The next, I lay on my bed, a wool blanket covering me. I felt hot all over, much as Bella had felt in the vision. Sweat drenched my hair and my clothes, and I shivered uncontrollably. Kate paced back and forth in my room, chewing her nails.

"Kate." My voice came out as a whisper, loud enough in my ears to make them pop.

"Bella is downstairs, working on a spell. Damn it, I wish I could do something!"

The halo of dying light around Kate extended out. Wherever she stepped, the bare wooden floorboards cracked and popped. Ice crystals spread in geometric patterns across the surface of the tall mirror. Her frustration leaked out of her, freezing the room, and reminding me of the ghost that just wanted to find her baby.

I wanted to say something to reassure her. No words came to mind. Coherent thoughts would not form consistently. I closed my eyes, still seeing my room and Kate. Tears ran down my cheeks and my nose ran with snot. I was in no position to reassure anyone.

I must have said something. Kate stopped her pacing and looked at me.

"What did you say, Mel?"

"It's cold." I didn't know if that's what I said before, but the words left my lips with a familiar taste.

"I'm not helping you by being here. I'll go wait in the car."

Kate disappeared. Soon after, Bella entered the room with a cup and one of the books from the library. She set the book on the bed next to me. Still holding the cup, she forced me to sit up.

"Drink this."

"What is it?" Steam wafted up from the mug. It smelled sweet.

"Tea with honey."

I took a sip. Aside from the hint of sweetness from the honey, it didn't have much flavor. "I thought you brewed a potion, like that reverse of the nasty elixir we drank yesterday."

"I could do something like that. I did find something. But if we go that route, you might not be able to open the Third Eye again."

My eyes widened. I turned to regard Kate, but she wasn't there. I turned back to Bella. "You said 'might.'"

"I told you before. There are no hard rules, only guidelines. From what I've read, you're going through something called 'The Awakening.' Some people have headaches. Some people crave strange foods. Some people don't experience any problems at all. For most people with a gift, this starts—"

I interrupted her. "Too many words."

"If we stop this, you will likely be shut off from your gift. Permanently."

As difficult as I found it to think straight, I knew what Bella's words meant. It meant more than just giving up on something that made me special. It meant I would no longer be of use to The Society, and I would be back out on the street, on my own. More importantly, it meant that I would be closed off from Kate. I wouldn't be able to see her or hear her. She would always be there for the rest of my days, isolated and alone.

"No," I whispered. "I can't."

"Okay." Bella blew out a relieved sigh. "That narrows our options. The safest is just to wait it out."

An involuntary whimper escaped my lips. I covered my eyes with my forearm. It didn't block my vision, and it didn't bring any relief. The invisible drills continued to bore into the sides of my head.

Bella watched me, frowning. After several moments, she reached out and plucked the mug of tea from my other hand. She shut her eyes and her lips moved. Then the halo of power surrounding her head flared into renewed brightness. It lasted for a split second, like a flash of lightning on a dry, summer night. She looked into the cup and swirled the steaming fluid. Then she took a sip.

"Drink this." She offered the cup back to me.

I sat up and took the cup carefully. To my mind's eye, the amber liquid inside glowed with a reddish tint.

"What did you do?"

"I cast a spell on it that might help. It should make you feel better."

"Should."

"Just drink it."

I did as commanded. As far as I could tell, the tea didn't taste any different. It might have been a little sweeter. I drained the cup, feeling the warmth spread down my throat, into my stomach. I waited for the pain to magically disappear, but it remained the same, relentless and excruciating.

"You should get some rest." Bella started to rise to her feet, but stopped when I grabbed her hand.

"Please. Don't go."

Reluctantly, she allowed me to pull her down onto the bed next to me. She brushed hair from my face, then draped an arm around me. She held me, sometimes saying things reassuring in a voice too quiet for me to hear. She comforted me, and before I knew it, I fell asleep.

24

I DID NOT SLEEP WELL. The pain continued the rest of that day and into the night. Mark stepped in at least once and prayed over me. Ortega also checked on me, standing at the door, looking solemn. Bella stayed with me the whole time, just as I asked. I kept passing out, and every time I woke, I found her laying next to me, one of her arms draped over my chest.

When morning came, I woke to find Bella asleep on my right side. I rubbed my forehead carefully, trying not to wake her. My dreams from the previous evening were fading, but I remembered enough to know that they had been dominated by images from the vision of Bella and the demon. In my dreams, it had been my body, naked and bound and suspended in the room, not Bella's. It played out in different ways. One time, Sebastian struck with the knife with all his strength, piercing my breastbone, lungs, and heart. Another time, Sebastian's chest exploded and his blood ran over me. But instead of imaginary fire coursing through my veins, actual flames consumed me, starting from my temples.

I shook off the nightmares and some of my morning grogginess. Then I realized: I still had my mind's eye open, but without any of the pain. I lowered my eyelids and focused my thoughts on closing my supernatural senses. The shadow-less world of impossibly bright colors receded. I sat in the peaceful, comfortable darkness that came from having one's eyes closed.

Bella stirred and I looked at her. Her eyes, brilliant hazel beneath straw colored bangs, fluttered open and locked with mine. She smiled at me, and I thought her the most beautiful woman I had ever seen. Her rumpled clothes and mussed hair did nothing to detract from her beauty. If anything, the imperfections made her that much more appealing.

"Feeling better?" she asked.

"Yes. Thank you."

Bella swung her legs down and sat up on the edge of my bed. She cocked her head to one side, then raised her arms over her head in a long stretch. "I slept crooked. If I get a headache now, I'm holding you accountable."

"Believe me, I wouldn't wish that kind of discomfort on anybody."

Still stretching and rolling her shoulders, Bella got up and left. A few minutes later, I rose, closed my door, and stripped down for a shower. I enjoyed the hot water a bit longer than usual, letting the warmth and steam loosen muscles in my shoulders and neck that seized up during the previous day. I felt like a new man by the time I dressed and met up with Bella and Mark in the kitchen.

"You gave us quite a scare," Mark said. He stood at one of the counters, implements of sandwich making in each hand. Bella sat at the dining table, her legs crossed. She gave me another smile like she had when she woke up. Beautiful. How had I not seen her beauty before?

I took a seat across from her. My eyes remained on her as I spoke to Mark. "Believe me, I was scared, too. What time is it?"

"Almost noon," Mark said.

"Your fever broke in the wee hours of the morning," Bella said.

I reached across the table and took Bella's hand. "Thank you for staying with me. I don't think I could have gotten through that alone."

Bella nodded and gave my hand a squeeze. Her skin felt soft and warm. She didn't withdraw her hand from mine, though I knew my own hands must have felt rough from all the callouses. "If we can't rely on each other, who can we rely on?"

I let Bella's hand go when Mark brought three plates of sandwiches and chips to the table. Mark quartered them and removed the crusts. I didn't think anyone actually did that.

We talked about our plans for the rest of the day over lunch. Mark intended to visit the homeless, much as Bobby and I had the previous day, only Mark's intentions were more pure. Bella wanted to confine herself to the library again and continue trying to find a better demon hunting spell. Neither of them objected when I suggested I stay to help Bella.

After lunch, I followed Bella into the library. She had changed since leaving my bed, once more wearing baggy clothing that looked like it came from a different era. Both her skirt and her blouse were made up of lots of different layers of fabric, with the outermost being frilly wisps, with hints of tan, black, and red.

"Do you have one of the rooms upstairs?" I asked.

Bella began selecting books from the shelves. "No. I have an old Victorian not far from here. Would you get out the amber incense, please?"

As I placed the incense and set it to burn, I started to psyche myself up. I am never shy around girls, but Bella stood out from the rest. She radiated intelligence, beauty, and sophistication. A strong woman, not a silly girl. I knew her in ways I would never know any other woman, and she had been there for me during the worst pain of my life. She held me when I thought my life was over. I wanted her. I needed her.

"You were good to me last night," I said. Then I hesitated. I should have planned this out. Oh well. I've always had more bravery than brains. "You should let me take you to dinner. Give me a chance to be good for you."

Bella set her books down on the table. She looked me up and down with the kind of scrutiny I used when planning a repo. Her eyes narrowed, and she licked her lips. After an eternity, she said, "That's sweet, but you don't have to do that."

I smiled. Technically, she didn't turn the offer down, so I still had a shot. "It's not a matter of 'have to.' I want to. You're unlike any woman I've ever known before."

Bella shook her head and laughed. "I'm sure you say that to all the girls."

"Bella." I stepped around the table and took both of her hands. I could feel her heartbeat, quick like mine. "I have never known a woman's thoughts or feelings before. I saw the world through your eyes. I felt your strength. I felt your fear. For a moment, I knew you in a way no one has ever known another person. Let me get to know you more."

I'm a little taller than Bella. She rose up on her tiptoes to give me a light kiss on the cheek. "Alright. But only because you asked so sweetly."

The next few hours went by in a blur. Bella did her best to unravel arcane secrets of the past, but I kept distracting her with jokes or silly questions. Eventually, she set me in front of a pile of very old books and had me check for visions. I found one in every tome, but I didn't tell her. The few that I peered into were strange beyond description.

The sun set and Bella and I left the office together, arm in arm. She led me to her car, which I immediately recognized. A tan and silver Buick. The same one I saw in the vision. I tensed, feeling an impulse to run the other direction.

Bella must have sensed my apprehension. "It's okay, Mel. It's not going to bite."

I gave her the best smile I could muster. "Of course it is! Buicks are ravenous."

She drove us out of the downtown area, taking the freeway towards Reno. She said something about a steakhouse in Roseville that she liked and I made agreement noises. I could not focus. Even with the prospect of a nice steak dinner, with a woman I liked sitting next to me, I couldn't relax in that car. The memory of the vision sat too close to the surface of my mind, and I couldn't shake the feeling we were going somewhere to die.

Once my feet touched the steakhouse's parking lot, with the Buick out of sight behind me, I breathed a huge sigh of relief. The night air chilled enough to turn my breath to mist. I took a few hurried steps away from the Buick. Turning my eyes up towards the stars, I felt more relief with each step.

"Mel, are you okay?" Bella hurried to walk beside me. She took my arm. I couldn't help noticing how it mirrored the way she took Sebastian's arm, just before he led her to the cabin.

"I'm okay. It's just ... it's been over a year for you. For me, it happened last night. I don't think I could have kept the car after all that."

Bella gave my arm a squeeze. She craned her neck to give the Buick a brief glance. "It's just a car. And I have other memories with it that aren't so bad."

Once in the restaurant and seated, I started to relax. The steakhouse smelled of pepper and wood smoke. The dimly lit wood paneling gave the place a rustic ambiance. Bella said the restaurant belonged to a local chain that stretched all the way to Lake Tahoe, but it seemed fancy to my tastes. A fake candle cast flickering amber light on Bella's skin, and I found myself lost in the details of her face.

After placing our orders, I asked, "So what does a pretty girl like you do when she's not cooped up in a stuffy library?"

Bella laughed. "You don't want to know. You'd be bored."

"Try me."

Bella stalled by taking a sip of water. She narrowed her eyes at me, then shook her head. "Alright. Well, you saw what happened to me."

I nodded and my cheeks warmed. The face of the demon flashed in my memory, followed by the glint of candlelight on a descending silver knife. I shuddered.

"After Mr. Ortega took me home, he told me about the cycle. He explained how we were entering the end times, and I realized that I had a bigger responsibility to the rest of the world. The problem was that I was a widowed housewife with no clue what to do. I had to start from the very beginning. I spent most of my time studying different languages until I knew enough that I could study magic."

"Sebastian knew magic."

"He did." Bella cast her eyes down at the table and fidgeted with her silverware. "He had worked with Mr. Ortega for quite a while, but I didn't know what he did. He never brought his work home with him. I thought he was just an investment banker."

"So you've been studying magic for a while now. You can find ghosts and brew disgusting potions. What else can you do?"

A playful smile crossed her lips. "Did you have something in mind?"

"I'm starting to get some ideas." I grinned.

It wasn't one of my better lines, but it made Bella's smile widen. "You're terrible."

"You're incredible."

"Really, Mel." Bella shook her head. "You're laying it on a bit thick."

Dinner came and went. I joked and flattered throughout the main course. Bella protested with smiles sometimes, flushed cheeks other times. I hardly tasted the meal. Bella's voice and eyes took all of my attention. In Bella's company, they could have served us cold cheese sandwiches and it would have been divine. I felt completely smitten, and I wanted to win Bella over to me. With her eyes twinkling and her cheeks flushed, I knew I succeeded.

When we left, the car didn't make me nearly so uncomfortable. I held her hand as she drove. I hadn't had any alcohol, but her smile intoxicated me, as did the subtle, sweet scent of her perfume. It came as no surprise to me when we pulled into her driveway rather than the front of The Society's office.

She put the car in park, killed the engine, and I slid closer to her. I gently turned her face to mine as I closed the remaining distance between us. Her lips were soft against my own, the kiss sweet and tender. Our mouths opened, the kiss turning into something more playful and passionate.

When we finally pulled apart, Bella leaned back away from me, her face hot and her breath heavy. "Are you sure this is what you want?"

"Don't make me beg." My voice came out as a low rasp.

She opened her door and slipped out. The cold November air cut through my clothes as if I weren't wearing any. The contrast to the warmth we'd been generating in the car pulled a misty, shuddering gasp from me. The cold reminded me of something, but I couldn't put my finger on it. Something important, but in that moment, I couldn't bring myself to care.

Bella took my hand and led me up the walkway to her house. She lived in a Victorian as old as the haunted house we investigated, but where the other house had been cold and abandoned, its outer walls faded and chipped, Bella's home appeared warm and well maintained. A small front yard made for a modest first impression, the grass well trimmed and neat. A massive planter with huge green leaves flanked the path to the door.

Inside, I found the front room furnished more for comfort than for style. A large couch with puffy tan cushions dominated the space. A large flat screen TV hung on the same wall as the hearth, with an entertainment center in the corner of the room, all of its cabling neatly concealed. Rich paintings decorated two of the walls. Voluminous curtains covered the large, front window.

There were other details about Bella's house I might have noticed. I stopped looking when Bella grabbed me and drew me down to her, resuming the kiss we started in the car.

We remained just inside the door for a long time, our mouths pressed together and our hands roaming freely. She moaned softly into the kiss when I ran my fingers along the back of her neck and into her hair. Then we were moving, still kissing. She led me up the stairs, our clothes cast off and landing like litter on the steps. My jacket went first, then hers, the beginning of a breadcrumb trail leading from the front door to her bedroom.

Our shoes gave us pause, breaking the moment comically. We separated long enough to hop from foot to foot, hurriedly pulling ourselves free of our footwear. As many times as I've done this particular dance, I never found a graceful way to kick off my shoes before sex. Tall boots or anything with long laces wind up being a hassle. Bella had been wearing practical flats. I helped her remove them, caressing her calf as I did so.

Bella wore so many layers that getting her out of her clothes felt like unwrapping Christmas presents. When at last we reached her undergarments and I removed her bra, she stood back from me and let me feast on her with my eyes. She did not have a supermodel's body. Her hips were too wide for that, and her waist not nearly narrow enough. Her breasts were ample, no longer immune to the effects of gravity. She had a little bit of a belly, and the skin on her thighs dimpled ever so slightly. For all that, she exuded confidence and sexiness, and I wanted her more than I wanted anyone before.

She radiated beauty and sexual need. I closed the distance between us once again. The tips of her breasts responded to my hands. She pulled me down onto her bed, her hands exploring my body as I explored hers. Shortly after that, I lost myself to sweet sensations. I stopped thinking entirely, and let myself be fully in the moment.

25

THE SOUND OF A RUNNING SHOWER, like the insistent white noise of a radio between stations, woke me the next morning. Gray light peeked through the windows. I rolled over and pointed my bleary eyes at the clock on Bella's bedside table. A little after 8:00, the earliest I'd risen from bed in as long as I could remember. I felt good, but I also felt like I had sand in my eyes.

I rolled out of bed and stretched. Bella had straightened up a little before going off to shower. She'd folded my clothes and stacked them in a neat pile on a chair. I considered leaving them there and joining her in the shower, but I didn't know her well enough to predict if she liked sharing shower time or preferred to just clean up alone. I stepped into my underwear and pants and shrugged into my shirt. I may not have been clean, but I felt dirty in the way I liked.

Dressed, I went downstairs in search of the kitchen. By the time Bella joined me, I had scrambled some eggs with cheese, fried up some French toast, and put some bacon in the oven.

"It smells good," Bella said. She took a seat at the kitchen table and crossed her legs. Her off-white dress had a long skirt, a modest neckline, and a lot of hanging material around the sleeves. She sat with her back straight and a small smile on her lips as she watched me finish preparing breakfast.

"Thank you!" I prepared a plate for each of us and joined her at the table. "You look fantastic this morning."

Bella frowned and toyed with a piece of toast. "Mel. I don't want you to get the wrong idea about last night."

I paused in forking some eggs to my mouth. I knew this speech. I delivered it a time or two myself. I couldn't remember ever being on this end of it before. Playing into it, I said, "What idea would that be?"

"We had a good time last night, but it didn't mean anything." Bella's voice sounded sad and apologetic. "We both needed a release, and it was very nice. You were exactly what I needed. But I don't want you to think I'm making some kind of claim on you, and I don't want you to make any claims on me."

I set my fork on the edge of my plate and leaned back in my chair. I thought about all the things I said and felt the previous day. After the headache, I obsessed over Bella, right up to the point where we tumbled into bed. Pushing my eggs around my plate with my fork, I studied her face. I still found her attractive, but I didn't see her as the Venus de Milo made flesh anymore.

"What changed?" I said.

Bella took a deep breath and let it out in a slow sigh. "I cast a spell on you. On both of us."

"Go on."

"I couldn't stop your Awakening without damaging your gift. I told you that. With more experience, I might have been able to cast a spell that would have dulled your pain. But you were in bad shape and getting worse and … I didn't think you had a lot of time, so I did what I could. I gave you a distraction. A temporary love spell."

I spent some time studying the eggs on my plate while I mulled over the implications. Finally, I said, "You roofied me."

"I wouldn't put it that way. The spell altered our perception, but it didn't make us do anything we were completely opposed to."

"You roofied yourself, too?"

"I had to. I gave the tea to someone once without taking it myself. Never again."

I forked another bite of eggs in my mouth and chewed with my eyes on my plate. I couldn't really taste my breakfast through all the confusing emotions tumbling through my head and heart.

Bella reached across the table, took one of my hands, and gave it a squeeze. "I hope this doesn't hurt our friendship. I like you, Mel. You're a sweet boy."

I laughed. An age difference existed between us, but I hadn't really felt it until that moment. "I'm sure we can still be friends, Bella. And I gotta say … you're pretty flexible for an older woman."

She laughed, and actually managed to blush. After that, we dug into breakfast with renewed interest. For awhile, we joked and laughed, without a hint of flirting. Whatever intimacy we'd shared the previous evening faded into memory, taking with it the awkwardness that usually comes with the dreaded Morning After.

By mid-morning, Bella and I stepped into the office of The Society. I realized as we walked through the building that we were probably following Bella's normal schedule. Until that day, I simply slept in too late to notice her comings and goings. For as much as I might have entertained her the previous night, I didn't even disrupt Bella's normal routine. The thought humbled me more than I liked.

Mark sat in the kitchen, a steaming cup of coffee and a fresh box of bagels on the table next to him. He had a section of the *Sacramento Bee* in his hands. When we entered the kitchen, he folded up the newspaper, set it on the table, and gave us a broad smile.

"Good morning!" he said.

"Good morning!" Bella and I said in unison. She gave me a small smile before fixing herself a cup of coffee.

I took a seat at the table and snagged a bagel. Mark studied Bella with pursed lips and a furrowed brow. He shook his head and picked up his paper. Did he know? How? Perhaps he'd picked up some of Bobby Greenwood's tricks. Thankfully, if Mark knew what Bella and I had been up to, he didn't say anything.

"Have you seen Bobby this morning?" Bella asked.

"Not this morning, but I saw him last night. He was asking about the two of you, actually."

"What did he want?" I asked.

"I'm not sure." Mark put the newspaper down again and frowned. "He seemed worried, though he didn't say so. He asked where you two had gone, then sat and talked with me for at least half an hour. I think he just needed someone to keep him company for a while."

"Well, he's going to miss out again," Bella said. "Mel helped me find a spell yesterday that will let me distinguish between ghosts, demons, and other spiritual entities."

I didn't think I'd actually helped that much, but it seemed more polite to smile and nod. "So, are we going to try and find something today, go there, and get Mark beat up again?"

"That's not our primary plan," Mark said. For a priest, Mark demonstrated considerable skill at giving cold looks.

"We're just going to look," Bella said. "I know, that's what we said last time, but this time will be different. Besides, Mr. Ortega said that he wants to be with us the next time we go into a hostile situation."

"What does Ortega do?" I asked.

Bella and Mark both raised an eyebrow, their curious expressions identical.

"I mean, what sort of supernatural gift does he have?" I asked.

"Oh," Bella said. "He's no more gifted than Bobby, in that respect. He's managed to collect a number of objects with supernatural properties, which have been useful over the years."

"Like, magic wands and invisibility cloaks?"

"All sorts of things," Bella said.

"Nothing as blatant as that," Mark said.

"I see." I took another bite of my bagel.

We finished our brunch and coffee and relocated to the library. Bella fetched the map book, incense, and the dowsing crystal. Mark moved to one side of the room, his Bible open in his hand and his mouth already moving in silent prayer. I moved to a corner of the room to get out of the way.

I opened my mind's eye. The supernatural sights within the room revealed themselves to me as brilliantly as when my eye had been forced open by the crystal ball. When I felt no pain, I let out a sigh of relief.

With renewed confidence, I examined the auras around both Bella and Mark. Bella's silver aura surrounded her head as before, with other light tracing the air around her hands as she started to cast her spell. Mark's aura shifted between brilliant white and gold, colors that made me think of the noonday sun. Mark's aura emanated from the center of his chest and his brow, coalescing and surrounding him like liquid smoke.

I looked around for Kate but did not see her. I turned in a complete circle, then peered out into the hall. I couldn't find Kate, and worry hit me like a bucket of ice water. My chest tightened and my stomach flip-flopped. I hadn't given Kate a second thought the entire night I spent with Bella. Had she returned from the car while I was under Bella's spell? It would have been uncomfortable for her, being around us while we flirted and kissed. Maybe she went back to the car to get away and give both of us some space.

Bella stopped chanting. She frowned at me. "Are you upset, Mel? This spell is sensitive to the emotions of people nearby. It's not going to work right if you're afraid of getting sick again."

"No, it's not that. Kate's not here with us. It's the first time we've really been apart since this whole thing started."

"Perhaps she has finally found peace," Mark said.

I shook my head. "I don't think so. It doesn't feel right."

"For those left behind, it never feels right. If she has moved on, then there is nothing left that can harm her."

His attempt to reassure me had the opposite effect. My jaw tightened and I gritted my teeth. I walked to the door. "Keep on with your spell. I'll get out of the way."

I went upstairs to my room and sat on the edge of my bed. I hunched forward, leaning my elbows against my knees. I couldn't remember the last time I felt this angry with myself. Kate had always been so sweet. And I ignored her in my pursuit to get laid. She deserved better than that.

I tried to convince myself that she went to the car and stayed there, waiting until it felt safe enough to come back. She wouldn't want to find me and Bella in bed together. That would be awkward for everyone involved. With the way I kept sleeping in the last few days, she might stay away until early afternoon.

"If she's just off somewhere else, then why do I feel like something is wrong?"

I drew open the desk drawer and reached inside. My fingers didn't find what I was looking for.

"What the fuck?" I leaped to my feet and yanked out the drawer. I upended it, spilling a few pens and a pad of stationery onto the floor next to my shoes. The triangle of material from the Nova was gone.

159

26

I RAN DOWNSTAIRS AND SLID into the library. "Bella! I need your help."

The dowsing crystal floated on its own in the air above the atlas, no longer attached to a string. It rotated slowly, glowing with a soft blue light. Bella's eyes also glowed. Once my words reached her ears, her concentration broke, and the light went out from both her eyes and the crystal. The crystal fell, and Bella lunged forward to catch it, just above the table.

"Damn it Mel, I almost had it."

Mark gave Bella an admonishing look. He opened his mouth to say something, but I stepped forward and didn't give him a chance to speak.

"You said the material from the Nova wasn't an anchor. You said she was bound to me. Could you have been wrong?"

"No." Bella shook her head. "No. I've held several anchors. They're always different, but they have a very distinctive energy to them."

"Well, it's gone, and so is Kate."

Bella carefully placed the dowsing crystal on the table. "Are you sure?"

I drew in a deep, calming breath. I didn't want to snap at Bella, but panic made my temper short. Something happened to the strip from the Nova and we were wasting time. I took another deep breath before speaking. "Would you like to come upstairs and see for yourself?"

Bella reached up and held my cheek with her hand. Her touch calmed me more than breathing. "Don't worry, Mel. We'll find her."

We went back to my room and Bella helped me look for the scrap of vinyl. Mark followed, but stayed at the door, frowning. We couldn't fit all three of us into my tiny room to look around. Also, there just wasn't that much stuff in the room to go through. After a few moments, Bella stopped poking through my belongings and shook her head.

"Alright, so the anchor that was not an anchor is missing." Bella cast her eyes once again around the small room. "And you can't see Kate anywhere, either. It probably isn't a coincidence, but … I just don't believe it was an anchor. If it were, she wouldn't have been able to follow you out of this room."

We pushed the dressing mirror out of the corner during our search. I glanced at it. My black eye and bruised cheek stood out, making my angry expression more fierce. My expression softened as I remembered how I received the bruises.

"Mark, do you remember what you and Bobby talked about last night?"

"We talked about a lot of things." Mark sounded confused.

"Did he tell you about his huge gambling debt?"

Mark hesitated before answering. "No, he didn't say anything about that. I've known for some time that he has money problems, but he's never sought to confide in me on the matter. Last night, all we talked about was The Society, and how you joining us might open up unique possibilities."

"You two talked about me? What about Kate, did you talk about her?"

"Yes. We talked about her as our newest 'unofficial' member. It was nothing serious. I did not think I'd betrayed a trust."

"You didn't betray a trust, Mark." I tried to give him a reassuring smile, but with my jaw clenched, it looked more like a sneer. "If neither of you took the vinyl, then it had to have been picked up by Ortega or Bobby. And Bobby was here last night."

Bella stiffened. She brushed past me and stepped around Mark, moving to a door across the hall from my room. The door, like many others in the building, was closed and locked. I hadn't had a chance to explore and had no idea what lay on the other side.

"What's in there?"

"Mr. Ortega keeps a number of artifacts in the office," Bella said. "Some of them we know what they do, some of them we don't. Some of the ones we've figured out are kept in here. Mark, do you have a key?"

"I do not."

I bent and picked up a pair of paper clips that fell from the desk drawer. I knelt in front of the locked door. I didn't have a lot of skill picking locks, but these weren't that tricky. They were a step up from the lock on a bathroom door, but not a huge step. I folded the clips into usable shapes and asked, "You have an idea, Bella?"

"Maybe."

The lock surrendered, the knob turned, and the door opened with an ominous creak. Beyond, I found a room twice as large as mine, lined with mismatched shelves. Boxes and chests and various other containers filled the space, most with placards written in a firm, neat print. A thin layer of dust covered a few of the boxes.

Bella pushed past me and pulled down one of the cardboard boxes sitting on a shelf made out of particle board. She pulled off the lid, set it aside, and leaned into the box, rummaging with less care than I expected. After several moments she straightened, her hands balled into fists. "The glasses are gone."

"What glasses?" Mark and I asked at the same time.

"There were a pair of reading glasses Pedro and I studied a few months ago. They let you see a ghost as long as you were holding its anchor. We didn't see a lot of use for them since we usually destroy anchors, so we put the glasses in storage. I thought about them when you first showed up, Mel, but since you could already see Kate, there didn't seem to be any reason to retrieve them."

"So the vinyl is an anchor," I said. "And Bobby took it and the glasses so that he could see Kate."

"I don't think so." Bella turned and moved deeper into the room, checking labels as she went. She stopped at a wooden chest that looked like it would be at home on a pirate's ship. Bella lifted the lid and it opened with a long creak. Instead of revealing piles of golden coins, the chest contained a set of scales made of silver

163

and bronze. The scales contained three bowls instead of two, with the third being smaller and towards the center of the device.

"What is that?" I asked.

"It's the Scales of Anitu. It is a device for creating anchors."

My shoulders slumped and I let out a sigh. "Fuck."

"Language," Mark said. He leaned forward, scrutinizing the scales with a frown. "Bobby doesn't have the gift. How would he make those work?"

"You don't need a gift. Anyone can use these." Bella gestured to the device as she spoke. "In one scale, you place something with a sympathetic connection to the deceased. Something to draw the *semangat*, or soul. In the other scale, you pour blood. When enough has been sacrificed, the *semangat* is pulled into and bound to whatever is placed in the center bowl. You don't need magic. You just need fresh blood."

"So, that's how you know so much about anchors," I said. "You've made them, using that thing."

"No." Bella shook her head. "Creating anchors is the opposite of what we're trying to do. Like I said before, we destroy anchors. I know about them as I do because we've come across several in the last year."

"Why would Bobby bind Kate to an anchor?" Mark asked. "How do we even know that he used that thing? Maybe the glasses are just missing. Or maybe Mr. Ortega took the glasses."

Bella pulled her crystal ball from a pouch at her waist. The orange light of the ball brightened the room, illuminating Bella's face from beneath, like the prelude to a campfire horror story. She closed her eyes and said, "*Animadverto.*"

With my mind's eye, I watched the silvery aura around Bella's brow move down and fill her eyes. Objects on the shelves around us reacted to her, glowing and pulsing in various colors. Some seemed to respond to her spell, others to the presence of the crystal ball. For a moment, I felt like we were surrounded by kegs of TNT, and Bella just struck a match.

"I see," Bella said. "He cleaned the scales, but there is still blood there."

Bella's hand holding the orb started to drift towards one of the boxes to her right, which yawned with a hungry, crimson light.

Bella didn't seem to notice. I reached forward and pulled Bella's hand away, careful not to touch the crystal ball.

"You should probably put that away in here," I said.

"Oh." Bella looked down at the ball, then to the box with the red glow. She shuddered before letting the crystal ball slip back into her pouch. The red glow faded. "Right. Thanks."

"For the sake of argument, let's say that Bobby is responsible," Mark said. "He came in the night, used the piece of the vinyl to bind Kate to an anchor. Then he took the glasses. To what end? He doesn't need a real ghost to help him with his show."

"I don't think that's why he wants her," I said. "He needs sixty thousand dollars before tomorrow. The thugs sent to collect from him dropped that hint around the same time they gave me the black eye. He's got a gambling problem. He's probably going to try and get her to help him cheat at cards or something."

"Would that even work?" Bella asked.

"Not at a regular casino," I said. "But maybe a private, high stakes game? Kate could walk behind the other players and let him know what their cards were, and he'd be the only one that could see her. For something like that to work, though, she'd have to be in on it. I know Kate. She wouldn't go in on something like that."

"He might be able to compel her, using the anchor," Bella said.

I shook my head again. "It doesn't matter. Bella, can you just use the spell you used before that found her?"

"The old spell is too clumsy and random."

"Come on, we have to do something!"

"Let's not do anything hasty," Mark said. "Right now, all we have is speculation. Bobby's been a friend for years. Let's not jump to conclusions. He deserves the benefit of the doubt."

"Fine." A few more words that would make the priest frown curdled on my tongue, but I bit them back. I wanted to punch Bobby. Now that Mark was coming to Bobby's defense, I wanted to punch the priest, too. But none of that would bring Kate back. "You want to give him the benefit of the doubt? Sure. After we find him. And after we figure out what he's done to Kate."

We went back down to the library and Bella reset the spell she'd been about to cast before. She lit the candles, started fresh incense to burn, then picked up the dowsing crystal.

"How long will this take?" I asked.

"Not long. If you're going to stay in the room, you can help by staying calm. Picture her in your mind. Imagine her in as much detail as you can."

I had a hard time staying calm, but I could picture Kate's face easily. Bella began chanting in more pseudo Latin. I lost track of the words. Mark closed his eyes and began to pray. I folded my arms across my chest and continued to imagine Kate.

The dowsing crystal lifted out of Bella's hands and floated over the table. It spun in the air, glowing with a soft blue light. Bella's eyes began to glow again. The atlas on the table opened, the pages flipping, moved by an invisible hand. A high-pitched whine sounded in my ear, faint enough that I wondered if I heard it or just imagined it. The air felt charged, like a summer day back home, just before a lightning storm.

The whine stopped. The dowsing crystal plunged towards the atlas, moving faster than I could blink. It stopped just over the page, quivering and pointing at an address in El Dorado Hills.

"Found her," Bella said. "Let's go see what our friend is up to."

27

ATER JOTTING DOWN THE ADDRESS and gathering our jackets, we headed out to Bella's Buick. My empty hands longed for something. Tools. A weapon. I needed something if we were heading into battle, whatever that meant. Not that we were likely to get into an actual fight. Still, I would have liked grabbing my old tool bag I used to use when boosting cars. My hands needed to be doing something.

I stepped out onto the sidewalk in front of the office and glanced at the throng of traffic rolling down the street. Several businesses hung their shingles in the area, which meant a pretty much continuous stream of moving cars during the day. By pure luck, I spotted a familiar face in a black SUV as it passed by. Special Agent Bennett, of the FBI.

"Damn it." I watched the SUV round a corner.

"What's the matter?" Bella asked.

"Hopefully nothing."

We slid into the Buick, with Bella behind the wheel and Mark taking shotgun. Bella eased her way into traffic and navigated towards 50. I watched for the FBI. After several minutes, I started to think I'd imagined seeing Agent Bennett. When we turned onto the east bound on ramp, I stopped doubting. A black SUV changed lanes and pulled onto the freeway behind us.

"Okay, it's not nothing," I said.

"Is it the guys Bobby owes money to?" Bella asked.

"No, it's the FBI. They want me to spy on you for them."

Bella and Mark exchanged incredulous looks.

"I appreciate your sense of humor," Mark said. "But is this really the time to—"

"They think you covered up murders."

"Oh," Mark said, his voice suddenly quiet. "You're not joking."

Bella frowned. Her grip tightened on the steering wheel. When she spoke next, her voice quavered a little. "You didn't tell them anything, did you?"

"About your ex-husband? Hell no. I wouldn't have, even if I had the chance."

"Did they ask about Father Philips?" Mark asked.

"They did. They said he'd been stabbed in his home."

Mark shook his head and looked out his window. I shifted in the backseat until I could see his face in the rearview mirror. Mark wore a pained expression, his cheeks flushed. He looked more than just sad for his friend's death. He looked guilty.

"Why are they following us now?" Bella asked.

"I don't know. They said they'd check in on me in a couple of days. For all I know, they've been following me ever since they picked me up. It was just dumb luck that I noticed them this time."

"If we're going to an illegal poker game," Bella said, "it would be better if we didn't arrive with a car full of federal agents behind us."

"We don't know that we're going to a poker game," Mark said. "And even if we were, how would the FBI know what's was going on inside?"

"They're the FBI," Bella said. "They'll investigate."

"Bella's right," I said. "It's a bad idea to take the feds to where Bobby is. Hell, it might be bad for us to show up. These kinds of games are usually invitation only, and they don't appreciate crashers. If two cars pull up, and one of them is full of guys in dark suits, it's going to be bad."

"So where should I drive?" Bella asked.

"I'm thinking," I said. "Just keep going, for now."

We continued east on 50, with Bella driving just above the speed limit. That meant most of the other cars flew past us. The black SUV continued to tail us. We were being followed, and there wasn't anything we could do about it. Not together, anyway.

"Alright," I said. "Here's what we'll do. When we get to El Dorado Hills, let's find some place to pull over and split up."

"Split up," Bella repeated.

"There's only one SUV. Mark and I will get out first. You go on with the Buick. If they follow you, Mark and I will keep going to the poker game. If they stay on us, we'll each take a cab and go different directions. They can only follow one of us. Besides, it might be better if we didn't all show up at the poker game at the same time."

We passed Folsom and traffic thinned. The FBI's SUV stood out about a dozen car lengths behind us, matching our geriatric speed. Before long, we began a steep incline, the freeway surrounded on both sides by hills made up of golden fields. After a short curve, the highway began to descend into the city of El Dorado Hills. Shortly after that, Bella turned off of the highway and cut into a bustling shopping center.

Bella circled a labyrinth of parked cars and disinterested pedestrians. She stopped in front of a supermarket and let me and Mark out.

"Be careful," Bella said.

"May the Lord watch over us all," Mark said, his voice solemn.

The Buick pulled away. Mark and I stayed near the door of one of the super markets. A Salvation Army worker stood nearby, ringing his bell. He smiled at me, a pleading look in his eye. I ignored him while I watched for Agent Bennett's car.

Mark spotted it before I did. He tapped my arm and nodded his head towards the SUV. "There. They're following Bella."

I followed Mark's gaze. A short distance behind Bella's Buick, a nondescript black vehicle prowled through the parking area. A few minutes after Bella turned back onto the main road, the SUV followed, cutting off a sedan in the process.

"That wasn't so bad," I said.

I dug out my cell phone and thumbed in a search for a cab company. Mark and I waited several minutes to be picked up. The charity worker's hungry stare burned into the back of my neck, making the wait drag on with awkward slowness. I'm not sure what I looked like to the man, but even without a collar, Mark had the bearing and look of a priest. The Salvation Army worker's pleading look eventually turned sour. He probably thought we were there to poach his territory.

The yellow cab pulled into the shopping center and Mark flagged it down. We gave the cabbie the address we received from Bella's spell. The cabbie made me repeat the address while looking me up and down through narrowed eyes. After a brief hesitation, he pulled the car out and navigated onto the road north.

Mark and I rode in the back of the cab in silence. I watched as we passed a golf course, a school, and an upscale residential area. After several minutes, the cab turned down a long, private driveway that climbed one of the tall hills. From the main road, opulent homes could be seen, ringing the top of the hill like a garter circling a stripper's thigh. We appeared to be headed for one of those houses.

"Maybe we were wrong," I whispered to Mark. "Maybe he's seeing a client after all."

"We'll know soon enough."

The cabbie pulled into a circular driveway bordering the immaculate yard of a mansion. The expensive home appeared to be made mostly of glass and white stone. Wide and tall, with massive windows, the main building appeared lavishly furnished even from the driveway. The mansion sat in a recess in the hill, gleaming in the light like a gem set in a crown. The manicured front yard adorned the front of the property, locked away behind a black cage fence. Several expensive cars sat in the circular driveway. Bobby's Ford truck stood taller than the sports cars and sedans that surrounded it. Next to the other cars, it looked cheap and dirty.

A thick-chested, no-necked guard stood on our side of the gate. Our first obstacle. He wore charcoal gray slacks and a blazer over a black shirt. With brown skin and a hooked nose, he wore his hair short enough to be a shadow. He watched us step out of the cab, folded his arms in front of his chest, and looked down at us with a clenched jaw and a furrowed brow.

"Do you want me to wait?" the cabbie asked.

"Yes, please." I paid the fare along with a tip. "We won't be long."

"Not long at all," Mark said, pitching his voice low. "We're probably not getting in."

"Give me a second."

I opened my mind's eye and tried something I hadn't tried since I first met Kate. I turned without turning, rewinding my vision of time. It came easily, as if I'd been doing this sort of thing my whole life. Apparitions of Mark and I walked backwards away from us, ducking to get back into the cab. The cab's echo backed away, separating from the vehicle inhabiting the present. As I watched, the guard from the past stared at us during our approach. When he saw the cab pull into the driveway, he checked the gun concealed under his coat.

I continued turning back time, increasing the speed of the rewind. The guard walked around, never far from his spot near the gate. He stood there when each of the cars pulled up, spilling out their passengers. He had been there when an enormous black man came out of the mansion to greet each of his guests. I took note of as many details as I could, then let my mind's eye close and return to the present.

With as much confidence and swagger as I could muster, I approached the guard. I had a weak plan. We needed to seem like we belonged, like we had been invited. That meant acting more confident than I felt. That meant bluster.

"We need to see Robert Greenwood." I nodded towards the house. "Let us through."

"I don't know any Greenwood," the guard said. For such a huge man, he had a soft, almost squeaky voice. "You and your buddy need to turn around, get back in your cab, and get out of here."

"Oh, you're not good with names," I said. "Let me try descriptions and see if that jogs a memory. I'm not here to see the short man in the track outfit that arrived in the silver Spyder. I'm not here to see the white man in the tan suit that showed up in the Aston Martin. I'm not here to see the mustached man, nor his blond escort, that pulled in driving the red Ferrari. I'm not even here to see the huge black man that lives here, that came out wearing a gray sports coat and t-shirt. I'm only here to see the guy with the deep tan and cocky smile that got out of that F-150."

The guard narrowed his already squinty eyes to the point where I wondered if he could see anything at all. He looked me up and down several times. "What are you, paparazzi?"

I held up my hands, palms out. "Do you see any cameras? Just let us through. We're here to see Bobby, not make a scene."

The guard reached into his jacket pocket and I thought for a moment that he was going to draw his gun. He brought out a cell phone instead. He hit a number on speed dial and pressed the phone to the side of his face.

"Mr. Jason," the guard said. "Sorry to interrupt, but there's men here at the gate asking for Mr. Greenwood." The guard paused, nodding his head. "Yes, sir." He dropped the phone back into his pocket. He looked me up and down one more time. Just when I thought he would turn us away again, he said, "Follow me."

The guard lumbered ahead of us, leading us through Mr. Jason's home. Occasional splashes of color on paintings or decorative vases contrasted with sterile white walls and carpet. The ceiling stretched high above us with occasional ceiling fans so far away that I wondered if they served a function at all. We passed through rooms and hallways, all spacious and decorated with a touch that only an interior decorator could achieve and appreciate.

Our journey through the mansion ended in what I assumed to be an entertainment room. Along one wall hung a TV larger than some of the screens at a multiplex theater. Along another wall, glass shelves held trophies and signed basketballs. A basketball jersey flew near the same wall, suspended by invisible wires. The number "43" marked the jersey in purple and white.

At the far end of the room, the men I saw in my vision outside sat around a poker table. Bobby sat with his back to me between the mustached man and the man in the track suit. A cloud of cigar smoke wafted over their heads. A professional dealer stood on the far side of the table, prim in his suit. He stood with a straight back and a blank expression.

I opened my mind's eye. There, just on the other side of the table, stood Kate. She frowned, walking around the table with her hands clasped behind her back. She watched the cards in each of the players' hands. I stamped down an impulse to rush forward and call her name. Neither she nor Bobby had noticed our arrival, and I didn't want to give anything away yet.

Mr. Jason turned towards us from where he sat at the circular table. He held up a hand, bidding us to stop where we were. With my mind's eye still open, I rewound time. I watched the last several hands from a distance. Bobby won the last five or six hands in a row, raking in chips and increasing his substantial lead. Kate helped him, but she didn't look happy about it.

The current hand ended. Bobby used one hand to rake a meager pot towards his stacks of chips. The man with the mustache had been the last to fold. The blond woman that arrived with him, sitting to his left with a modest stack of chips of her own, squeezed his arm. As they shared a kiss, the man in the tan suit fished out another cigar, tapping it against his palm with a little more force than necessary. The man in the track suit sat back in his chair and shook his head, staring at his chips. His stack stood smaller than anyone else's, and from the haunted look in his eyes, he wouldn't be at the table much longer.

"Let's take a short break," Mr. Jason said. The host of the party, he was very tall, even sitting down. He wore his black hair short, though not as severely trimmed as the guard that escorted us. A thin mustache and a bit of chin fuzz decorated Mr. Jason's face. The gray sports coat he had been wearing before sat slung over the back of his chair. He pushed the chair back and stood up. "Robert, you've got some fans waiting to get your autograph."

Bobby turned. His smile evaporated as soon as he saw us. He wore thin, wire-framed glasses with round lenses, like something John Lennon might have envied. A moment later, Kate noticed us, and her face lit up with a wide smile. I had to fight to keep my expression neutral. As much as I wanted to bust a chair over Bobby's head, I needed to stay calm. Just like any other repo, this would only play out in my favor if I stayed cool.

"Mr. Greenwood," the man in the tan suit said with a thick Russian accent. "Will your friends be joining us? Maybe you could take their chips instead of ours for a while, no?"

"They could take my spot," the man in the track suit said. "I'm almost out, anyway."

"You keep your ass in that chair," Mr. Jason said, smiling. "I'll float you a few gee's. I know you're good for it."

"It's not the money," track suit said. "It's the losing."

"Excuse me a minute, gentlemen," Bobby said. He stood and and turned to the host. "Tommy, would you mind if I took my friends out on the deck to talk with them?"

"Be my guest," Mr. Jason said. He turned to Mark. "I'm Thomas Jason. Any friend of Robert Greenwood is a friend to me. If you need anything, you just let my man know and it's yours."

"Thank you, Mr. Jason," Mark said.

The guard left. Bobby, Mark, and I went through a glass door onto a huge redwood deck. The Sacramento Valley stretched out below us. Rays of sunlight slashed through holes in the clouds, illuminating the tops of trees. I continued to keep my cool, but if something happened and I lost it and threw Bobby over the balcony, I couldn't have picked a more idyllic place.

"What are you guys doing here?" Bobby asked.

"What are you doing?" I jabbed a finger into his chest.

"Winning." Bobby took a step back from me and gave Mark an apologetic look. "I know I shouldn't have made the anchor, but my back was against the wall. Mel, you saw those guys. You know what's at stake. I didn't have a choice."

"That doesn't justify what you've done," Mark said. "We destroy anchors. We don't bind ghosts to our will. We don't use our gifts to help us steal from the rich."

"I'm not stealing from them," Bobby said. "They're buying entertainment. It was Tommy's idea to invite some of his friends over for some high stakes poker against a psychic."

"But you're not a psychic," I said. "I am. And Kate is my friend."

Bobby's expression darkened. "And Izzy is my friend. But that didn't stop you from fucking her, did it?"

"This isn't helping," Mark said.

"No, you're damn right it isn't," Bobby said. "This little shit shows up and everyone starts kissing the ground he walks on. Well I've got news for you, Mark. He's nothing. He's a bigger sham than I am, and none of you see it. I saw it, and I did something about it. I stole his toy." He drew a bound stack of bills from his suit jacket pocket and pushed the money into my hands. "Here. Take this and get the fuck out of my sight."

"Robert, this —" Mark started.

"No!" Bobby said, cutting the priest off. "Enough is enough. This guy has been using Kate to fool you this whole time. I've put an end to it."

"Put an end to it?" Mark said. "By binding Kate to you instead?"

Kate stepped through the door and stood near Mark. She chewed on her lip, looking between me and Bobby. Bobby still had the glasses on. He gave her a pitying look.

174

"You're right. That was probably a mistake." He pulled a handkerchief from his jacket with one hand, a lighter from his pants pocket with the other. "A mistake I can correct. The difference between you and me, Mel, is that I don't need her."

Bobby snapped the lighter into life and set the flame against the edge of the handkerchief. The cloth caught fire. Kate screamed. Bobby let the burning handkerchief drop. Kate flickered and disappeared, her tortured scream echoing in my ears.

"You bastard!" I yelled. And then I lunged.

28

I CAUGHT BOBBY BY SURPRISE. My fist connected with his jaw with a loud smack. His head rocked back. Saliva sprayed from his mouth. Pain lit up my hand and my knuckles throbbed. I fell forward with the punch, crashing into Bobby. We both tumbled towards the rail.

For a moment, we teetered on the brink of going over the edge. Bobby clutched it and heaved with his arms. We slipped sideways, falling to the floor. I landed on top of him. His breath went out in a grunt. I hauled myself up, straddling his chest with my legs. Then I reached for his throat.

Kate's scream echoed in my mind. This man burned my friend in front of me. He destroyed her. I lost control. In my blind rage, I'm not sure I could have stopped on my own. I've never been a violent man, but in that moment, I think I would have murdered Robert Greenwood.

Fortunately for all of us, Mark intervened. He pulled my hands away from Bobby's neck and hauled me off of him. I struggled against Mark for a moment, my blood still hot in my veins. He pulled me away from Bobby, gripping my upper arms and holding me back.

My rage subsided enough for me to regain a little bit of composure. I stopped fighting against Mark, and he loosened his grip on me. Then I looked behind us. Thomas Jason and his guests stood on the other side of the glass door. He held his phone in one hand at his side. He had already placed a call. I hoped it was to summon his guards, and not the police.

"Mark, I'm done," I said. Adrenaline continued to course through my body, and I shook uncontrollably. I still wanted to tear Bobby's arms off, but the blind rage passed. "Let me go."

Mark released me. Bobby climbed to his feet. He leaned against the railing while rubbing his jaw. I stooped and picked up one of the stacks of bills he'd given me before I attacked him.

"You can't buy my friend from me." I started to throw the money at him, then changed my mind. Instead, I stuffed it into the waist of my pants. "So I'll take this as an asshole tax. You're still short."

Mark and I stepped back into the play room. Jason and his guests moved back, giving me space. They looked at me like tourists at the zoo, staring into lion's cage. I took several deep breaths and tried to give them a smile. I don't think I managed it very well.

"Sorry for the disturbance," I said.

"Don't be sorry," Jason said. "Just go."

We went.

The cab sat parked in the driveway where we left it. We told the driver we wouldn't be long, and we were true to our word. It had only been a few minutes, but with all that happened, it felt like much longer. After Mark and I ducked into the backseat, Mark gave the cabbie the address of The Society's office. We pulled away from Thomas Jason's house, the rough crunch of tires marking our escape.

We rode in silence. Mark stared out his window, his expression pensive. I looked out the other window, my mind's eye open. I hoped to see Kate rematerialize next to me. On highway 50, somewhere near Folsom, I started to cry.

She died once already, hours before I met her. We already faced the tragedy that she would never grow old or have a real life again. But even as a ghost, she had been bright and funny and thoughtful. Her death may have been painful, but this destruction at Bobby's hands? I couldn't think of anything worse. No one deserved such a fate. As the cab left the freeway and entered the downtown area, I started imagining ways I would make Bobby pay for what he'd done.

The cabbie dropped us off at the office. I paid him with what I had left of my stipend. I left the "asshole tax" bundled and tucked into my pants, the way a movie hero keeps a gun when he doesn't have a holster.

Bella sat in the kitchen, a cup of steaming coffee on the table in front of her. I sat across from her. Mark went to the counter and started preparing sandwiches. I told Bella everything that happened after she dropped us off. It took me a moment to get started, but once begun, the words spilled out of me like coins from a shattered piggy bank. By the end, my eyes blurred with tears again. Bella held my hand, her hands warm and comforting.

"I should have known what he was going to do," I said. "I should have moved. Done something. Oh God, what have I done?"

Bella patted my hand. "You couldn't have known what Bobby was going to do. You shouldn't blame yourself."

"But Kate's gone." The tears I had been holding back ran down my cheeks. "Kate's gone. Bobby destroyed her."

Bella's eyes narrowed. She cocked her head to one side, studying my face. "She's gone, sure, but she's not destroyed. You can't destroy a ghost by destroying its anchor. You just release it."

"What? She's still out there somewhere?"

"She's probably back in the car where you found her."

I stood up. I began to pace around the kitchen. I felt a need to move. I wanted Bella's words to be true, but she didn't see what I saw. I watched her go.

"Bella, I heard her scream."

"It probably wasn't pleasant for her," Bella said. "It's never pleasant for a ghost when their anchor is destroyed and one of their connections to the living world is destroyed. But she should be, well, 'fine' isn't really the right word, but she should be as well as any ghost ever is."

"You're saying that she's stuck in a car. Alone."

Bella sighed and stood up. She wrapped her arms around me. "She's gone, but not destroyed, Mel. There's nothing more you can do for her."

Mark set plates of sandwiches on the table and took a seat. He'd cut off the crusts again. I sat down and picked up a sandwich. Bella had been sweet and supportive. Mark had been stolid and consistent, supportive in his own way. He kept the faith and made the sandwiches. For all of their support, I couldn't accept the comfort they offered. I kept imagining Kate far away, alone and trapped in a car. I ate the sandwich, unable to taste it.

As we ate, Bella told us about what happened with her after she dropped us off. She headed east on highway 50, driving as far as Cameron Park before the black SUV disappeared from her rear view mirror. She turned around and drove for awhile longer, watching for the FBI. When she couldn't find them, she returned to the office and waited for us.

I heard her words, but my thoughts remained on Kate. After a moment, I asked, "Did Bobby know that destroying the anchor wasn't going to hurt Kate?"

Bella nodded. "Pedro and I taught him as much as we could about ghosts and crossing over. Bobby thought it would help his show if he knew all of the real details. That's how he knew about the glasses and the scales."

It made me hate Bobby a little less. When I finished lunch, I walked up to my room and sat on the edge of my bed. I looked into the floor mirror. My own reflection looked back at me, alone.

I already knew what I had to do. It scared me to leave, but I couldn't just let Kate remain stuck in a car for the rest of her existence. I needed to fly back to Louisiana, break into the lot where they impounded the Nova, and drive off with it. It meant leaving the comfort of The Society, where I had a place to sleep and the support of friends. I never knew any place before where I felt so accepted. A place where I could make a difference in the world. A place where a priest made sandwiches with the crusts cut off.

I would need to dodge federal investigators and local police. If they caught me, they would throw me in jail for killing Kate. It didn't matter whether or not I committed any crime. I knew how they saw me.

On the bright side, it also meant the FBI would have to find a different stooge to spy on Ortega's organization. Go or stay, I would never be able to spy on The Society. That narrowed things down to a simple choice.

I pulled out a backpack from the closet and started stuffing it with my clothes. I didn't have much to pack. I needed to go as soon as possible. If I waited, I might not be able to bring myself to leave.

Mark, Bella, or maybe even Ortega would say something that would stop me. This could be my only opportunity to leave.

Shouldering my backpack, I stepped out of my room without looking back. I needed to go, without hesitation. Kate needed me.

29

I TIPTOED DOWN THE STAIRS, pausing at the bottom to look around the corner. When I didn't see Bella or Mark, I went the rest of the way down the hall, past the library. I stopped at the front door and pulled out the cell phone Ortega gave me. I regarded it a moment, running my thumb across its darkened screen. Then I set it on a table and opened the door. No time for farewells. If I stopped and said goodbye, I wouldn't be able to leave.

Once outside, I stood on the sidewalk with my back to the door. I watched the passing cars, waiting to see if one of them would be the FBI. I stalled, drawing the moment out longer than necessary. I wanted to go back in, because I knew that no matter how well I managed to avoid the police and FBI, at the end of this journey, I'd be in jail. My feet felt heavy.

The FBI were nowhere to be seen. I turned and started walking, shrugging my backpack up higher on my shoulder and hugging my jacket closer to me. The weather turned cold, and the gray clouds deprived me of the warmth of the sun. The weather suited my mood.

A number of crazy plans for evading the FBI rolled through my head as I walked. At the airport, when I needed to show my ID, maybe I could bribe the person behind the counter to look the other way. Maybe I could take a car or bus to San Francisco and fly from there instead of the Sacramento airport. It would cost me extra time, but it could throw off my pursuers.

I considered stealing a car. How many times had Kate suggested I do just that? I knew she'd been joking half the time. The other half, I couldn't tell. It didn't matter. Stealing a car remained a terrible idea.

In the end, I climbed onto the Yolobus from downtown and rode to the Sacramento airport. If the FBI pursued me, it didn't matter which way I went. They already found me once, here in Sacramento. They probably had someone watching the airport. If they were serious about apprehending me, they might have someone waiting to nab me when I got off the plane in Louisiana. The best thing I could do is take the quickest, most direct route.

While riding to the airport, I pulled out the stack of bills Bobby gave me. After looking around the bus to make sure no one watched me, I pulled off the rubber band and leafed through the money. They were all hundreds. The stack was a little thicker than my thumb. I counted it. Then I counted it again. Ten thousand dollars. I couldn't believe so much money took up so little space. This changed things. I didn't have to mess around with teller machines or dodge cameras. With this much money, maybe I would be able to get away, after all.

At the airport, I shouldered my backpack, moved through the ticket line, and bought my ticket. It cost a little over three hundred dollars and about two hours of my life, waiting for take-off. After everything else that happened, it felt like a bargain.

I shuffled through airport security along with other ticketed passengers. I looked around at the other people. A couple of businessmen in suits stood a little way off, pulling laptops out of bags to send them ahead on the conveyor belt like digital scouts. Behind me in line, a mother carried a sleeping baby. The child seemed calm now, but I bet the baby would find her lungs once the wheels left the ground.

Just as I set my pack on the conveyor belt, a heavy-set security guard with tired eyes and a thin mustache stepped up to me.

"Come with me, please," he said.

"Is something wrong?" I could feel sweat forming between my shoulder blades. Maybe I could still run away and find a different way back to Louisiana.

"You have been randomly selected for extra screening," the guard said.

"Extra screening?" I asked.

"Come with me, sir."

I expected the guard to take me to some dark, secret room. Perhaps the FBI would be there already, waiting to question me, or torture me, or both. Well. I'd had a good run. But now they had me. They would throw me in a cell and life as I knew it would be over.

Instead, the guard took me past the x-ray machine, off to one side. He squatted down, an impressive feat considering his girth. Then he began to pat me down, his fingers squeezing my legs through my jeans. The search reached my waist and became personal enough that I wondered if I should turn my head and cough. He continued up my torso, padding my pockets, the small of my back, and my armpits.

"Alright," he said. "Go to the bench and put your shoes back on. You're free to go."

I didn't argue with him. I gathered up my things and put myself back together, both physically and mentally. Nothing had happened, but I felt like I just dodged a bullet. As I tied my laces, I thought about my future. If I spent the rest of my days looking over my shoulder and flinching whenever a security guard looked at me, they wouldn't have to throw me in jail. I would already be a prisoner.

Once aboard the plane, I started to relax. I put my backpack in the overhead compartment, took my seat, and stretched. As stressful as my day had been, I looked forward to catching a nap on the plane. I reached the easy part. I'd worry about the next hurdle once I arrived in New Orleans.

Before the plane finished boarding, two large, sweaty men, one Hispanic, the other black, sat on either side of me. The Hispanic seemed to only know a few words of English. They both gave me sympathetic looks, trying to give me as much elbow room as the cramped seating would allow. In the end, they could only do so much. When the plane took to the sky, I found myself sitting crooked between the two larger men, with one shoulder raised and pushed out from the seat.

Six hours later, we arrived in Louisiana, my muscles sore and my eyes heavy. In California, I'd been some sort of supernatural investigator. In Louisiana, I became a repo man once again. And my next job would be the most difficult of my career.

30

I FOUND THE AIRPORT in New Orleans almost the same way I left it: quiet and nearly empty. No police waiting at the gates with handcuffs. No federal agents watching the halls, talking into their sleeve-microphones. Just a handful of janitorial staff pushing mops and running vacuum cleaners.

I walked slowly through the concourse area, a handful of other passengers moving past me. I felt so relieved and surprised to have made it that I stopped in the middle of the terminal for a moment with my eyes closed, just breathing. The Gestapo didn't surrounded me or cart me off to a cold, dark cell. Instead, busy travelers from my flight streamed past me, ignoring me the way a river ignores an immovable stone. It felt good knowing the universe did not revolve around me.

The cold slap of a Louisiana winter caught me by surprise as soon as I left the shelter of the airport. I forgot how much warmer Sacramento felt compared to New Orleans. The brisk air woke me up, putting a spring in my step. I shivered as I hailed a cab.

I resisted the urge to go straight to the police impound and try to rescue Kate. Even through the fog of travel weariness, I knew it would be a stupid thing to do. For one thing, I didn't know which impound held the Nova. Would I try to make the cabbie my accomplice, driving me from police lot to police lot? Even with my stack of Benjamins, I probably couldn't pay him enough.

When it came time to break into the impound, it would be better to go during the day. The dark of night could hide me, sure. It could also hide the cops. To pull off a job like this, I needed to know where the opposition patrolled. Daylight would also help me find the Nova quickly, which meant less time fumbling around, drawing attention.

More importantly, to steal the Nova from an impound, I needed to be fresh. I thought about this at the same time I realized the cab hadn't moved. The driver stared at me in the rear view mirror. He asked me a couple of times for a destination, and I still hadn't answered him.

I needed to crash for a little while. Would my silver bullet trailer still be there? Probably not. If it still squatted at the edge of the city, chances were good it would be watched. More likely, the police swung by, hitched it up, and hauled it off to impound. It did have wheels, after all. How strange would it be if Kate sat in the Nova, right next to my old home?

Snapping back to the present, I gave the cabbie an address. The cab's tires gripped the road and I leaned back in my seat. When it came to places in New Orleans I could visit in the middle of the night, I only had one choice. My time in California had been brief, but I made more friends there than I ever knew here. No wonder I left Louisiana so easily, but dragged my feet when it came time to leave California. I wondered if I would ever see my California friends again.

The cab stopped near a garage on the eastern edge of New Orleans, not far off of highway 90. A chain link fence surrounded the property, with the gate closed and secured with a heavy padlock. Past the garage sat a single-wide trailer up on cinder blocks. I paid the cab driver with change from the flight, then stood on the sidewalk. The dim lights of the trailer looked warm and inviting.

I tugged on the chain securing the gate, then looked around the street. Certain no one watched me, I hopped onto the fence and pulled myself over, quick as a fox stealing chickens. Before my shoes settled on the other side, a huge dark blur slammed into me, knocking me on my butt.

The blur resolved itself into the shape of a shaggy black mutt. Standing, the dog would have come up to my mid thigh. On the ground, with my back against the fence, the mutt loomed over me. His breath filled my nostrils. I pulled away from him, but he moved with an animal's speed, his mouth darting in and finding my face. I pushed him back, but he continued his relentless assault, his tongue covering my face with saliva.

"Easy, Jack!" I laughed and pushed him away again. He took the hint and sat back on his haunches, his tail wagging like it meant to escape and set out on its own. I stood and leaned over to give his fur a good rub.

Jack escorted me to the back of the property, panting cheerily, his black tongue hanging to one side. He smelled like he needed a bath. He kept stopping in front of me, begging for more rubs. When I bent to oblige, he tried to poke his nose into my crotch. I laughed as I pushed his snout away. Jack had a pure and effective way of making me feel welcome. I scratched behind his ears and made appreciative sounds at him.

Though it must have been close to 2AM, the trailer's lights pushed back the darkness. I stepped up onto the rickety stair and gave the plastic and particle board door a sound knocking. When I heard sounds of movement in the trailer, I stepped back, onto the ground. Jack moved around my legs, eager for more attention.

The door opened a crack, allowing more light to escape. The man on the other side of the door peered out briefly, then opened the door wide. In the doorway stood my former employer and mentor in the repo business: Marshal Smith.

Marshal had more years on him than any of my friends in California. I guessed him to be in his mid to late forties, but then again, I've always been terrible at guessing someone's age. His thin white hair stood up all over, and stirred in the evening breeze like tall grass on the prairie. He had a ruddy complexion, a face full of wrinkles and scars, and pale blue eyes like faded jeans. He stood with a slight stoop to his back, which seemed more pronounced since the last time we met. He raised a shaky hand and beckoned me in.

"Hurry up, Mel. Get in before my house gets cold."

I stepped into his trailer, grinning. Jack bounded up the stairs with me. Marshal tried to stop the mutt, but the dog slipped past him. Not the first time Marshal and Jack performed this dance.

Marshal scowled at Jack before closing the door, leaving the dog inside.

A bit larger than my silver bullet, Marshal kept his home clean and neat. A brown and orange shag carpet straight out of the seventies covered the floor, and wood paneling adorned the interior walls. Marshal took a seat in his Lazyboy. I sat across from him on a squat, square couch.

"So, what's the trouble?" Marshal asked.

"Do you remember the Nova you had me pick up?"

"No. You never brought it in."

"Well, someone was killed in it. And the cops are half convinced I did it."

Marshal winced, either in pain or disgust. "And they caught you? You've been in jail the last month over this?"

"I've been in California. It's kind of a long story."

"Shit." Marshal pronounced the word with two syllables and a long e. "If you got away, why'd you come back?"

I shook my head. "Like I said, it's kind of a long story."

"Son, I want you to quit foolin' around with me. What did you come here for? What do you need?"

"I was hoping you'd let me crash on your couch for a night or two, until I got back on my feet."

"That's not a problem. Is that all?"

I thought about it a moment. "Actually, I could use some information. Who wanted you to repo the Nova?"

Marshal rubbed his chin. "I'll have to look it up. I've got a file on it, somewhere in my garage. If it didn't get thrown away. You're not thinking of going to see them, are you?"

"No, I don't think so. I just want to know what happened. Things have gotten a little crazy the last few weeks."

"Tell me about it. Hey, do you want a beer?"

"I'd love a beer."

"Well, you know where they are in the fridge. Bring me one, too."

I fetched us each a bottle, popping the tops and flinging the caps into the trash from across the room. I retook my seat on the couch and we started chatting about business and old jobs. Before I knew it, half an hour had passed. Though the time got away from me, I did notice a couple of things while we sat and talked. First, I observed Marshal's hands shaking worse than I remembered.

Second, Marshal hadn't done any repo work all the time I'd been gone. In spite of that, he didn't seem to be hurting for money.

"Why did you stay in the repo business so long?" I asked, once the shop talk wound down.

Marshal raised his bottle and tipped it towards me. "A young man's gotta have something to keep him busy. Besides, I knew you could use the money. We made a good team, kid. Maybe when things are settled with the police, we can be a good team again."

"I'll drink to that." And we did.

Marshal drained the rest of his bottle and let out a satisfied sigh. He gestured with the empty, like a professor wielding a yard stick. "Say, are you going to be able to sleep if I run the TV?"

It turned out I didn't have problems falling asleep at all.

31

I WOKE UP THE NEXT MORNING with Jack curled up on my legs. It would have been early for me in Sacramento but with the time difference, I was back on my wake-at-the-crack-of-noon schedule. I stretched, my joints popping their protest for having slept on the couch. I didn't feel too bad, but I only spent one night on the couch so far. Many more like this and my back would be more bent than Marshal's. I needed to get my own place before too long.

Though I never owned my own car, I never had a problem getting around Louisiana. After dropping off a fresh repo at Marshal's, I usually hitchhiked to get home. Louisiana law states that you can't stand on the road to solicit rides, but I've never been content to just stand around. I walk, stick out my thumb, and someone would usually pick me up before long. Maybe I'm lucky, or maybe the people of this great state are just friendlier than most.

Heading into town from Marshal's, I hitchhiked. An older woman, probably Marshal's age, pulled over for me in her little Mitsubishi pickup. She had a full load of something in the back, covered over with a tarp. She didn't say what she carried and I didn't ask. She said I reminded her of her grandson. I smiled and made pleasant conversation with her until she dropped me off near Canal Street.

The thing about New Orleans, or any major city for that matter, is there are a lot of police stations. In fact, one stood within walking distance of Marshal's place but I knew better than to go there. It didn't have an impound yard. My best bet for finding the Nova would be to start with the cluster of stations a few blocks off of Canal.

Chain link fences topped with double strands of barbed wire surrounded the impound lots. The physical security kept people from climbing the fence and getting in at night. During the day, however, the gate stood open, with a security guard manning a small booth to keep people honest. I knew all of this because I considered repo'ing a car out of an impound lot once before. It didn't take long for me to realize how stupid I would have to be to try something like that.

The day felt like a good one for doing stupid things. I walked around the corner, through the gate, and gave the security guard a single nod. The guard gave me a curious look. He started to rise from his chair to stop me. The chilly November air saved us both the hassle. The breeze picked up, curling around the pane-less window of his booth. Rather than leave the warmth of his space heater, he returned the nod and turned back to watching the street.

I did a full circuit of the lot but didn't find the Nova. I walked a few miles to the next lot, entered it with similar ease, and didn't find the Nova there either. Half a mile further away, trying to enter a third lot, I hit my first snag.

"You can't go in there." The guard addressing me was a bit younger and thinner than the guards at the other two lots. This one didn't seem to mind the cold. His breath misted in front of him like a dragon breathing smoke. The cars and trucks behind him were his hoarded treasure. No one would stroll in off the street into his lair. Not on his watch.

"I was told I needed to make sure my car was in the lot before I could lodge a complaint." I didn't have to fake sounding annoyed or upset to make my story believable. I guess I'm a method actor.

"That's not how it works." The guard crossed his arms across his chest. "No unauthorized access is allowed. End of story."

I looked longingly towards the cars, hoping to see the Nova from the street. I didn't see it, but enough vehicles were hidden from view that I couldn't rule the place out. I hugged myself against the cold, drawing my denim jacket in a little closer, and walked away.

It occurred to me I might be wasting my time. A month had passed since they picked me up from that gas station. After this much time, they might not have the car in impound any longer. Then again, if the murder investigation remained open, the car could be evidence. They probably needed to keep it until they closed the case. I looked back towards the guard shack and considered my options.

Two squat office buildings stood on either side of the lot. A street and an alley completed the square around it. I rounded the corner and walked to the mouth of the alley. From this side of the lot, the guard wouldn't be able to see me. Maybe I could just climb over the fence and hope for the best.

I looked at the barbed wire twisting along the top of the fence posts. If I had the right tools, I could cut the wire or make a hole in the chain links. I double checked my pockets. Empty. I felt the leatherman clipped over the top of my waistband. I also had a spare slim jim from Marshal's garage stuck up the back of my shirt. Not the right tools for getting through a fence, even if I had time.

Further down the alley, I saw a small parking lot for one of the surrounding office buildings. I approached and examined the handful of vehicles parked there. One of them stood out from the others. A large, black truck with red striping and a recently waxed finish. It wore over-sized tires, and its suspension had been lifted to the point where its passengers would need to duck to avoid passing aircraft. The kind of vehicle a complete asshole would drive. Time to get to work.

Standing on one of the front tires gave me enough height and leverage to make the slim jim work. The thin sliver of metal slid into the door like a surgeon's scalpel, and the lock lifted with an audible pop. I opened the door a crack and reached in to snag both floor mats. My heart raced. This would be the perfect time for someone to come upon me unexpectedly and ruin my day. My luck held and no one came. I closed the door behind me and took the floor mats back to the fence.

It's easy to underestimate the effectiveness of barbed wire, which is why I used two floor mats. This wasn't my first rodeo. While technically easy, a bad toss or a simple slip could result in serious injury. I felt sweat forming between my shoulder blades, in spite of the winter chill. Standing at the fence for several moments, I breathed slowly while trying to psych myself up.

I threw the first mat up. It landed where I wanted, flopping to drape across both lines of barbed wire. Then I launched myself at the fence with the second mat slung over my shoulders. My fingers and the tips of my shoes caught between the links. The fence rattled and rang beneath me. I climbed, skittering towards the top like a squirrel flying up a tree. Once I reached sufficient height, I slapped the second mat over the first. I climbed higher, then rolled bodily over both mats. I caught myself on the other side, momentarily upside-down. I lowered myself, reorienting with the ground. Then I took hold of the mats above me. With a whipping motion, the mats came free of the wire. I pushed away from the fence and dropped into a crouch. I stayed there a moment, my knees bent, my heart racing.

Waiting to catch my breath, I listened for approaching footsteps. When I felt safe enough to move, I left the mats at the base of the fence. I shuffled from car to car, crouched as low to the ground as I could go.

This lot dwarfed the first two I visited. Unlike the others, it contained several trailers and larger vehicles. Which made it easier for me to hide from the guard, but more difficult to find a particular car.

Slipping around a dusty SUV, I found the Nova parked between an old Trans Am and a Volkswagen mini bus. I breathed a sigh of relief. My hands shook with nervousness and excitement, making it difficult to open the door. I managed to get it open and slid into the driver's seat. I didn't bother opening my mind's eye. I twisted to my right and turned the rearview mirror.

Kate sat up straight in the backseat. She took several slow, deep breaths, and the temperature in the car plummeted.

"Mel."

I opened my mind's eye and turned to face her. "What's the matter?"

"I didn't expect to see you again." Her voice sounded as frosty as the wintry air in the car. "You're free of me. Now you can sleep with whoever you want without worrying about me hanging around."

I hung my head. "I'm sorry about what happened with Bella."

A long pause stretched between us. Kate broke the silence first. "Thank you for coming for me. Both here and at the poker game."

She leaned forward in the backseat. Her yellow dress stood out, compared with the monochrome image of her I saw in the mirror. I drank in her pale blue eyes, her blond hair pulled up off her shoulders. She reached forward to touch me. My skin grew cold and the bones of my arm ached where her hand passed through me. We both winced. She withdrew her hand, and I rubbed my sore arm.

"Sorry." Kate lowered her head.

"No, I'm the one that should be sorry. I shouldn't have let that asshole steal you away."

Kate shook her head. "What's done is done. It's not your fault, anyway. What are we going to do now? Does your girlfriend have a spell to reattach me to you?"

I shook my head. "I don't think so. And she's not my girlfriend. Bella cast some spell on me and we … it doesn't matter. I'm here on my own. I'm not sure I'll ever see anyone from The Society again."

"That's too bad, but okay. Do you have a plan?"

Good question. I turned back forward and looked around. I couldn't drive the Nova straight out. An old Plymouth blocked the way. I looked past the Plymouth, and an idea blossomed in my mind. I opened the door and started to get out.

"The plan is to get us the hell out of here," I said.

I shuffled over to the Plymouth and found it unlocked. Unfortunately, it had an automatic transmission. It would have been much easier if it had been a manual, but we work with the vehicles we have, not the ones we wish we had. I pulled out a flathead screwdriver on the leatherman and started prying off the plastic beneath the steering column. I hated to do it, but the steering wheel would not unlock without the key. The plastic cracked, the ignition assembly went slack, and I slipped the vehicle into neutral. I cranked the steering wheel until I had the car aimed more or less in the direction I wanted it to go. Then I returned to the Nova.

"This is going to suck, but it should work." I bought the Nova's engine to life, then let off the brake, enough that it rolled up against the Plymouth. The bumpers scraped with a crunch, and the Plymouth moved a little. Then I stepped on the gas.

Both cars lurched forward. I gave the Nova some more gas, the jungle cat purr of the engine swelling to a roar. I took my foot off the gas and slammed on the brakes after a car length and a half. The Nova stopped, and the Plymouth continued to roll.

My aim could have been a little better. The Plymouth glanced off a minivan, rebounded off a sedan, straightened, then crunched through part of the guard shack. It slowed, but kept rolling, entering the busy street. A Dodge slammed into it at full speed. Fortunately, the guard managed to get out of the hut before the Plymouth pulverized it. Unfortunately for him, he stood alone near the wreckage. The driver of the Dodge leaped from their car and started yelling at the guard.

With the guard's attention fixed on the Plymouth and the shouting driver, I gave the Nova some gas. I rolled out onto the street, turned, and headed off before anyone could stop me.

"Holy hell, Mel." Kate rubbernecked to watch the commotion behind us.

"I've done this sort of thing before." I had been aiming to create a distraction. Mission accomplished, though I did a bit more damage than I anticipated.

"So now what?"

"Now we solve your murder."

32

I STUCK TO SIDE STREETS and alleys as I made my way back to Marshal's garage. I hoped the commotion with the Plymouth would delay any reaction to the missing Nova. With the angry driver yelling at him, maybe the guard didn't notice me pulling away. Whether he noticed or not, I didn't think we'd be lucky enough to get off scot-free. Once they traced the Plymouth back to where it started before crashing through the gate and entering traffic, they would find the Nova missing. An investigation of the lot would find the floor mats I left behind as evidence of a break in. Aside from the guard being able to identify me, I could have left other evidence. The safest thing I could do is assume they would pick up my trail sooner than later. I hoped I had enough time to solve Kate's murder before they caught up with me and threw me in jail.

"How do you plan on solving my murder, Mel?"

"I thought we'd start with whoever had this car before I repo'd it. I mean, it's possible the murderer stole the car and I stole it from them, but if that were the case, why bother trying to clean up the back seat? They could just ditch the car and be done with it."

"That's a good point. What are you going to do if you do figure out who murdered me?"

I rubbed the bridge of my nose. My friend Kate, asking all of the tough questions today. "I guess that's when I'll go to the police."

Kate sat back in her seat, stunned. After a moment, she threw up her hands. "I guess that's better than becoming a murderer yourself. If you come face to face with him, I don't want you to die, but I don't want you to kill him, either. It's not worth it."

"It won't come to that." I tried to sound reassuring. If I came face to face with Kate's murderer, I'd probably wind up a ghost just like Kate.

I pulled into Marshal's lot and slipped the Nova into an empty stall in the garage. Marshal had a Volkswagen Beetle raised in the next space over. He slid out from under it and rose to his feet. He placed his hands on the small of his back and stretched. Then he stared at the Nova for a full minute before spitting.

"Son, there's a helluva big difference between crashing on a man's couch and making him an accessory in grand theft auto."

"I had to pick up the car."

"Why? Did you leave evidence in it? Son, the cops have had this thing a month. If you left anything in it, they'd have found it by now."

"It's not like that." With my mind's eye still open, I looked into the backseat, making eye contact with Kate. She regarded me with her blue eyes, her mouth partly open.

I turned back to Marshal. "I have reasons for getting this car back. You wouldn't believe me if I told you."

"If you're going to bring a stolen vehicle in my garage, you're going to have to try me." Marshal folded his arms across his chest and his face became stony. I'd only seen that look on his face a few times before. It meant no amount of bullshit would sway him.

I looked back at Kate again. She shrugged. What did we have to lose?

"Alright, Marshal. You asked for it. The Nova has a ghost stuck in the backseat, and I can see her. It turns out I'm psychic. I can read visions off of objects and look into the past now, too."

"God damn it, Mel." Marshal paused to spit again. "Have you been on the weed again?"

"I can prove it."

"Fine. Prove it."

We spent the next half hour in a kind of battle. Marshal kept trying to find different ways to stump me, while I kept trying to demonstrate my gift. He blindfolded me with several layers of cloth. With my mind's eye open, I could still see. I described for him anything he held up or touched. He sent me into the trailer for a few minutes while he did something in the garage out of my sight. When I came back, I could have looked backwards in time, but Kate told me not to bother. While I was out, he pulled down his pants and sat in the back seat in just his underwear. With each test, his brow became more and more furrowed. By the end, he was squinting at me so hard I didn't think he could see at all.

"Bullshit," Marshal said. "It's some kind of trick."

"I don't need you to believe me. I just need you to help me keep the Nova out of sight for a while. And I need all of the information you can get on the previous owner."

"Oh yeah. That." Marshal shuffled over to a filing cabinet set against a wall next to one of the toolboxes and started rifling through loose files. I turned back to Kate. She shook her head as she looked towards Marshal's back.

"Is he your father?" Kate asked.

"No. My sperm donor is in Northern California somewhere."

"He keeps calling you son."

"He's like that. That's just his way."

"Ah ha!" Marshal straightened, holding a file folder in the air like he just won a prize. He turned back to me with the folder open and starting reading in a voice a little louder than necessary. "Seventy-four Chevrolet Nova, originally purchased in Michigan, yadda yadda, restored and rebuilt in ninety-five, yadda yadda … Here. Marshal Dean Smith is hereby granted repossession rights to reclaim vehicle Chevrolet Nova to the possession of Felix Werner from Joshua Werner, for failure to meet fiscal responsibility." Marshal clapped the file shut. "The dad sold the car to the son, and the son stopped making payments. It happens."

"Josh Werner?" Kate said, leaning against the window. "Holy shit. That's my ex-boyfriend!"

"The one you caught banging your roommate?" I asked.

"Now you have my attention," Marshal said.

"And you didn't recognize this car?" I asked Kate.

"No! He's from a rich family. He went through two different cars just while we were dating."

"And he's a student at Tulane?"

"Yeah. But Mel, if the police had the Nova, they should have known all of that. They should have already investigated Josh. If it could be proved he did it, they would have found something by now."

I shook my head. "No. No, they didn't go down that angle."

"Why not?"

"Because the car had been reported stolen. I don't think Marshal was hired to repo the car. He was hired to be the scapegoat. The police were already out looking for the car, well before they picked me up from the gas station. Marshal was supposed to take the fall for the murder, but since I picked up the car, I was the one that got caught."

"God damn it," Marshal said.

I lowered my head, my face feeling hot. I looked down at my hands. I saw calluses and scars. Working man's hands. I was never that great a mechanic, but I could usually fix a car up enough to get it to move. I had always been good with my hands, able to fix things if I just put my mind to it. But this situation went beyond anything I'd ever done before. I didn't see any way to fix this.

"We need to find his motive," Kate said.

"How do you propose we do that?"

"I don't know. But if we're going to clear your name, we're going to have to give the police everything they need. If they could have pinned a motive on you, they probably would have come after you a lot harder."

I thought about that a moment. "They had my records unsealed. You think they did that so they could find a motive?"

"I don't know," Kate said. "Maybe? Let's focus on Josh. How do we figure out Josh's motive?"

Marshal ran a hand through his thinning hair and turned to leave. "If you need anything, I'm going to be in the back, getting drunk. I'm too old to start believing in ghosts."

"Marshal, wait," I said. "Would you mind making a phone call for me?"

The old mechanic turned and gave me a questioning look.

"I'm going to need you to talk to Kate's former roommate."

"I'm not interested," Marshal said.

"It'll help us solve Kate's murder."

"I'm not the police! I don't want to get involved, and neither should you, son."

I sighed. Then another thought struck me. "The person I need you to call. She's a smoking hot model that's on her way to becoming the next Ms. Louisiana."

Marshal grimaced. "Damn it, Mel. You probably should have led with that. Fine. Let me get a phone."

33

MARSHAL FETCHED A CORDLESS from the front office. I waved him over to stand with me next to the Nova. Kate rattled off the phone number and I relayed it to Marshal. Whether from frailty or nervousness, his hands shook while trying to dial the number. He mis-dialed, swore under his breath, then started over. Finally, the phone started ringing. With his brow furrowed from concentration, he pressed the receiver to his ear.

"So what am I going to tell this Jen girl when she picks up?"

"We probably should have thought of that before you started dialing," I said. "Shit. Let me think a moment."

The phone had the volume turned all the way up. I could hear the phone ringing, right up to the point Jen answered. The phone made her voice sound like an AM Radio DJ. "Hello?"

Marshal froze. Silence stretched across several frantic heartbeats. I panicked and grabbed the phone from Marshal.

"Hey, Jen. This is Tim." That name didn't sound right. What name did I give her before? My mind raced and then I remembered. I cleared my throat and tried again. "Jim. This is Jim. Please don't hang up."

Another pregnant pause filled the garage. I could hear an electric buzz on the line while I waited for Jen to respond. When she finally did speak, her voice blasted painfully loud in my ear. I flinched and held the receiver away.

"I thought we had an agreement."

"We do! We do. Just. Uhm. I wanted to ... I couldn't bring myself to destroying the pictures. I want to give them to you. With some money. I just feel so bad for blackmailing you. I want to make it up to you."

Another uncomfortable silence gave me time to sweat and play back my words in my head. I should have planned out the story before we called. I wondered for a moment if I missed the click, and if the phone would start complaining about being off hook.

"Alright," Jen said. "But let's meet in a public place. And you better not be doing this just to stare at my boobs again."

"No, this isn't about your boobs. You name the time and place, and I'll be there."

"You said you were going to give me money? How much?"

I looked at Marshal. He shook his head.

"Five hundred?" I asked. "A thousand? How much do you need?"

"A thousand," Jen said.

"A thousand it is." I would have agreed to anything.

"Alright. Tonight, nine PM. Be at the corner of Bourbon and Conti."

"Bourbon Street. Got it."

Jen hung up. I handed the phone back to Marshal.

"Real smooth, son. And here I thought you needed me to talk to a supermodel."

"You froze."

"I paused to gather my words. You should try it sometime."

I opened my mouth to fire off another retort, but stopped. Kate's laughter from the back of the Nova distracted me. I looked at her and said, "Alright. That's enough from the peanut gallery."

Marshal turned to go again and I didn't stop him this time. He probably planned to head back to his trailer, crack open a beer, and turn on the television. I wanted to go with him and get a bottle of my own. I had the time. Instead, I climbed back into the Nova and shut the door.

"What are you going to do now?" Kate asked.

"Now? I'm going to take a nap. Would you mind waking me before seven?"

•　　•　　•

I knew better than to take the Nova out of Marshal's garage. The police would be looking for it. They demonstrated their ability to find it once already when they picked me up that fateful Halloween night. If they caught me with it again, they'd throw me directly in jail. As much as I wanted Kate with me, I knew the best thing I could do would be to leave the car hidden in the garage.

Besides, the French Quarter isn't a fun place to drive. The area around Bourbon Street is a rat's nest of narrow, one way streets. Bourbon Street itself is closed to vehicles every night. Even if I managed to sneak the Nova past the police, I wouldn't be able to get the car to the corner where I planned on meeting Jen.

With all of that in mind, and knowing I would be meeting Jen several hours after the sun set, I decided to head out early. Jen didn't strike me as the sort of person that would wait long. I probably had one chance to get some information from her, so I needed to be there before her. I called a cab and had the driver get me as close to Conti and Bourbon as possible.

I had half an hour to spare when I walked into the intersection. With it being a chilly November evening, there weren't quite as many people walking the streets. Not every night on Bourbon Street is Mardi Gras, but there's a little bit of that Mardi Gras feeling every night. I stood with my arms crossed on a corner and did some people watching.

Adults of all ages walked the street, though most were people my age. A group of girls glided down the street away from me, laughing a little too loudly to be sober. Some army boys, probably from Keesler judging by their short haircuts and wolfish gate, followed the girls. The military boys looked more hungry than drunk. A trio of college-aged boys bartered with a girl wearing several beaded necklaces. Despite the chill in the air, another strand of beads went around the girl's neck, and she raised her shirt, exposing her breasts for a few seconds. I loved this town.

I stood and watched and waited. I didn't have anything to do, but I never felt bored. The legal drinking age is 21, but I saw boys stumble past, blitzed out of their gourd, that looked like they didn't have to worry about shaving yet. Public nudity is not legal in New Orleans, either, but I caught another show a bit further down the street. Bourbon Street is all about knowing what you can get away with, and when you can get away with it. I might have been wanted by the police, but I knew I could get away with standing out that evening if I didn't get caught up in other people's trouble.

When it finally started to feel late, I started asking people for the time. Nearly 10 o'clock, and Jen still hadn't shown up. I felt cold and my feet were starting to hurt from standing so long. Had she stood me up? If I were in Jen's shoes, I probably would have. I deserved it. The thing is, Jen didn't strike me as the type to play it safe and smart. She already demonstrated enough bravery or stupidity or both to meet me once before.

I waited until well after 10 before leaving. I walked several blocks away and flagged down a cab. I gave the cabbie the address to Marshal's garage and sat back, warmed by the car's heater. The cab helped me get over feeling cold, but it made me uncomfortable in a different way. I felt defeated. Somewhere along the lines, I missed something critical, and I had a feeling that something bad would happen as a result.

I looked out the window and wondered how I could have misjudged Jen. I took her for vain and greedy. The promise of money should have been enough to get her to come out. She called me a creep for staring at her boobs, but how bad could she really feel about that? Her chosen career involved getting men like me to stare at her. Once back at Marshal's, I would talk to Kate. She lived with Jen. Kate would know what went wrong and what I should do next.

"Wait a minute," I said, my train of thought derailing. I sat up straight.

"Pardon?" the driver said through a thick Indian accent.

"She told her boyfriend. Holy shit, she told her boyfriend!"

The cab driver looked at me in his rear view mirror, his face twisted with confusion and agitation. A wave of nostalgia rolled over me. I looked back at the driver in the mirror. In that surreal moment, I realized what it must have been like for Kate, waking up in the back of the Nova and finding me. I came back to my senses and thought about what I needed to do next.

By trying to get Jen to come talk to me about her boyfriend, I set her on a course to talk to him. If he had been the one to kill

Kate, why wouldn't he be willing to kill Jen? She could be dead already. I was the one that set her up for that confrontation. The responsibility for her death lay at my feet.

"Change of plans," I said. "Take me to Tulane. And hurry!"

34

WHILE THE DRIVER didn't lay rubber or blow through any red lights, he did make good time getting to the campus. He may not have broken any speed limits, but he went as fast as he legally could. I appreciated him not getting pulled over and ruining my whole night. I gave him a hundred and ran off without waiting for change.

Scared and amped up on adrenaline, I ran for a few minutes before I realized I had no idea where to go. Maybe the dorms? I turned in that direction, still jogging. I didn't know which room belonged to Jen. She could have gone to Josh's room and I didn't even know what he looked like. She could be anywhere. Her body could be cooling, discarded in an alley, just like what happened to Kate. I gritted my teeth and ran harder.

I needed to see what Josh looked like. If I could find a place where I knew Josh had been, I could look back in time and find him. I considered this, then slowed to a walk. I knew one place I could go to see him in the past. The Howard-Tilton Memorial Library, the last place Kate remembered before her life ended. If I could look far enough into the past, I'd be able to see the face of Kate's killer.

Panting and wheezing, with my skin freezing and my lungs burning, I stopped running once I reached the front of the main entrance to the library. I looked up at the gray building. It loomed over me with square pillars and long rectangular embellishments. The dark interior turned the glass windows into black mirrors. Yellowish lights attached to the building face illuminated the space around the library.

Standing in place, I looked at the surrounding area. A narrow parking area stretched away from me in both directions, empty. Moss-covered, wiry trees punctuated the lot. Across the parking area stood a red bricked building facing the library. The space felt very open and exposed. Not a very good place to murder someone.

I turned and walked, keeping the library on my left. I reached the end of the building and found a walkway running between the library and another red bricked building. A set of bike racks occupied the narrow space, along with a short run of stairs leading up to the library's side door. None of the yellow lights from the front of the library illuminated the space. I looked up. The fixture that should have filled the alley with light sat as a dark square blemish on the side of the building.

"This is more like it," I said. I took a deep breath, trying to calm my fears and my nervousness. If I had guessed the location correctly, I would see something I didn't want to see. For Kate's sake, I needed to look.

I opened my mind's eye and glanced down the path. The shadows and darkness dissolved into the stark reality that came with supernatural vision. I willed the sensation of turning without turning, so similar to the queasy spinning that came after drinking well past the point of drunkenness. My senses shifted, and my perspective of time rolled backwards.

It had been almost a month since Kate was murdered. I paid attention to the sun while forcing time to slip backwards faster and faster. The sun ascended in the west, raced across the sky, then set in the east. Students whipped around me and through me, streaking by as indistinct blurs. My stomach writhed. Vomit came up to the back of my throat, and my grip on rewinding time faltered. I swallowed, refocused, kept going.

The further back from the present I spun, the more difficult it became to rewind time. It felt as though I pulled and stretched an

212

elastic band, which wanted nothing more than to snap me back to the present. I gritted my teeth and kept going. The sun, moon, and stars streaked across the sky.

I counted twenty-two transitions of the sun before my progress began to slow. The resistance became a weight on my mind, slowly overcoming my ability to turn back time. After twenty-seven days, I started to shake with the effort. Sweat beaded my brow and ran down my back. Progress slowed enough that the people moving around me were no longer indistinct.

Twenty-nine sunsets. The rewinding became erratic, like the wobble and dance of a spinning coin coming to rest. The moon jerked and spasmed across the sky. I knew I had to be close. I kept turning. My chest felt tight and a headache pounded inside my skull.

I saw the Nova. It backed into the space between the buildings with its lights off. A man got out of the car. He wore black clothes and gloves.

I stopped rewinding time and held the moment still. I walked to where the man stood, frozen in time. I regarded his flat gray eyes and his blank expression. Blood smeared his cheek and nose. I never saw this man before, but I knew who I'd found. Kate's killer. Josh Werner.

With an effort, I continued rewinding time. The night of Kate's murder unfolded in reverse. Josh walked backwards to the trunk of the Nova. He placed his hand on the blue metal, lifted his hand, and the trunk opened as though stuck to his flesh. A bucket handle lifted, and Josh grasped it. A plastic jug leaped from the trunk to his other hand. Continuing his backwards walk, Josh moved to a slowly retracting puddle a few yards from the library's side door. Josh upended the jug, and the puddle receded into a stream of clear fluid, pulled up and into the plastic container. With the jug full, Josh set the bucket and jug on the ground. Then he went back to the trunk where a dustpan and a broom leapt to meet him.

I wanted to skip all the clean up and go straight to the point where Josh killed Kate. I couldn't. It took everything I had to coax the vision to keep moving backwards. It would have been easier to pick up the Nova and carry it on my shoulders than to force time backwards any faster.

With my head throbbing and my breathing heavy, I looked around while Josh did his business. Neither of us had witnesses, past or present. I stood as alone in the present as Josh did in the past. Above us, two nearly full moons stared down while we did our work.

Josh returned to the scene of the crime. He appeared to be pushing a mixture of kitty litter and wood shavings onto the ground with the dustpan and broom. He spread the mixture in a wide circle, covering the place where the puddle had been. He walked around, moving the litter and chips with his feet, turning the smooth, even distribution of the mix into clumps. Then he upended the bucket. The wood and cat litter lifted from the ground, filling it just as the fluid had entered the jug. With the mixture out of the way, I could see dark streaks and puddles on the concrete. Kate's blood.

While Josh took his equipment back to the car, I knelt next to the largest pool of blood. I reached out to touch it, but my sense of touch remained in the present. The concrete felt dry and cold. A lump formed in the back of my throat. I swallowed it down. I didn't have time to cry over Kate's murder. Not now.

I turned my attention back to Josh. He put the cleaning materials away and moved to the backseat of the Nova. Kate's feet lifted up to his hands, her legs unfolding. I wanted to turn away, but I forced myself to watch, just as I continued to force time to rewind. From my perspective, it looked like she sat up and climbed into his arms. The illusion of life disappeared as he moved back to where I knelt. Blood stained her dress, and her arms hung limp.

I stood and moved out of the way. Josh stooped and lay Kate on the ground. Her face turned towards me, her head settling in the center of the slowly shrinking pool of blood.

The moment in time froze as I looked into my friend's face. I started to shake, and the vision of the past nearly slipped out of my grip. Some part of me knew that Kate still lived in the moment I was viewing. She died later, in the car. I closed my physical eyes to hold back tears, but my mind's eye remained fixed on Kate's eyes, half lidded, unstaring. I turned my attention back to Josh. He wore the same blank, emotionless expression I witnessed before.

Gritting my teeth, I rewound time a little bit further. I had to see it happen. I needed to know what weapon he used. I needed to know for sure. More importantly, I needed to see Josh's face when he did it. What did this man feel when he stole my friend's life away?

Josh returned to the Nova. A tire iron flew up out of the trunk, into his outstretched hand. It stood out as a dull black shadow in his hand. One end of the iron split into a forked claw, the other end bent at a sharp angle, bulbous and shaped to cover a tire nut. Josh walked back to a place near the library's stairs. He'd hid behind one of the square pillars near the door. He held the tire iron in front of him a moment, looking at it with a slight frown. A moment later, Kate lifted from the ground. She floated up in slow motion, her hair and her dress preceding her until her feet reached the lowest step of the library stairs. Josh's arm moved, and the bent end of the tire iron came up to rest at the back of Kate's skull.

I couldn't go back any further. I pushed, but I reached the end of my ability to go back through time. Kate stood on the steps, her face turned towards the Nova. Her blue eyes shone beneath a frown. She hadn't seen Josh or the tire iron. She just noticed the strange car parked there, out of place. She couldn't have known she was looking at the place where she would eventually die and be bound as a ghost.

Josh stood behind her, descending from the shadows. He had the emotionless expression of a man setting himself to do some mundane work. He could have been swinging a hammer to repair a fence, or swinging a bat to hit a baseball. Looking in his face, I couldn't read any discernible emotion in the moment this man committed murder.

With an effort, I closed my mind's eye. My body shook with relief. The vision faded, and I collapsed back to the ground, breathing hard. Sweat soaked my hair and my shirt. I felt both hungry and nauseous in waves.

After a few moments of slow breathing, I sat up. I slouched, sitting on the cold concrete. Shivers from the cold shook me and my head still ached, but I felt better. I took stock of my situation. I saw what happened, but I couldn't go to the police. What friends I had that could help with this were thousands of miles away and I couldn't call them for help. I didn't know which dorm Jen lived in, but now I knew what Josh looked like. I had a place to start.

I got back to my feet and started running again. I arrived a month too late to do anything about Kate's murder. But maybe I could still do something to save Jen.

35

I N THE MOVIES and on television, the police use footage from security cameras the way Bella uses magic. Their cameras are always pointed at just the right spot. The footage starts only a few moments before the crime takes place. In some shows, they can zoom in and find critical details, like a face in a reflection, or the missing digits of a license plate. All it takes is the investigator to say with a stern voice, "Enhance."

My gift proved to be more powerful than the magic security cameras of fiction. I didn't have to worry about focusing a lens. If I wanted to look at something more closely, I could just get closer. As amazing as my abilities are, I still had the problems of time and space to overcome. I had too much space to cover, and not nearly enough time.

I needed to find either Jen's or Josh's face in a crowd, moving in or out of one of the dormitories. It had been several hours since I talked to Jen on the phone, so wherever I went to look for their faces, I had all of that time to comb through. That amounted to a lot of time to cover and a lot of faces to check.

Fortunately, a guy hanging out in front of the dorms with his hands in his pockets isn't all that strange. I stood in front of the Butler dormitory for a while, my mind's eye open, looking into the faces of everyone that came and went through the main door that day. After the difficulty of turning time back a month, looking through the last several hours felt effortless. Unfortunately, I didn't find Josh or Jen at the Butler dorm. I repeated the process at the J. L. Dorm and didn't find them there, either.

In front of the Sharp dorm, I got lucky. In the afternoon, probably while I napped at Marshal's, I found Jen. She wandered in my direction from the nearest parking area. As she walked, she drew out a cell phone and pressed it to her ear. She walked stiffly, gesturing emphatically with her free hand. She looked agitated as she entered the dorm.

So she lived in Sharp. Probably the same dorm where she shared a room with Kate. Somewhere up there, more than a month ago, Kate walked in on her boyfriend and set in motion a series of events that led to her murder. Depending on the dorm security, I could probably follow Jen back to the room where all that took place, but that wasn't going to help anyone. I had been watching time in reverse. I could keep following Jen along that path to her room, but it seemed unlikely I would find her there in the present.

I let my view of time move forward. Jen walked out of her dorm, her attention fully on her phone conversation. A girl in a green and white tee shirt had to step out of her way. The look the girl gave Jen's back could have curdled milk. I ignored the girl and followed Jen. She hung up and put her phone away. Then she turned and walked to the parking area.

Jen slipped into the passenger seat of a new BMW. I held the vision in place and walked around the car. The metallic gray vehicle shone like polished stone. I checked the plates. Instead of a metal platter with raised letters, I found laminated cardboard printed with a dealership's logo. I continued around to the driver's side. The rolled up windows were tinted dark enough I couldn't see the driver from the outside. I stuck my face through the glass. Josh Warner occupied the driver's seat. He wore a baseball cap and dark clothing, and he gripped the steering wheel through gloved hands.

"Damn it." I let the vision play out a little further. The BMW pulled away, cutting off someone else trying to leave the lot.

If Josh meant to kill Jen, it looked like he meant to do it off campus. The problems of time and space grew. I could try to follow the car, but the vision in front of me took place hours ago. Following a BMW on foot, it would be that many more hours before I caught up to where Josh took her.

I needed a better plan. I needed to get back to the Nova. Maybe Kate would have an idea where Josh might have taken Jen.

First, I needed to get back to Marshal's. I had no car, no cell phone, and none of my tools. I wracked my brain as I jogged away from the school. With my tools, I could steal a car. There were many parked along the street. The law doesn't matter all that much when you're already a suspect in a murder investigation and you're trying to stop another murder.

Desperation started to settle in as I jogged down Freret street. But desperation is the grease that makes it easy to do stupid things and take unnecessary risks. I started looking at houses. I couldn't steal a car, but maybe I could sneak into a house and use a phone.

I turned down one of the side streets. A white two story home with a short chain link fence stood out to me. It had a green door, and all of the windows were dark. No cars parked in front. I hopped the fence and approached the entrance.

I pressed my ear to the door and listened for several moments. My heart pounded in my ears, and my breathing came in gulping rasps, but I couldn't hear anything else. I tried the door. Locked. I looked around. Checked under the door mat, a potted plant, and a small porcelain statue of a dog holding a "Welcome" sign. No key. No obvious way in.

With a sigh, I put my shoulder down and slammed into the door. On the second shove, the weathered wood gave way. I pushed into the house and closed the door behind me. I leaned against the door, holding it shut, waiting for the sound of an alarm. Maybe a policeman would drive up, their lights flashing and sirens wailing. Maybe a helicopter would descend on the neighborhood, hovering overhead with a spotlight on me. After an eternity, I relaxed. I eased off the door and slipped into the darkness of the house. The door, unable to latch, creaked open behind me.

Moonlight crept in through the windows. It gave me just enough light to see by. I stood in the living room, a coffee table in front of me, a couch to my left. I could see a dining area ahead of me, just beyond the couch. The adjoining rooms gave the impression of a much larger space. I tip-toed forward, finding a kitchen around the corner next to the dining room. A phone hung on the wall along the invisible line that separated the dining area and the kitchen. A cork board and note area were mounted on the wall next to the phone.

I picked up the receiver and started dialing for a cab. Each dialing tone seemed loud enough that it should echo through the house. I pressed the receiver against my ear with force, as though to crush the sounds of the phone against my face.

"Yellow cab," a disinterested male voice said.

"Hey, I need to be picked up at ..." I paused long enough to look at the cork board. Several bills were affixed with push pins. I plucked off a phone bill and read off the address. "As soon as you can make it, please."

I hung up. The silence of the house held the weight of deep water. I waited in it, breathing slowly through my mouth, trying not to drown. Time crept. I felt afraid to move. What if I tripped a silent alarm? I desperately hoped for the cab to show up before the police.

A car pulled up. No red and blue lights. No siren. The car bleated a single, short honk of its horn. I released a sigh of relief. I started for the door, then stopped. I had an idea.

I picked up the phone and dialed 9-1-1.

"Nine one one, what's your emergency?" a woman's voice said at the other end.

"Kate Lynnwood was murdered by Josh Warner," I said. "And now he has her roommate, Jen." I hung up and ran.

I hopped in the cab and rattled off Marshal's address before I even closed the door. The driver regarded me in the mirror, his eyebrows climbing towards his scalp.

"Ah! You again! The big tipper!"

Emboldened by the hundred I gave him earlier, the driver tried to make small talk all the way to Marshal's garage. I did my best to uphold my end of the conversation, talking about the weather and sports. I didn't do a very good job of it, though. I couldn't relax. I kept thinking of the vision of Kate's murder. Had I taken too much time? Would I find the place where Josh took Jen, only to find another vision of another murder? Maybe my call to the police would help. Or maybe it would just get them looking at me again. Now they had a recording of my voice, tying me to the whole mess.

At Marshal's, I gave the driver another hundred dollar bill before getting out of the cab. The driver rolled down his window and called his thanks after me, but I didn't hear him. I slid into the garage, opened the door to the Nova, and fell into the driver's seat, my mind's eye open before my butt hit the vinyl.

"What did she say?" Kate asked.

"She didn't show. Do you know where Josh lives?"

Kate hesitated. "He's in the Monroe dorm. Why?"

I shook my head. "They've gone somewhere else, then. Josh has Jen. I think he's going to kill her."

"Holy shit!"

"Do you have any idea where Josh would take her?"

Kate hesitated again. After a long, thoughtful pause, she said, "If she went willingly, he could have taken her to a cabin his family keeps on the bay. It's pretty remote, especially this time of year."

I started the Nova and backed out. "We're probably already too late, but we have to try. Tell me where to go."

Kate provided directions and I followed them. With the pregnant moon in the sky and the crisp chill in the air, it felt like the first night I met Kate. The Nova's engine purred as the tires swallowed the road. We left the city and entered the wet, green areas that surrounded it. The further we went, the narrower the roads became, and the fewer cars we saw. Soon, we were alone on a two-lane road.

Kate directed me to turn down a single lane access road. After a few yards, we were surrounded by gnarled trees covered with limp leaves and moss. Foliage overhead blocked the moonlight. The Nova's headlights exposed a countryside covered with rough, gray-green brush and shallow puddles. A bend in the access road ahead of us concealed whatever lay beyond.

"Park over there," Kate said, pointing to a narrow a pull-off area. "If you go much further with the car, he'll see you coming."

I pulled over and killed the engine. I looked back at Kate in the rear view mirror and shook my head. "If it goes badly, I'll try to make it back out to the car so you'll have some company."

"Don't say that." The temperature in the car dropped a little. "You don't have to do this. Just back the car up and go back to the garage. Let the police sort this out."

"If Josh has taken Jen, then I have to go. It's my fault."

"You're not responsible for this."

People talk about near-death experiences where their life flashes before their eyes. In that moment, something similar happened to me.

I saw myself taking gigs from Marshal, living in the silver bullet and sliding through life. Never getting too involved or attached. Not until that night I met Kate in the back of a repossessed Nova.

"That's the problem, Kate. I'm never responsible for anything."

I got out of the car and headed back to the trunk. It opened with a creak, revealing what I saw that first night. A donut to serve as a spare tire. Some jumper cables. A stray crescent wrench, its wheel rusted to uselessness. And a coal black tire iron, one end forked for scraping, the other end round for cupping lug nuts. It had been there the whole time. The weapon used to murder my friend.

36

MY BLOOD CHILLED WHEN I SAW IT. I hesitated before reaching for it. I knew what would happen when I picked it up. I would find a vision inside. Like every other vision, I would go into the head of a person, seeing through their eyes, hearing their thoughts and feeling their emotions. This time, the subject of the vision would be a murderer. If I let the vision take me over, I would know him as intimately as I came to know Bella and Mark. More importantly, I would see why he killed Kate. I'd learn his motive, beyond any shadow of a doubt.

The tire iron felt cold against my palm. The vision pressed against my hand, eager to take over. I held it back, hesitating while I considered the journey that led me to this moment. If I opened the trunk earlier and picked up the tire iron, I wouldn't have had to contact Jen. More than ever, I knew that whatever happened to Kate's old roommate would be my responsibility.

I took a deep breath. Then I let the vision overwhelm me.

Josh stood next to the library beneath the light he just disabled. His cell phone rested in his left hand, the tire iron in his right. He looked between the two, his brow furrowed. He had a very important decision to make. He could call it off, or he could go through with it.

He looked around the campus, feeling comfortable in the shadows. The Nova sat a few yards down the path, its trunk open like a hungry mouth. A third choice presented itself. He could get in the car and just drive. He could go somewhere else. Become a different person. Forget the life he'd been born to.

"No chance of that," Josh said. He thumbed a number into his phone, hit send, and pressed the phone to his face. He grimaced, thinking of the oils from his skin dirtying the glass. He would have to clean the phone again. He preferred things to be clean.

"Josh?" a male voice said. The man at the other end of the connection stood apart as the biggest influence in Josh's life. In person, he commanded the presence of a giant, though in stature he stood shorter than Josh himself. The man on the other side of the phone would always would be Josh's hero. The phone reduced his voice to something small and insignificant. Josh hated the phone for the insulting reduction.

"Hello, Dad," Josh said. "Remember what we talked about?"

"Let's not talk about it," Felix Werner said. Josh knew what his father meant. He meant they shouldn't talk about murder over the phone.

"I'm having second thoughts."

"Nonsense. Listen. It's perfectly natural. College is a time for experimentation and self discovery. Move decisively, be true to yourself, and you'll be fine."

"It doesn't seem that simple."

"I felt the same way my first time. But, then I got through it. After that, I found that I could do anything I set my mind to. You can do this, son. The apple doesn't fall far from the tree."

His father used those words before. The sentiment always filled Josh with pride. There could be no greater aspiration than to be like his father. The greatest sin would be to disappoint the man. He took a deep breath. "Alright, Dad. I'll call you later."

"Alright, son. I love you. I'm so proud of you."

Josh hung up. He wiped the front of the phone with two gloved fingers before slipping it into his pocket. He looked up at the broken light. So far, his crimes amounted to some minor vandalism. Before long, he would be guilty of quite a bit more.

He stepped over to the stairs leading up to library's side door. Kate would come out here. She would see him. There would be a startled look on her face, and in that moment of surprise, he would cave in her skull.

"No, that won't work," Josh said, shaking his head. "If she sees it coming, it might get messy."

Josh didn't like the thought of making a mess. He walked back to the Nova and checked the trunk. He had everything he needed to clean up any blood. First, he'd use the dry mix that his father told him about. Next would come the bleach, which washed everything clean. He had some rags, some rope, a hacksaw if it came to that. He had all of the materials he needed. But did he have the courage? The ability to follow through?

He looked back up to the door and tapped the tire iron against his thigh. Did he really need to do this? It seemed so wasteful. Kate had been a decent friend. He always appreciated her prettiness, though she didn't hold a candle next to her roommate. Jen had better connections and looked better on his arm. Choosing Jen over Kate had been an easy choice. The transition had been sloppy, but he'd done it. But did Kate really have to die?

Josh turned and slammed the trunk. He left his hand on the trunk lid and steadied himself. He needed to clean the mess up. He gave Kate weed, which could be problematic on its own if that ever came to light. A problem, but not a major one. As his Dad said, people experiment in college. No one cared much about weed these days.

The photograph presented the real problem. When Kate came into the room that night, catching him with his pants down and his dick inside Jen, things got out of hand. Josh hadn't seen a phone or a camera, but Jen said she saw Kate take a picture. He could not allow photographs like that to exist.

"Dad's first advice: 'Do what you want, but do not let them take any pictures.'" Josh shook his head and walked back to the stairs. Kate would be coming out soon. He needed to get ready.

Something else his Dad had said. Power follows sacrifice. There had been more to it. Special words to be said. Some sort of ritual. Josh couldn't say if this act would fulfill the requirements, but it didn't matter. As soon as Kate found him with Jen, she became the target.

He hopped up onto the ledge and put his back against the square pillar closest to the stairs. He held the tire iron in a relaxed grip. He needed to remain calm. Steady his breathing. Don't seize up. He ran the plan through his mind again. He imagined Kate stepping out, starting down the stairs. He would take one swing, once she put herself in the right position. He imagined the place at the back of her skull where the strike would be most effective. Then he imagined it again. And again.

When she finally emerged, he did the deed so quickly he couldn't be certain if he murdered her, or if he'd just imagined it. He looked down at her body, the dirty blood spreading around her. Time to finish the cleanup. His father would be so proud.

37

I PUSHED THE REST OF THE VISION AWAY with a shudder of revulsion. The muscles in my hands spasmed, and the tire iron slipped from my grasp. I looked down at it where it landed in the mud at my feet. Dirty. I wanted to scoop it up and put it back in the trunk, or throw it into the woods. I rubbed at my elbow. I felt an echo of the reverberation that ran up Josh's arm in my own, as if I had been the one to deliver the killing blow. I could still feel the swelling of Josh's pride, knowing he had seen the deed through to the end. It made me want to tear my own heart out.

Panting, I stood behind the Nova for several moments. I tried to separate my feelings from Josh's. The foreign feelings and thoughts infected me, made me sick. I felt like I dirtied my soul, stepping into Josh's mind. The dirty feeling triggered a need to clean, a reaction purely of Josh's mind.

I took a deep breath. I bent down, scooped up the tire iron, and began the walk down the access road. I held the tire iron at my side. It felt heavy and cold in my hands. It might have been a poor weapon choice. After what I just witnessed, as heavy as it felt, I didn't think I had the strength to wield it against anyone.

The fishing hut squatted amongst the mud and trees, a drab structure made of wood and chicken wire. An angular roof topped the hut like the slash of a stab wound. Light lanced out from two glassless windows next to a closed door. When I saw the hut, I froze in my tracks. Someone stood near one of the windows. I couldn't see them clearly. As far away as I stood, the surrounding darkness should have concealed me. I couldn't be sure, though.

I opened my mind's eye. Darkness and shadows disappeared, the world becoming a perfectly illuminated place within my mind. Ahead of me, I could see leaves and bare twigs that would have sounded my approach. Behind me, I found Kate, standing right behind me. I clamped my mouth shut. I stared at her, blinking my surprise.

"I know," she said. "I didn't think I was still attached to you, but here I am. Let's do this."

My grip tightened on the tire iron. I looked at it. It must have been an anchor. Maybe it had always been the anchor and not the car at all. I remembered watching Josh clean the blood from the ground, and I knew he cleaned the backseat. Maybe he overlooked the tire iron and some of her blood still clung to it.

Whatever connection existed between Kate and the tire iron, we couldn't talk about it just then. I couldn't risk the sound carrying to the cabin. Instead, I gave Kate a nod and continued moving forward, placing each step as though crossing a minefield. After walking what felt like a hundred miles, I drew up close enough to hear someone talking.

"Where are the pictures, Jen?"

Jen's response came in the form of wordless sobs. I felt the weight of the tire iron, and the muscles in my arm tensing. I forced myself to relax. I steadied my breathing. I needed to remain calm. Don't seize up. Just like Josh, when he held the crowbar before killing Kate. My stomach twisted, and I wanted to throw up, but I kept moving. Slow and steady.

"Where are the pictures, Jen?"

I placed my back against the outer wall of the hut. I leaned, twisting my neck to peer in through one of the windows. Josh stood with his back to me. He wore the same black clothing I saw him wear when he murdered Kate. Jen sat in a chair facing me. Mud covered one side of her face, caking her hair down on that side in clumps. Ropes wrapped around her chest and neck, the tension of the line pulling her back into the chair. Zip ties secured her hands and feet behind her. Rips in her clothing revealed pink and muddy flesh. As I watched, she shivered with cold or fright or both.

"Where are the pictures, Jen?" Josh's inflection and tone were identical to how he spoke the question before. He stood with his arms crossed in front of him, implacable. Patient as stone. He looked like he could keep this up for hours.

Lit candles surrounded Jen. They were pressed into puddles of wax on the wooden floor so they would stand on their own. Circles and arcane patterns had been carved into the floor, with Jen's chair at the center. Josh stood just outside the circle, his feet planted far enough away so as not to disturb the ritual markings. He didn't need to bother. With the Third Eye open, I could see no magic in the room at all.

I looked around the rest of the room, stalling. Gas lamps burned on a narrow table along one wall. A twin bed stood against another wall, the blankets pulled tight and the corners squared with military precision. Another table with a bucket for a sink rested just past the bed.

Though the window contained no glass, it could have been shuttered. Josh must have opened the window to watch for people approaching. Or maybe the cold November air helped with this sort of long, patient interrogation.

I lifted a leg and began climbing in. I kept my eyes fixed on Josh. Halfway into the hut, I saw Josh lift his head. He started to turn towards me. I froze, unable to breathe. I pulled the tire iron into the hut, preparing to defend myself. Then I saw the gun in Josh's right hand.

Jen saw me. Her eyes widened. Before Josh could turn to fully face me, she yelled.

"Alright!" Jen said. "I'll tell you where they are! Just let me go!"

Josh turned back to Jen. I moved, pulling myself the rest of the way into the hut. No turning back now. I surged forward, swinging the tire iron overhand. Like trying to drive a nail. Or smash a spider.

From Josh's vision, I knew how to swing the tire iron to kill with one blow. I experienced his thoughts. Riding behind his eyes, I imagined doing it, over and over. I had the opportunity to deal Josh the same killing blow he gave Kate. I gritted my teeth and twisted at the last moment. The tire iron swung past Josh's face. The socket end struck the wrist holding the gun. Bones crunched. Josh screamed.

The gun fired. The explosion of sound filled the hut. A tiny hole appeared in the wood near Josh's feet. The gun slipped from his grip and clattered to the ground. Josh clutched his arm and stumbled. At the same time, my lunge carried me forward. I flew past Josh, falling into Jen's lap. Her chair toppled and smashed into splinters beneath us. I heard another loud pop, not as loud the gunfire. Jen screamed, her cry replacing Josh's voice.

In spite of whatever I did to Josh's arm, he recovered before me. I had enough time to disentangle from Jen and get to my hands and knees. Josh brought a booted foot up into my gut. The wind went out of me. The kick lifted me a few inches off the ground. I fell back onto the floor and folded into the fetal position.

Josh stomped and kicked me. I tried to protect my face and head. My arms and legs absorbed most of the blows. One booted heel slipped past, sinking into my ribs. My world went white with pain. I rolled, trying to get away. I slipped under Josh's raised boot, colliding with his other leg. He lost his balance and almost fell. He staggered back, keeping his footing.

Kate floated up behind Josh. Her light-consuming aura flared, and the room cooled so fast that the walls creaked. The color drained out of her. Her face contorted in rage. I thought of the ghost named Mary, endlessly looking for her child, killing people that got in her way. I thought of Bella's warning. All ghosts turn into monsters. Even Kate.

"You did this to me!" Kate screamed. She swung a fist at Josh. Ice formed in the air around her hands. The ice smashed into the side of Josh's face. Kate's fist continued, passing through Josh's head. He clutched at where Kate's hand struck him. He turned to face his new assailant, his eyes wide and seeking.

Kate hung in the air in front of Josh. She looked down at her hands, then back at her murderer. To my vision, her eyes glowed with a cold blue light. With those cold, killer's eyes, she stared at Josh's chest. Her fingers twitched. She raised her arm and reached towards Josh's heart.

Bruised. Winded. Desperate. I rose to my feet, scooping up one of the chair legs on my way. I thought I knew what Kate was about to do. Her hands would sink into his flesh and the blood would freeze in his veins. She would murder Josh, and then she would be lost forever.

I swung the chair leg with all the strength I could muster. The wood struck the back of his head, knocking him forward. It sounded like a baseball bat connecting with a fastball. Josh crumpled to the floor. I followed him down and swung again. And again. And again.

Josh lay beneath me, his body still. I staggered back away from him and dropped the chair leg. My vision blurred. It had been a choice between letting Kate become the monster, or take her place and become one myself. I couldn't stop the tears. I sagged to my knees, covered my face with my hands, and cried.

38

AFTER A FEW MINUTES, I pulled myself together. I sniffed and wiped my nose with my sleeve. Then I noticed the sounds of someone else in the room crying. Jen lay still in a crumpled mess, her hands and feet still zip tied together. One of her shoulders looked sunken, turned at an odd angle. The popping sound I heard when we fell must have been her shoulder dislocating. Or maybe it could have been her collar bone breaking.

Kate stood next to me. Her aura diminished and color returned to her, replacing the darkness and shadows that filled her. She continued to look at her hands.

"I was going to kill him."

Before getting to my feet, I checked Josh for a pulse. My hands shook too much for me to find it, but I did notice the slow rising and falling of his chest. I hadn't killed him after all. Looking at the blood running from his nose and head, it might still happen. Maybe he was in the process of dying, the way Kate slowly died after Josh put her in the back of the Nova.

Next to the door sat a green denim tool bag. I knelt and rummaged through it. I found more zip ties as well as a box cutter.

The Repossessed Ghost

I looked back at Josh. For a sickening moment, I couldn't tell which I should use on him.

I grabbed a fistful of ties and went back to kneel next to Josh. I had to loop them together to make them long enough to go around his wrists and ankles. Josh let out a pained groan when I moved his broken wrist, but he didn't open his eyes or struggle as I bound him.

I took the box cutter to Jen and cut her ties. Once freed, she turned and held me, burying her face into my shoulder. We stayed that way for several moments, her tears soaking through my shirt while she sobbed. I tried to comfort her as best I could. I felt on the verge of crying again myself.

When her crying subsided enough for her to speak, she pulled away from me and scrubbed her face with one hand.

"He was going to kill me."

"I know. I'm so sorry."

"He said he wouldn't kill me until he had the pictures." She looked into my face then, and her eyes hardened. Before I could stop her, she started hitting me, punctuating each blow with a word. "Those. God. Damn. Pictures!"

I caught her fist and held her arm away from me. "Jen, stop! I'm sorry. There never were any pictures. Kate didn't have a camera that night."

Jen twisted and pulled her arm out of my grip and started hitting me again. It hurt, but not because she hit me with any strength. Bruises covered me all over from where Josh kicked me. My left side in particular burned like fire. I held up my hands and shuffled back from her, getting to my feet awkwardly.

Jen cradled her dislocated arm against her side as she pulled herself to her feet. Her rage shifted from me to Josh. She let out a low growl. Then she kicked him where he lay, driving her foot deep into his abdomen. He grunted, but didn't move.

"Take it easy!" I put myself between Jen and Josh. "You don't want to do this."

"Yes I do!" She tried to get around me, but I blocked her and pushed her back.

"Maybe you should let her at him," Kate said. "She could do the whole world a favor."

"No, you don't want to do this," I said to Jen. I turned and fixed Kate with a stare for a moment. Then I turned back to Jen. "And I

234

don't want to stand by and watch you kill him. He's the murderer, not you. If you kill him, he wins."

She relented, though her eyes still burned with fury. After a few moments, she let me lead her out of the hut. Everything hurt. The night air seemed to make it worse. Jen and I leaned against each other as we walked up the access road, back to the Nova. I opened the door for her, then got in myself. I rested my head on the top of the steering wheel, letting my mind's eye close. After a moment, I looked up to the mirror. Kate sat in the backseat, scowling with her arms crossed.

"I think we did it," I said. "He's not going to hurt anyone again."

Before Kate could respond, a pair of headlights cut through the darkness. The lights reflected into my eyes, obscuring Kate from my vision. Two police cars rolled past the Nova, one of them proceeding on to the hut, the other angling to block the Nova from going forward. A third police car blocked us in from the back.

"Thank God," Jen said.

"Shit," I said.

I angled the mirror so I could see Kate again. She shook her head.

"Typical," Kate said.

•   •   •

The police were efficient in securing us, but an age passed before they carted us away. When the police realized we were all injured, they called for paramedics. Jen and I were pulled out of the Nova and separated, with Jen allowed to sit in one of the police cars. They gave me a wool blanket and had me lean against one of the trees along the access road. When the paramedics arrived, a pair of them went on to the hut to pick up Josh. Another attended to Jen, and another attended me. He said I had at least one broken rib, but nothing else to worry about. Not medically, anyway.

The paramedics cleared me to be taken into custody. Instead of taking me to a hospital, the police brought me in to the police station. Once again, I found myself in an interrogation room. Yellow tinged linoleum covered the floor. A thin layer of vinyl covered the plain chair under my ass, providing the barest hint of a cushion. Across the table in front of me sat two men in drab brown suits. The first, a Hispanic man with a proud black mustache, stared at me with sharp eyes. The other, an older man with blotchy white skin and graying hair, tried not to look at me directly. One-way mirrored glass dominated the wall behind them. I had never been in this room, and yet, it felt the same as all the rest. I took comfort in the familiarity.

"I'm Detective Martinez," the Hispanic officer said. "This is Detective Winchester."

"Pleased to meet you." I rested a hand on my left side where the paramedic wrapped my ribs. Pain pulsed from the place Josh kicked me, flaring to life like a stubborn alarm clock. Instead of hiding the pain, I made a show of it. It's important to stick to the truth when being interrogated by the police. It also helps to play up for any sympathy you can get.

"Are you going to be okay to answer a few questions?" Martinez asked.

I winced before nodding.

"Alright. We'll try to keep this brief. What is your relationship with Joshua Werner and Jennifer Billings?"

"I honestly don't know either of them very well," I said.

"But you were in an altercation with Mr. Werner on Mr. Werner's property. That fishing hut is pretty remote."

I frowned. That hadn't been a question. I opened my mouth to retort, but stopped. Something moved in the mirror behind him.

As I watched, Kate rematerialized behind me, her reflection monochromatic. She smiled and reached for me, her hands stopping just short of my shoulder.

For a moment, I forget about the interrogation. I sat up straight, my eyes locked with Kate's. She smiled. I opened my mouth to say something to her. How did she get out of the Nova, or away from the tire iron?

Then I looked back at the detectives. Martinez raised an eyebrow. Winchester cocked his head to one side, looking more directly at me than he had all evening.

I decided to play it straight. It didn't really matter what I said at that point. Whatever story I came up with, no one would believe me.

"Someone very special to me told me where to go," I said. "I followed her directions."

Winchester looked over his shoulder to see what I had been staring at. He turned back to me and said, "Who told you?"

I leaned back in my chair. I reached the end of my journey. As soon as the police pulled up behind the Nova, I knew there would be no escape. I couldn't talk my way out of this. I didn't have money to buy my way out. I didn't have a prestigious family name or connections that would trade favors for my freedom. Josh Werner would probably recover and walk. They'd pin the murders on me and I'd go to jail, no matter what Jen said. I ran a good race, but whatever I said or did now, the only place left for me to go was a prison cell.

I looked back at Kate and smiled. Prison or not, it looked like I would have an opportunity to do something right by Kate, one last time.

"Kate Lynnwood told me where to go." I turned back to Winchester.

Winchester and Martinez exchanged looks. Winchester pushed his chair back and said, "I'm going to get some coffee."

"Sounds good," Martinez said. "I've got this, for now."

Winchester left and Martinez and I regarded each other for a long moment.

"Do you have any more questions?" I asked.

"Plenty. But you're either stupid or crazy, so I'm not sure where to begin."

"Well, I'm not crazy. So pretend I'm stupid, if that helps."

"You came back to New Orleans. Why did you come back here? You had to have known you'd be arrested as soon as you turned up."

I looked back at my friend in the mirror before answering. "I came back for Kate."

"The dead girl."

I didn't have a response to that, so I just shrugged.

"You could have stayed in California," Martinez said. "You could have gone anywhere. When we patted you down, we found thousands of dollars on your person. So why come back here?"

"I already answered that question," I said with some annoyance.

"Okay. Then why did you go out to the Werner fishing hut?"

"I didn't want Josh to kill Jen."

"Why didn't you go to the police?"

"Because I'm apparently not as stupid as you think I am."

Martinez wiped his brow and ran a hand through his thick black hair. He pushed his chair back and rose to his feet. "Let's take a break. I'm going to get a coffee. Do you want me to bring you something when I come back?"

I shook my head and Martinez left. I opened my mind's eye, turned in my seat, and regarded Kate.

"How?" I asked.

"I'm not sure," Kate said. "I tried to come to you so many times. I tried again after some detectives put the tire iron in a plastic bag, and it finally just worked."

"They're going to throw me in jail, you know."

The temperature in the room dropped. Kate knelt next to me and looked up into my face. "Don't let them. Tell them anything they need to hear. Don't let them lock you up!"

"It's okay. Listen. I've been giving this some thought, and I need to tell you something. If I'm going to prison, I need to go alone."

Kate frowned. "What, do you think I'm just going to wait in the car until you're free? That's a smaller prison cell then where you'd be going. Don't try to be noble. You don't have to go suffer alone."

"I didn't mean it like that. What I mean is, Bella warned me that the longer you're with me, the more likely it is you'll lose the part of you that makes you a person. I saw it start to happen in Josh's hut. I want to help you move on. To the next world, as Bella put it. Kate, what I'm trying to say is ... I love you."

Kate's eyes narrowed for a moment. "I love you, too, Mel. You're one of the best friends I've ever had."

"No, I mean, I really love you. Like, true love. Isn't that what you've been waiting for? The thing that's been holding you back?"

Kate sighed. "You think that's what I've been waiting for? True love?"

"Well, with the way you reacted after Bella and I—"

"It's not that. I've been in love before. Or I thought I was in love, once. That's not my issue."

"What is it, then?"

Kate straightened and began pacing the room. "It's stupid."

"Try me."

She stopped pacing and turned to face me. "I wanted to change the world."

I cocked my head to one side as I studied her. "What?"

"I was going to be a doctor or a lawyer. Something important. I was going to do something that mattered. I wanted to help people, but instead ... nothing. Dead before I had a chance."

I shook my head. "I don't understand."

"I told you it was stupid."

"No, it's not stupid." I leaned back in my chair. "I meant, I don't understand what's holding you back now. You have changed the world. You've changed my world. You made me care about something bigger than myself. You made me a better person. Maybe that isn't much, but to me, it's everything."

"Don't be so melodramatic."

"Kate, listen to me. Finding you in the back of that car is the best thing that ever happened to me. You saved my life, more than once, in more ways than one. Before I met you, all I did was skate by. But you changed me. Made me a better person. The kind of person that wants to get involved. You're the strongest person I've ever known. You changed the world, Kathryn Lynnwood. Believe me."

Kate closed her eyes. The chill in the room disappeared. Through my mind's eye, I watched the nearly invisible aura that surrounded Kate change. Instead of consuming light, the halo circling Kate's head began to radiate with a soft, golden glow. Kate opened her eyes, and I saw something I'd never seen before. A single tear rolled slowly down her cheek.

"I believe you," Kate said. "Thank you, Mel. Maybe you're right."

The glow around Kate began to wash out the colors of her skin and her dress. Warmth spread from Kate's aura, like sunlight stretching beyond the boundaries of a shadow. She looked up, her eyes wide and moving. She could see something in the air between us that I couldn't see.

We witnessed this before. At her funeral, when the old woman moved on. Something fundamental shifted inside Kate, and whatever held her to this world no longer mattered. In a few moments, she would be gone.

"Looks like this is it," I said. Though my supernatural vision remained clear, I could feel tears welling up in my eyes.

Kate closed her eyes, breathing in the light and warmth that surrounded her. When she opened her eyes, she gave me a strange look. She leaned forward and placed a kiss on my lips. I felt the warmth of her pass into me. I closed my eyes, both physical and supernatural. I sat still for several minutes, feeling the energy of her pulse through me with the beat of my heart. Her kiss stayed on my lips. Real or imagined, I felt as though some part of her stayed with me, and would remain with me for the rest of my days.

I cried silent tears, alone in the interrogation room. Eventually, Martinez and Winchester returned. I answered the rest of their questions woodenly, the answers slipping from my mouth without any hesitation or taste. When they finished, they placed me under arrest, and led me to a cell.

39

LATER THAT NIGHT, I lay on my cot feeling sorry for myself. After everything I'd gone through, I had a hard time letting Kate go. She had been the best friend I had ever known. Losing her overshadowed any dread I felt for my future in prison. The next day would come, and I'd handle it. For the moment, I let myself miss my friend.

As I lay there, I heard a strange sound coming from the corner of the cell. At first it sounded like a high pitched whine, starting low and climbing into dog whistle territory. Then came a sound like glass shattering. I got up and went towards the sound. It came from the toilet. I looked in the bowl. The water had been frozen solid.

I opened my mind's eye. Kate knelt next to the toilet, a gold and silver aura surrounding her.

"You didn't think you'd be rid of me that easy, did you?" she said.

"But, I saw you move on!"

Kate stood up and smoothed the front of her dress. "I did. Sort of."

My knees felt weak. I moved back to my bunk and sat down. "What happened?"

Kate followed me to the bed and sat next to me. "We can talk about that in a moment. First, I want to ask you something. When you and Bella talked about ghosts turning evil, did she tell you why?"

"Something about losing touch with humanity. It was a long time ago. I honestly don't remember."

Kate nodded. "What do you think it is that makes us human?"

"A lot of things." I smiled. "Language. Religion. Football."

"While I was away, I had a moment to give it some thought. I think what makes us human the most is the ability to choose."

I studied Kate's face, enjoying the little details. The blue of her eyes. The shape of her cheeks and her nose. "You liked hanging out with me more than heaven, huh?"

Kate laughed. "Maybe. I don't know if I made it all the way to heaven or not. I just knew that I wasn't done yet. So I came back. I made a choice."

That's when I knew. Whatever Bella said before, I didn't have to worry. Kate would never turn into a monster, ever again.

•   •   •

The next three days slipped by quicker than I could count. They kept me in an orange jumpsuit, free of belts and shoelaces and anything else I might harm myself with. They made sure I ate and they had someone tend to my bandages every morning. Every once in a while, one of the detectives would tell me something about attorneys I had access to, or rights I possessed. I didn't pay much attention to any of it. I kept to myself when others were around. The rest of the time, I talked to Kate.

In the middle of the fourth day, a huge guard with dark skin and squinty eyes opened my cell. It broke the daily routine. I braced myself for the worst.

"Walk, Walker," He'd used that joke before. It hadn't grown any funnier. I got up and walked. He followed, directing me to one of the interrogation rooms.

"More questions?

"Nah. It's just your lawyers."

I opened the door and blinked in surprise. Sitting at the table were two men I recognized. At one end sat Marshal dressed in a new suit and as cleaned up as I'd ever seen him. Mr. Ortega sat at

242

other end of the table, as dapper as usual. I could see why the guard would think they were my lawyers.

"Ah, Mr. Walker," Ortega said, getting to his feet. "Please have a seat. We have much to talk about."

I entered the room. Before I could sit, Marshal got up and gave me a hug. I groaned in pain. My ribs were still tender.

"Look at you," Marshal said. His eyes were bloodshot and watery. Then his voice dropped to just above a trembling whisper. "I hoped I'd never see you like this."

"I think we both knew it would happen eventually." I clapped Marshal on the shoulder and gave Ortega an apologetic look before taking a seat across from him. Marshal sat back down. Both men looked at me with identical concerned frowns.

"Let's talk about your case," Ortega said.

"Let's not," I said. "There's nothing really to discuss."

"Actually, there is," Ortega said. "They have a long list of charges against you, including battery, grand theft auto, and attempted murder. How much of it is true?"

I leaned back in my chair and thought about it a moment. "I don't know if I ever really meant to murder anyone. I had good reasons to do what I did, and for a minute I thought I did kill Josh. I guess everything else they say I did is true."

Ortega and Marshal both let out relieved sighs.

"Good," Ortega said.

"I didn't think you were stupid, son," Marshal said. "And I tried to convince your friend here that you had more sense than that."

"What does it matter?" I said. "The rest is enough to put me away for a really long time. And I can't prove my innocence on the attempted murder charge, anyway. I was on Werner's property. I beat him half to death with a chair leg. It doesn't take a psychic to tell you how this is going to play out in court."

"Well, you are psychic," Ortega said, shaking his head. "I'm not, but I can still tell you how this is going to go. You won't have to see the inside of a courtroom. I'm getting you out of here. Today, if I can manage it."

I narrowed my eyes as I studied Ortega's face. "How? I don't think your briefcase is big enough to smuggle me out."

"Don't be a wise ass, boy," Marshal said. "Use your mouth less and your ears more."

"Mr. Felix Werner isn't the only man with government connections," Ortega said. "He's a congressman that's pissed off more than a few people during his rise to power. As we speak, a backhoe is rolling into his backyard. There, it will dig up and reveal the bones of a girl. We suspect Congressman Werner had been about Josh's age when he killed her."

"The apple doesn't fall far from the tree," I said quietly. "How'd you find the body?"

"Ms. Theroux is getting more precise with her scrying spells," Ortega said.

"Well, that's all good news. But that doesn't prove Josh killed Kate. It just means Josh's dad will have a cell near mine."

"Don't be silly," Ortega said. "If you were bound for jail, which you are not, Felix Werner would be headed to a much nicer facility."

"I guess that's probably true," I said.

"Ms. Billings ..." Ortega stopped when he saw confusion in my eyes. "Ah. Jennifer Billings, the girl you rescued, has stated that you saved her from the younger Werner, and that the injuries he sustained were a consequence of you trying to keep her from permanent harm. She has spoken on your behalf, and her parents have been making their own case for your release."

I licked my lips. It all sounded too good to be true. "What about Kate's murder? They're not going to pin that on me?"

"Actually," Ortega said, raising his eyebrows, "you are no longer considered for her murder. They found the murder weapon in the hut where you rescued Ms. Billings. With her statement, they believe they have motive and means enough to prosecute Joshua Werner for that crime."

I sighed, relieved. "Then ... that just leaves the car. Grand theft auto."

"Yeah, about that," Marshal said. He reached down to a brief case next to his chair. From the case, he drew out two papers. He laid them on the table and slid them towards me. I looked at the top one a moment before I recognized it.

"That's the authorization to repossess the Nova," I said. I squinted at it and frowned. "Wait. It's not the same letter. This one has my name on it. Marshal, this isn't going to work. It's clever, but you're the repo man, not me."

"Not anymore, kid," Marshal slid out the bottom page and stacked it on top of the first.

It looked like Marshal's repo license. I'd seen it in a frame on his wall a million times. But like the letter, Marshal's name had been replaced with mine. I shook my head.

"Forgery?" I asked.

"Before Mr. Greenwood took his show on stage, he had a talent for paperwork," Ortega said. "He sent this, along with his apologizes for what happened at the poker game."

"The poker game. What happened to Bobby after I left?"

"He went on a tremendous losing streak and lost all his money to the basketball player. A short time later, he had some sort of mishap. Fell down some stairs, he says. Somehow wound up with two broken knees. He had to do the paperwork from a hospital bed."

I looked at the papers and frowned. "He did this in the hospital? He's not in New Orleans, is he?"

"No, he's still in Sacramento."

"I brought them with me, when Mr. Ortega flew me out to California," Marshal said.

"I'm confused," I said.

"We found Mr. Smith when we were looking for you," Ortega said. He gestured towards Marshal. "Mr. Smith and I share a mutual concern for your well being. It seemed prudent for us to have a face to face meeting, and discuss options for your future."

"My future."

"You're too talented to leave in jail," Ortega said. "You have a rare gift."

"We both agreed that if you had set out to kill the Werner kid, you were better off in jail," Marshal said. "Mr. Ortega thought if you were a budding murderer, it'd be immoral to let you out. I agreed, but I also thought that if you had set out to kill the Werner kid and he lived, then you probably ought to rot a little while for incompetence."

"Thanks," I said. "But at the risk of sounding ungrateful, I'm thinking that maybe you're both wasting your time. I don't want to go to jail, but I'm not too keen on you two deciding my future for me. I'm my own man, and I'd rather stay that way."

"We're not making decisions for you," Ortega said. "We're presenting you with options. You can decide for yourself what is best. But if it is all the same, I'd like you and Kate to come back to Sacramento with me and continue to help The Society prepare for the end of The Cycle."

"How'd you know Kate made it back to me?" I asked.

Ortega paused. "Is there some reason Kate would not be with you?"

I shook my head. "I'll tell you about it later."

"Very well. What's important is that you have talent, Mr. Walker. With no training whatsoever, you single-handedly brought at least one ghost to some sort of peace. It seems you're becoming something of a specialist with the undead. Think of the good you can do, with my resources and the support of a team. Ms. Theroux and Father McAdams like you, and even Mr. Greenwood had pleasant things to say on your behalf."

"But we all know what you really want to do," Marshal said. "Stay here in New Orleans and work with me. We both know how much you love the cars. Heck, Mr. Ortega said he might even be able to get you the Nova. We can get your trailer out of impound, get you a couple of cars to pick up. It'll be like old times."

I looked between the two men and shook my head. They both offered me lives I enjoyed. Both were exciting choices. I had new friends in Sacramento, but New Orleans was where I was from. Neither place would be the quite the same after what I went through. The whole world shrank, and I didn't think I would ever quite fit in it the same way again.

I turned in my chair, opening my mind's eye to find Kate standing patiently behind me.

"What do you think?" I asked.

"I think you already know where we should go," Kate said, smiling.

And she was right. I knew what I needed to do. I needed to go where I belonged. Where we both might be able to change the world.

ABOUT THE AUTHOR

Hailing from sunny Sacramento, California, Brian C. E. Buhl is trying to save the world. Formerly enlisted in the U.S. Air Force, Brian now spends most of his time writing software for the solar industry. When he's not engineering technical solutions, he can sometimes be found playing saxophone with local community bands. Also, he writes science fiction and fantasy.

YOU MIGHT ALSO ENJOY

CORPORATE CATHARSIS
THE WORK FROM HOME EDITION
compiled by Water Dragon Publishing

The pandemic came and the world changed. The boundaries between reality and fantasy have become as blurred as those between life and work.

THE INSANE GOD
by Jay Hartlove

A meteorite fragment cures a teenaged trans girl's schizophrenia, but leaves her with visions of ancient warring gods annihilating each other in space.

POSSESSION IS NINE-TENTHS
by J Dark

Possession might be 9/10th of the law. But no one mentioned 9/10th of what.

Available from Water Dragon Publishing in
hardcover, trade paperback, and digital editions
waterdragonpublishing.com